Just Em

on her own

ROSE O'CONNOR

Just Em

on her own

ROSE O'CONNOR

Also by Rose O'Connor

Footpaths: Love, Adventure, and Finding Home Within

Dedication

To my faithful Doppelganger

and to my mother Margie

both always in my heart

Published in the United States by Rose O'Connor
ISBN: 978-0-9985732-3-6

Cover design by Eva Polakovicova

This book is a work of fiction. Unless otherwise indicated, all the names, characters, businesses, places, events, and incidents in this book are either the product of the author's imagination or used in a fictitious manner. Any resemblance to actual persons, living or dead, or actual events is purely coincidental.

∽ Prologue ∾

December 21, 2015

Em was starting her day like she always did with several sun salutations in front of the wide windows that looked out over the lake while the tea water boiled. It was a cool December morning and the promise of snow was in the air. Em was always doing at least two things at the same time. She moved fast inside her head although it appeared to others that she moved slowly... easily... through life.

But appearances weren't everything, she thought, as she caught a glimpse of herself in the mirror—ignoring her thick copper-red hair and fair skin, instead fixating on the puffiness under her usually bright green eyes. She'd tossed and turned the night before, worrying about her father's declining health. Family was everything to her, and aside from her husband Pete and her sister Sophie, her dad was all the family she had.

After she'd finished her cup of tea, she began to wonder what was keeping Pete upstairs so long. It seemed like ages since he'd gone into the bathroom for his shower, though, unlike her, he did like to do one thing, thoroughly, at a time. It was one of the things that she loved about him.

She began formulating a list in her head of what needed to be done that day, and after another ten minutes, she could wait no longer. She called to him as she put her foot on the first step.

"Pete?" she called. As she reached the top of the stairs, she called again, "Pete?" more loudly this time. But she knew that he wouldn't hear her anyway, no matter how loudly she spoke. His work in construction had made him hard of hearing at 40, though he denied it, insisting that she was too soft-spoken. Moving quickly down the hall now, she could hear the shower still running. She knocked on the bathroom door.

"Honey? Are you okay in there?" No answer. She turned the knob to open the door. It seemed like it was locked but Pete never locked the door. Something heavy gripped her chest, and she started banging on the door now, shouting his name. "Pete! Open the door! Pete!!" She stopped to catch her breath and it was then that she felt it. Her feet were getting wet. What in the world? She looked down to see water running out from under the bathroom door. "Oh my god oh my god oh my god." She felt as though she were hyperventilating. Her heart was pounding and she couldn't breathe. She heard someone screaming "PETE!!" as she slid to the floor. She didn't realize then that the scream was coming from her.

PART ONE

There are, in fact, no beginnings and no endings; just the eternal spiral that continually weaves in and out like the waves of the sea.

Unknown

Sophie pushed her head around the door of the bedroom where her semi-conscious boyfriend lay with his head covered up by a pillow to block the constant sunshine that seemed to stream into Boulder most days—unless there was a snowstorm. It was the thing that she loved most about living in Colorado—daily sunshine you could almost bank on, a welcome change after growing up in the mountains of western North Carolina, where the weather could be, well, unpredictable. "I'm going, Myles. For real this time."

Myles groaned and peeked out from under his pillow. "Are you leaving without a proper goodbye?" His British accent, which at one time turned her on, suddenly grated on every nerve in her body.

There might have been time for a "proper goodbye" if you would have bothered to get your British arse out of bed one of the four times I told you I was leaving, she thought, but aloud she simply said, "I'm not really in the mood, Myles."

"Alright then, if that's how you feel. Have a good trip to...ah... wherever you are going. And when will you be back? I might have found a different girl by then." He laughed as though he found himself very amusing.

Four months ago, a remark like that would have crushed her, but now, oddly, she felt nothing at all except anger at his utter selfishness.

"You know full well where I'm going." Her jaw clenched to hold back the scream she felt wanting to burst from her throat. "I'm going to be with my sister whose husband just had a heart attack. You do remember my sister Em?" She felt nauseated, both at having to deal with such an incredibly self-centered boyfriend and thinking about what Em must be feeling right now.

Myles sat up then. "Of course I remember, darling. I remember everything. And I'm sure I'll manage while you are gone so don't worry about me." That was his way of apologizing but it irked Sophie. He actually thought his well-being was the only thing she ever thought about.

"Now be a good girl and give us a kiss." He closed his eyes and puckered his lips in an exaggerated fashion and suddenly Sophie found it hard to remember what she'd ever seen in him at all.

Myles Richardson had charmed her from the very beginning of their relationship, with his flashy looks, charm, and high-profile job as a big city editor. He seemed to know all the "important people" and had that knack of perfect timing, able to say just the right thing at the right time, a skill she'd never learned. But the more she got to know the real Myles, the less his charm seemed to work on her. In fact, this morning, she was seeing him in a whole different light.

She sighed and made a huge effort to focus on what she

needed to be doing. She didn't have the time or mental energy to think about him right now. She had a plane to catch. In an effort to simply keep the peace, she strode over to the bed, gave him a quick peck on the cheek, and left the apartment without saying another word.

"Give your dear sister my best," he called after her. Right. As if Em would want to hear anything that came from Myles's lips. Em might not have the city slicker savvy of a man like Myles, but she could smell a skunk a mile away.

As the door slammed behind her, she suddenly wished she weren't so headstrong and had to learn everything the hard way.

Em sat on the couch, staring into space, acting as if she were talking to herself. "I don't understand, Chloe. Please explain it to me again." Chloe, Em's friend and colleague at the large animal hospital where Em was a vet tech, wondered if she should call someone else, do something more.

She gently took Em's hand. It was ice cold as though her blood has just stopped circulating from the shock. "Honey, look at me."

Em turned towards her friend with no expression on her face, her fair skin paler than usual. Chloe held her hand tightly. "You've received a terrible shock, Em, and it's understandable that it doesn't make sense. When someone... when someone we love dies so suddenly it never makes sense." Em turned away, looking straight ahead and started shaking her head from side to side, as if to dispute what had happened.

"But he is...was," she choked on the word, "only 40 years old, Chloe! 40! He's strong, young, active. Men just don't have heart attacks that are...." She couldn't say the word fatal but they both knew how that sentence ended. They both knew what had just occurred, so... unexpectedly, so abruptly. Em closed her mouth and continued staring blankly into space.

Chloe gently put the sedative that Dr. Chavez had given her at the hospital into one of Em's hands and a glass of water in the other. Just then the phone rang and Chloe grabbed it quickly, hoping for something, anything to comfort Em. It was Em's sister Sophie, calling from the Denver airport. Chloe had left a second voicemail for her, this time telling her that Pete was gone.

Em took the sedative numbly and put the phone Chloe handed her to her ear but said nothing into the mouthpiece. A sigh escaped her lips, letting Sophie know her sister was on the other end.

"Em, is that you? It's me Sophie."

Still Em didn't say anything—just nodded her head as if Sophie could see her.

"I'm on my way, sweetheart. My flight got delayed because of some heavy snow here in Denver, but I'll be there first thing in the morning. Em?"

"Uh huh." Em's voice was a monotone.

"I'm so very sorry, Sis. I... I don't even know what to say. I can't actually believe it."

There was silence for a long moment before Em spoke. "Go see Dad."

"What?"

"Go see Dad first when you get here." Her voice became stronger and even insistent.

"But why? I mean I want to see you, to hold you, to be with you and..."

"Just do it, Sophie. Please. See Dad and tell him. I need him to know."

"But he won't..." Their father, Jonathan Watts, had dementia and likely wouldn't be able to process the information. Sophie didn't understand Em's request. She was desperate to get to her sister as soon as possible.

"Just promise you'll go there first."

"Ok, I'll go there first. See you in few hours. Please try to get some sleep. I love you!"

Em couldn't answer. She wasn't capable of feeling emotion of any kind at the moment. She handed the phone back to Chloe, who walked into the next room so she could speak privately to Sophie.

"Sophie? I'm sorry. She is in major shock right now. It's all been too much for her. She's just taken a sedative the doctor prescribed and I'm hoping that she'll be able to sleep."

"I've never heard her sound like that."

"Yes, well, she just lost the love of her life." Chloe's voice was choked, as she held back the sobs that Em could not seem to muster at all.

"I just cannot believe this is happening." Sophie's voice was shaky now as well.

"I better get back to her. Just get here as soon as you can, and travel safely, okay?"

"Thank you, Chloe, you're the best."

When Chloe went back out to the living room, Em, looking up at her friend with a hollow, tired expression, said, "I'd like to lay down now." She stretched out on the couch.

"Wouldn't you be more comfortable in your bed?"

Em bit her lip and for the first time her eyes filled with tears. "No?" She said it like a question but there was no question about it. An empty bed without Pete was more than she could bear.

Chloe got her a blanket and a pillow and gently tucked her in on the couch. Em's eyes were already closing. *Thank God for sleep and sedatives*, Chloe thought. "I'll be in the guest room if you need me."

Em just nodded her head without opening her eyes. "Thank you for..." She stopped mid-sentence, exhaustion overtaking all else.

Butter, Em and Pete's golden retriever, came out of the bedroom where she usually waited every night for Em and Pete to come to bed. Without asking for any explanation of this change of events, she walked up to lick Em's face very gently, just one lick, and then laid down quietly beside her. Fudge, their calico cat, jumped up and stretched out on top of the back of the sofa.

"Right." Chloe spoke to the animals. "You've got things covered I see." Butter looked up as if to say goodnight and waved her thick tail once before laying her head down between her paws with a massive sigh.

"Whoever thinks that animals don't understand everything we say and do must just not be paying attention, Butter." Chloe walked with weary footsteps down the hall to the spare bedroom, trying not to turn her head as she passed Em and Pete's empty room.

$$\sim 3 \sim$$

Sophie was outside waiting for a taxi after a long night of trying to sleep sitting in an airport chair followed by spending another three sleepless hours on the plane. She was tempted to ignore Em's request to visit their dad, as it felt more urgent to get to her sister, but Chloe reassured her over the phone that Em was still fast asleep. The prior day's events had hit her square on.

As Sophie sat in the backseat of the cab on her way to the assisted living facility where her father had been living for the past two years, she thought about her relationship with her only sibling and everything she was going through right now.

Em and Sophie were born seven years apart but sometimes they felt more like twins, even though they were nothing alike. Em had red hair and green eyes, was tall and slender, and a worrier by nature or maybe by circumstance. Sophie was blonde with brown eyes like their father, was short and curvy, and never failed to take a risk when it appeared. Despite their differences, they read each other's thoughts from long distances. They knew, just as twins do sometimes, when the other was hurt or sick or lonely. If Em fell in a puddle Sophie got wet. That's just the way it was with them and they didn't question it.

As the cab stopped in front of Quiet Acres Assisted Living, Sophie took a deep breath and got out. Once inside, she approached the petite, dark-haired woman sitting behind the reception desk.

"You're looking well, Maria," Sophie greeted the woman who smiled up at her in return. She made a habit of being friendly and kind with everyone who crossed her path, a quality she'd learned from her dad. She sighed as she headed down the hall to her father's room. It always pulled at her heartstrings to visit him here. It was a beautiful place and they took excellent care of him, but just the fact that he was here was something Sophie found difficult to accept, even now. Her steps felt heavy with the weight of the news she had to share with him.

She knocked gently at the door to her father's room since it was partially closed. "Dad? Are you decent? I'm coming in now." Even though her dad was not in charge of his mind anymore, he still carried a deep sense of privacy about himself. He wouldn't want her to see him even a little bit disheveled in appearance or partially dressed. It was the officer in him she supposed. Bounce a dime on his sheets and all that.

"Hi, Dad, it's me, Sophie. How are you doing?"

"Sophie, come here and let me look at you. It's been such a long time." Sophie let out a big sigh. At least today he knew her. When she'd been there a few months ago, he'd thought that she was one of the attendants at this "establishment where he had been detained" as he put it. No matter how many times his daughters explained it to him, he didn't seem to grasp the idea that he was in a care home to help keep him safe. He thought he was back in the army and that he was being detained for some reason. Fortunately, he had no sense of time, so every day to him was another day when he might be "discharged."

She sat with him for a while, looking out the window at a light snow that had fallen over everything the night before. Her father looked at it as if he'd never seen snow before. She reached over and took his hand.

"Dad?"

"Mmm? Yes, Em?"

"Dad, look at me. It's Sophie, not Em. But I have to tell you something about Em."

Her dad looked at her then. "She's not hurt, is she? My little Emerald didn't end up in a car accident driving that fool Mustang, did she? I told her that 16 was too young for her own car."

"Dad. Em is grown up remember? She lives down the road with her husband Pete."

Her father said nothing but nodded.

Sophie swallowed hard, twice. "Dad, Pete is, well, he's gone."

"Gone where? Has he joined the service? I always told that young man you're not a man until you've joined the service."

"No, Dad, he's gone..." she choked back tears as she spoke, "... to heaven. He had a heart attack yesterday."

Her father said nothing at first and Sophie thought maybe he hadn't heard her. She just watched him staring at the snow. "My little girl is going to be very sad. She loved that boy. Loved him from the first day they met."

Sophie, eyes bright with tears, urged him to tell the story once more, a story she'd heard him tell a thousand times. "Do you remember that day, Daddy? Do you remember the story?"

She could see him searching his brain, but the storyteller in him was lost. He shook his head as he struggled. She took his frail hand in hers.

"She met him at the bowling alley... remember, Dad?" Her tears were flowing freely now but his eyes were on the snow and he nodded. "You always said she came home all rosy cheeked and eyes glittering, telling you that she'd met the man of her dreams. You asked her how old he was, and when she said 18, you laughed and said, 'He's no man, he's a boy!'"

Her dad smiled then. "I think that was some time ago now?"

"Yes, Dad, it was some time ago." Sophie choked back the urge to sob, forcing herself to finish the story. "You said they were stuck together like glue after that first night. They wanted to be together all the time and when Pete asked for her hand in marriage, you told him they had to wait until she was 20, which they did. She finished school and he started building their house on the land by the lake that his aunt and uncle had given him." *The house where they still live*, thought Sophie. *The same house where Pete had a heart attack yesterday.*

Sophie thought then about Uncle Walter and Aunt Patricia, Pete's adopted parents, and how they must be taking the news that they'd lost their only child. She could no longer hold back her sobs, sobs that would not stop. Her father squeezed her hand tightly.

"It's okay, honey. You just cry it out. It doesn't hurt forever. At least that's what your mother says." This made her cry even harder. The fact that, in his mind, her mother still lived, even all these years after her death. Her mother never knew Pete at all. She'd died when Em was 17, just a few months before she met Pete. And Sophie had only been 10. In all the ways that mattered, Em was the only mother figure Sophie had ever known.

For a moment, she wished with all her heart that Dad wasn't mixed up, that her mother was still alive somehow and that maybe she could really get to know her. Just then, the smell of lilacs filled the air around them, though the window was closed and there were no flowers in the room.

Sophie looked up from her tears, puzzled. "Do you smell that, Dad?" she asked, but her father didn't answer, lost in his own mind. Suddenly, for no reason, Sophie shivered. Em always told her that lilacs were their mother's favorite flowers.

Finally in the cab on her way to Em's house, Sophie couldn't stop thinking about her dad, seeing his face looking so lost and confused. Though he was much worse than the last time she saw him, oddly she felt a sense of peace about his situation, at least in this moment. There was a strange mixture of relief and sadness in times like this when someone doesn't remember everything. They seem to go along, like he did now, existing in the moment, unaware of what had gone before or what was to come. He didn't have to hold onto the hurt, and for that she was grateful—grateful for the knowledge that, although in those moments she had been with him he might have been thinking about Em, by now he likely would have already forgotten their conversation. He didn't have to breathe every breath, knowing his son-in-law was dead and his daughter heartbroken. Instead, he could just exist in his world of forgetfulness... unlike her, who felt as if her heart was going to break in two.

She allowed herself to think now about the relationship she had lovingly envied for so long; that of Em and Pete. She always told them that they were like pie and ice cream—one without the other was good, but when you put them both together, it was perfection. Somehow, over the nearly two decades that they were married, they learned to strike a perfect balance, enjoying their individuality but equally cherishing their time together. Em had her work as a vet tech and Pete his construction work. On Saturdays, Em taught horseback riding and Pete coached Little League. They both loved working with kids and Sophie thought, not for the first time, what a shame it was they were never able to be parents themselves. She sighed, thinking about all the other people who would be affected by his death. It felt so unreal, almost unthinkable.

She leaned more deeply into the back seat of the cab and couldn't help feeling soothed by the beautiful scenery rolling out before her, as she gazed at the light snow covering the hills and trees. It felt good to be here, despite the reason... good to be away from Myles, who hadn't stopped leaving her texts and calls since she'd left Denver.

She closed her eyes for a moment and suddenly Pete's face came into full view in front of her. Though he was technically her brother-in-law by marriage, he was in every way her brother by heart. And, like any good brother, he was the first one to tell her when she was dating a jerk... every single time, which, unfortunately, seemed to be quite often. She remembered the last time they were together in person. They'd been alone at the lake house while Em was finishing up at work, just a few months before. As they had been walking side by side through the kitchen, too famished to wait for dinner, laughing over something funny that had happened earlier that day when they'd been kayaking, Pete had suddenly changed the subject.

"Myles. What kind of name is Myles anyhow, Soph?"

"Stop it, Pete. It's just a name."

"Maybe so. But a name tells you a lot about a person. At least that's what my Aunt Patricia says." Pete's Aunt Patricia was the salt of the earth type who hung all her laundry, even her unmentionables, baked her own bread, and had a saying for every occasion.

"What's your point, Pete? You don't like his name? So what?" She tried to sound defensive but it was impossible to be mad at Pete. The

man had the heart of a giant.

"I mean, look kiddo..." Oh boy. When he called her kiddo there was definitely a lecture coming. "I don't want to butt into your life but..."

"But you are about to."

Pete stood behind her and put his hands on her shoulders as she turned to face the view of the lake. "It's just, Soph, you're like a kid sister to me, you know? And I want you to have what Em and I have. You deserve everything. And I just don't think Myles is the one to give it to you."

Sophie turned around then to look at him, her eyes filled with pain. "Not everyone can have that, Pete. Don't you know how special you two are? How rare that is?"

Pete reached up then and rubbed his head and sighed. For a moment he looked at the floor, as if willing the right words to come jumping out of the floorboards. Finally, he turned clear blue eyes to latch onto her deep brown ones. "Yeah, as a matter of fact, I do. But because of that, I know it's real. It does exist. And I just don't want you to settle, Sophie. Please."

This time it was Sophie who looked away as she felt her eyes well up with tears. "Point taken and noted, Pete, ok?" She forced herself to sound cheerful. "Come on, let's go sit out on the porch and have a beer while we wait for Em. It's too beautiful outside to be standing here in this kitchen!"

As Pete grabbed two beers out of the fridge, Sophie picked up the tortilla chips and salsa, already heading towards the sliding glass doors that led to the back porch.

Sophie literally shook herself then in an attempt to force her thoughts back to the present moment as the cab pulled up in front of Em and Pete's home by the lake. But even as she approached the front door, she couldn't help but wonder why, when it came to choosing men, she and Em were oceans apart.

〜 4 〜

*P*ete had always been just Pete—never Peter, which was his given name, not P.J., for Peter James, and most certainly never Petey, although Em sometimes called him that when she wanted to get him to chase her around the house. Sure enough, it always worked.

He was a loner in school and at home. He lived with his Aunt Patricia and Uncle Walter ever since he could remember. He had parents, that was true enough, judging by the photographs, but he never remembered meeting them. He'd long since stopped wondering if he ever would.

They were so young when they had him and they both had dreams of living their lives on the road. Way too adventurous to be taking a child with them everywhere, they left Pete in the kind care of his Aunt Patricia and Uncle Walter McAllister, two hard-working people who, as it turned out, couldn't have children of their own. Pete's biological father, Billy, was the younger brother of Walter but that was where the similarity ended. Unlike Billy, Walter was the type of man who kept his eyes on the task ahead and nothing in this world would deter him from it. He worked from Monday through Saturday building *and remodeling houses, and on Sundays he went to church with Patricia and spent the rest of the day tinkering in his shop, making furniture. It was his passion and he was very good at it.*

Pete thanked heaven for Walter and Patricia every single day. That was one thing they taught him as a child, to always count your blessings. He cringed to think what would have happened to him if they hadn't taken him in. So grateful was he that he devoted himself to them even as a young boy, and as he grew older, he began learning Walter's business. He worked on jobs with his Uncle Walt from the time he could hold a hammer. And he held joy in his heart for what he did in life and where he was. He missed not knowing what had happened to his parents, who never showed up or even called, and he felt an emptiness around it from time to time, but mostly he was just happy for the life he'd been given.

Aunt Patricia always said he was an unusual boy. He used to hear her talking to her women friends in the kitchen when they came over for coffee. "Pete is different than most boys. It's as if he was born a grown-up instead of a little boy. He has a light about him that I've only seen or felt before... well, when I pray. His parents have no idea what they missed. But I'm so thankful that he came to be with us."

Whenever Pete heard his aunt talk about him this way, a wise part of him understood, and was thankful too.

Before he knew it he was 18 and about to graduate from high school and go to work for his uncle full-time. It was then that he met Em. Although his growing-up years had been pleasant, nothing compared to the day he met her. Even before he knew he was looking for his true love, there she was and ever since she'd been the answer to all of his dreams and more.

It's just that now, since he no longer had a body, it meant that he couldn't touch her anymore, couldn't talk to her, at least not so she could hear him. All he wanted to do was be able to comfort her like he always did and to let her know everything was going to be alright.

Life was a strange thing, he thought—and death even stranger than that.

$\sim$ 5 $\sim$

Em could still hear the voices swirling around inside her head like dark clouds—the consoling words of her friends, her family, the parents of Pete's Little League team, his staff at work... so many words that had left her feeling empty and aching inside. The memorial service had been endless. The stoically sad faces of Aunt Patricia and Uncle Walter were the worst to bear. Em didn't know she could feel this tired.

When the family finally left for the day, Em sat mutely on the couch, mindlessly petting Butter, while Sophie took a shower. Initially, she had felt so much better after Sophie's arrival, but that had quickly worn off with the stress of today. Now she just felt annoyed that Sophie had left her alone, even though she didn't want to talk to anyone, or look at anyone, or in any way try to act normal. Not tonight, maybe not ever. How could anything be normal again?

Though her body was exhausted, her mind refused to quiet and pretty soon exhaustion turned to anger. This is how it was. Her emotions were like a Tilt-a-Whirl, one minute one way and the next spinning round in the opposite direction. "Pete, if you can hear me, I'm pretty pissed off at you right now. How could you go and do this to me?" She looked at Fudge, who sat on the chair near her, silent and blinking... somehow it made Em feel as if she were being judged. "That's just great, Fudge. Just for once you could agree with me you know?" She knew she was acting crazy and she didn't care. She felt as though if she didn't do something, she would break into a million pieces. She wished she could go to the barn where she taught lessons, get on one of the horses, and just go galloping through the fields, but it was dark outside, and besides, she didn't have the energy to go anywhere. Instead, she sat rocking to and fro on the couch, holding tightly to a pillow. It seemed there was no escaping the pain. She wished there was a way she could rip it right out of herself.

Just then she heard her sister's voice.

"Em? Are you still awake?"

Em made a low grunting sound like an animal in pain. "Sleep would be too easy right now. At least when you sleep you stand a chance of... forgetting. That is, unless it catches up with you in your dreams."

Em could always play it straight with Sophie, and after all the politeness she'd had to endure today when she'd felt like screaming every second instead, she wasn't about to pull any punches just now.

Sophie sat down next to her and put a hand on her sister's shoulder, but Em just brushed her away. "Sophie, why? Why in the hell did this happen? I just don't understand!"

"I don't know, Moo." Sophie hadn't called her sister Moo

in a very long time. When she was really little, she had a favorite stuffed animal, a baby calf that said "Moo" when you squeezed its belly. It had been Sophie's first word, even though at first it came out like "Ooo" until she learned to make the M sound. Then she started calling everything Moo, including Em. After a while the name just stuck.

It was that one little word that did her in completely. "It's just not... fair! I loved him so much. I love him so much still!" Em's face became soaked with tears, every single one that she had been holding back all day long. Amidst heavy sobs, she choked out, "He's... supposed to be... here. He... promised nothing... bad... would happen. He promised!" Her sobs subsided but then her whole body started to shake. Sophie reached out again and this time Em let her hold her close.

"I know, Moo. I know." Sophie stroked her sister's red curls. And after a while, she said, "I loved him too."

Her sister's words kicked Em into a different gear, one in which she stopped thinking just about herself. She sat up straighter and hugged her sister tightly. They stayed like that for a long time, sobbing together, until eventually they both started groping for some tissues.

"Where's your tissues, Em? You always have loads!"

"Used them all up I guess. Lots of crying going on." Em and Sophie looked at each other then and suddenly both burst into laughter. "Aw, come on, Em. We have to get out of here for a while. Let's take a hike around the lake."

"It's pitch dark and it's freezing!"

"We'll take a flashlight. And we'll dress warm. I'm sure Butter will like it. What do you say, girl? Would you like a walk?" At the word walk, Butter ran to the front door and began to spin in circles, carrying her leash in her mouth.

"How long can you stay, Sophie??"

Her sister just shrugged and smiled. "As long as you need me, Moo."

⚬ 6 ⚬

Pete had always imagined that heaven was a fun place, a place where everything was smoothed out and all you felt was love, not pain for the ones you left behind, not confusion about why you left so soon. Now he wasn't so sure. As if someone were reading his thoughts, he heard a voice behind him.

"It is a place of love here, Pete, but there is an adjustment period, both for you and for your loved ones. It's our job just to witness and help when we can." Pete sensed, without using his eyes, because he was seeing in a very different way now, a very large presence next to him. And there were colors too, colors that weren't on Earth. So much golden light mixed with all of these other colors. The words seemed to be coming from one of the larger swirls of golden light, and he recognized it as the same light he'd seen the day he left Earth. He realized then that he could speak without really speaking. "Excuse me, but how did you know what I was thinking?"

A sound that was like a hundred tiny bells tinkling in a soft breeze emanated from that light and Pete knew it was the Being laughing. The sound seemed to reverberate out into the Universe, again and again. "Do you think that such communication is so difficult? I could hear you when you were still in a body as well. You could hear me too. You just didn't always know how."

Something clicked and he knew the Being was right. He remembered the day in the shower just before he'd blacked out. He'd heard that same voice then, at the same time he'd started to feel pains in his chest and it was hard to breathe. He was scared, more afraid than he'd ever felt in his life, and then he'd heard the voice, only it was inside his head somehow. "It will soon be time to go, Pete. You don't need to worry though. Everything is being taken care of." He remembered thinking that maybe he was losing it, and then he heard the Being again, when he was in the operating room. He remembered looking down at his body on the surgery table and it all felt so strange, yet somehow comforting. And he'd sensed that the Being was beside him then too. And now he was here, and it was all so very beautiful—the colors, the love, the feeling of unity with all things—yet confusing too, because now he just didn't know how to help Em anymore.

"You and she will be able to communicate, Pete. It will just take some time for things to adjust. Trust, Pete. Have some trust." Then the Being was gone. If the Being was right, he knew he had to find a way to connect with his Em. He had to try and he would.

❧ 7 ❧

m knew after two weeks that it was time to go back to work though she was still carrying her sorrow heavily. Being with horses had always been very healing for her, not to mention that she needed something to do other than sit and think about Pete. On her first day back at the vet hospital, she worked hard all day, keeping her mind focused on one task after another, then went with Sophie and Butter for a long walk. Before bed, she reached up on tiptoe to get her journals from the shelf in her closet. It had been a long while since she'd allowed herself to write. Pete was always after her about writing, urging her to put words on paper.

"You have a gift, Em. Well let's face it... you have a lot of gifts. But the way you write, well, it's just a waste for you not to do it!"

Pete used to buy her beautiful journals, one each year for Valentine's Day or her birthday, or anytime he saw one that was really special. Em loved to write, even though she thought of Sophie as the writer in the family, by way of her job in journalism.

But she was usually too busy doing something for someone else. The horses. Pete. Her dad. Butter or Fudge. The kids she taught to ride on Saturdays. There was always something in the way of writing, and by the end of the day, all Em wanted to do was spend time with her precious Pete. And, if she were honest with herself, there were just things she didn't want to write down, because she didn't want to remember them. Yet somehow she'd accumulated a closetful full of journals, their pages filled with writing.

As she pulled down the box of journals and spread them out on the bed, she realized how much life was there. Ideas, stories of their lives, many happy times and some sad ones. She had each journal marked carefully with what she wrote about in them or the period of time they covered. The journal at the bottom of the box, the one she'd written in after her two miscarriages, was one she usually opened just to read a few pages, as if to remind herself of the pain, of what could have been.

She held that journal in her hands, but instead of thinking about her babies just then, it was Pete who filled her thoughts, her heart. The first time she'd met him was not long after her mother's passing, and she remembered how gentle he'd always been with her about it, even though he'd never really known his own birth parents at all. Pete was the most well-adjusted person she'd ever known, and he'd made her feel safe, like she'd found home.

From the very first, Em and Pete were inseparable. Even though he lived 30 minutes away, was out of school, and didn't have his own car, they found a way to see each other. He took the train to her town after work and she walked in the cold to meet him on many nights that first winter. There was a diner where they would go and sit side by side and talk for hours. The owner, Maggie, was a fan of true love and never kicked them out, despite the fact that they hardly ever spent any money in there. Sometimes she even gave them free donuts.

"Pete, what's going to happen when I graduate and go to vet tech school?" She chewed nervously at one of her long copper curls as she spoke. Pete had graduated the year before and was working full-time for his Uncle Walt in his construction business.

"Nothing is going to happen, Em. I will just be working and you'll be going to college. We'll still see each other as much as we can."

Em hated change. Change usually meant someone in her life went away. She liked the security of knowing things would always be the same. She looked at him and frowned.

He took her hand and stroked her fingers with his other one. "And in the meantime, I'll be saving my money and in a few years we'll get married... I hope?" He grinned sheepishly and she grinned back. "Just as soon as I can convince your dad to allow it, that is."

Em caught his sweet smile trying to wipe her worries away but it didn't work. "I know that's the plan, Pete. But what if..." and she stopped, afraid to even think about all the what ifs. Life had taught her at a very tender age that things could turn on a dime when you least expected it.

Pete took her face between his hands and touched his forehead to hers. "No what ifs, Em! Nothing is going to go wrong. Everything will work exactly as we planned. Two kids, a little house near your dad, the

whole thing. It's going to be perfect. We will live happily ever after."
Pete, just barely 19 years old at the time, wasn't as sure of himself as he
seemed. He knew that life could always change, just as Em did. But he
had to tell her this so she wouldn't worry. He hated when she worried.

Em had believed him then, but even so, deep down in her gut, she'd had a nagging feeling that things were going to turn out differently. She put down the journal about her miscarriages and picked up another—one that she'd written long ago, just after her mother died. Sitting down on the bed, Em spoke out loud. "Our happily ever after didn't last long enough, Pete. You promised me that nothing was going to happen. Not like it did with my mother." As she rubbed her thumb across the pages of the well-worn leather journal, her thoughts shifted to that of the woman who she'd known for the first 17 years of her life as her mother.

Even now, 22 years after her mother's death, there was much she didn't understand about her mother's life or her death. Eva Watts, in her younger years, had been a beautiful, joyful, captivating woman, full of life and hope. At least that's what her dad told her, though she herself remembered much more clearly the sad, silent woman who sat smoking in the kitchen and who slept a lot.

She also remembered the day she took to her bed and never left it again, not until the life was gone from her body. After that, no one really spoke of her in their house, not her dad and certainly not Sophie. Sophie was ten years old but it had been several years since Eva acted like a real mother to her. She was more like a ghost moving through the house. And Em unconsciously took over that job, even though she herself was but a young teen at the time.

Em held the journal tightly in her hands but refused to open it and unleash those memories. Not today, she told herself. Today her pain over losing Pete was more than enough, although the memories of the two of them, both gone from her life, were somehow mixing and swirling together in her head.

Pete had been right about one thing. He always said writing was her medicine and, though she'd often neglected it, she knew now it was just the medicine she needed most. "Today is the day," she declared to Butter, who lay looking up at her, and she reached into the box, picking out a fresh new journal, filled with beautiful blank pages, and sliding the box back up onto the shelf. She held the journal, smiling down at the front cover decorated with lavender and white wildflowers, grabbed her favorite pen, and padded out to the porch in her slippers.

She let out a heavy sigh, though, as she sat down on the wicker rocking chair. She looked over at Pete's empty chair and then back at the lake. She couldn't even begin to count how many hours the two of them had spent sitting side by side on this porch. It had always been her favorite spot in the house, but now it felt like the loneliest place in the world.

Butter sat at her feet and she could feel the soft swish of her tail, as if she were waiting. "Come on, Mom, snap out of it. Let's have some fun for a change," the dog seemed to say. Em bent down and kissed her forehead, pausing for a long moment, then sat up straight, picked up her pen, and began to move her hand across the page.

Dear Pete,

It's only been a few weeks since you've been gone from my life and it already feels like an eternity. I am going to go crazy if I can't talk to you anymore, so I will talk to you this way, even if it doesn't make any sense or if you can't hear me. But I think you can, right? I mean that's what they say anyway. I never thought I'd hear myself saying this, but I feel the need to learn more about what happens now. For you I mean. Like where you are and what you are doing and if you are okay.

I was thinking today about our wedding day. Do you remember, Pete? Well of course you do. I mean how could you forget that day! Everything that could go wrong did. Your best man had a hangover and didn't show up at all. Your Uncle Walter had the stomach flu and was throwing up during the service out behind the church. I ripped my dress on a nail on my way in the door. I was so upset! I thought it was a bad omen or something! I never told you this before, but when that happened I thought about turning around and running in the other direction. I was so scared to get married anyway. I mean because of my mom. I know my dad loved her more than anything, but marriage didn't exactly seem to work out for her so well. I never understood the look she had in her eyes when she thought no one was watching, like she was missing something. I swore growing up that I never wanted to marry and have that empty look she wore some days.

And then... I opened the back door of the church to peek down the aisle and I saw you standing there in your suit and tie. You hated that suit so much! And you didn't know I was looking at you but the expression on your face was so peaceful and happy and excited, as if someone just told you that you were marrying a Princess. And then you saw me, remember? You saw me peeking at you and you broke out into that big grin with those two dimples on one side of your face, and it was all over. I knew there was no place I could ever be except right next to you. No matter what. How I wish I could be there now, right beside you, wherever it is that you are.

Em had to stop writing for a few minutes because her paper was getting wet from her tears. She thought for a moment that this was too hard, writing to him, but she couldn't stop herself. It was as if it were her only solace, her only thread to him. She wrote and wrote as if she could extract him from the page somehow. A long while later, when her hand hurt from writing, she decided to finish the letter.

So I guess in some ways you got your wish. I'm writing again, even though it's probably a lot of emotional garbage. But I'm writing to you, so that can't be all bad, my dear Beloved. I will write again soon.
For now, for always, forever.
Your Em

$$\sim 8 \sim$$

Eight months later

Em changed her shorts for a pair of jeans before taking Butter for an after-dinner walk. She looked at the trees, so close to changing colors, and just couldn't believe it was almost autumn. It had been nearly eight months since Pete "crossed over" as they called it in the after-death communication books she'd devoured by the dozens. Unbelievable. So much had changed and yet so much remained the same.

Em still worked at the vet hospital though she'd cut back some of her hours to spend more time with her ailing father. Sophie finally broke things off with Myles over the summer and had moved to North Carolina permanently. It took Myles screwing up several more times, the last time being the worst, that made Sophie decide. While leaving Colorado had been difficult for her at first, it turned out to be a very good thing for both women at the end of the day. Living together had its perks and they could share the responsibility of looking after their father. He got many regular visits these days, though he communicated less and less.

When she got back from her hike with Butter, she poured herself a glass of iced tea and made her way to what was soon going to be her writing room. It was a small space upstairs that had been Pete's office once upon a time and it had one of the best views of the lake in the whole house. Em had finally found the courage to begin to clear out some of Pete's things and she was going through all of the piles of papers on his desk so that she could transform it into a writing space. She loved the idea of sitting where he'd sat and continuing to write to him.

Letters to Pete were the only thing that had saved Em from falling apart all of these months. Family and friends, especially Sophie and Chloe, helped a lot of course, as did the four-leggeds constant love and companionship, but in those moments when she thought she couldn't stand another day without Pete, writing to him was the only thing that eased her soul. Mostly she wrote down her memories of them, going through old photographs, cards, and other memorabilia... anything to spark her memory about something she might have forgotten.

Most of her letters started with, "Do you remember... ?" She knew that sometimes people didn't want the memories of someone they lost to remind them of their grief, but she, on the other hand, wanted to remember and record everything, bring every moment into fresh feeling so that somehow, if she could keep the memories alive, she wouldn't lose him forever.

She didn't tell anyone, except for Sophie, but she continued to hold onto the belief that if she wrote to him long enough, he would communicate with her. Aside from writing, she continued to read everything she could get her hands on regarding after-death communication and near-death experiences. Sometimes she knew that Sophie thought she was obsessed and possibly needed therapy, but for Em this was her therapy, her way through the dark hours. She wanted to learn as much as she could about where Pete was and what it was like there. If she just knew he was okay, maybe... maybe it would somehow ease the deep pain around her heart.

After three hours and several iced teas later, she was cleaning out the last of Pete's desk drawers, keeping what was important or particularly sentimental and shredding the rest, when she found it. A huge whoosh went out of her lungs until she felt there was no air left to breathe. She couldn't believe what she was holding in her hand. It was something they'd talked about, something they'd dreamt of doing. She thought of the many times they sat together on their back porch, imagining how wonderful it would be to go on a real second honeymoon for their 20th wedding anniversary. A trip to Ireland, the land where her mother was born. Em always thought it was just a happy dream. She never imagined they would really be able to do it. And yet, here it was in black and white, all the dates, the arrangements, the tickets, everything. She looked at Butter, lying at her feet. "How did he keep this from me, Butter?" The tears streamed down her face and onto the pages she held in front of her.

When Sophie came back from her walk, she found Em sitting in her favorite chair on the screened porch, the papers now in her lap, staring out across the lake. Before Sophie could speak, Em silently handed her the papers.

Sophie sat in Pete's chair and looked quickly through them. "Your trip? Your trip to Ireland? Your second honeymoon trip?" She looked up to see her sister nodding, tears streaking her cheeks. "Aww, Moo." She leaned in toward her sister, taking her hands. "You just found this?"

Em nodded through her tears. "He planned it all, Sophie. Every last detail is taken care of."

Sophie looked back at the papers now in her lap. "You're right. It looks like he arranged everything! There's even a note here about staying at a cottage in West Cork. That's where Mom grew up, right?"

"Yep. The cottage is on the farm where she grew up. Our Aunt Brigid lives there. You probably don't remember her. She was here for Mom's funeral."

"I kind of remember a stiff woman with a long black skirt. I remember she scared me and I didn't want to go near her."

That made Em laugh. "That was Aunt Brigid. She is rather formidable, though she can't be all bad because I know she and Mom were close. I don't really know her though. She never came to visit except for Mom's funeral, and we never went there. Mom talked about her sometimes but it always seemed painful for her to talk about anything to do with Ireland."

Sophie couldn't stop looking at all the details of the trip

Pete had planned. "And you didn't know anything about this?"

Em shook her head. "We'd been talking about this trip for simply years, but I had no idea that he'd planned it all out. He must have wanted to surprise me. What surprises me most is that he managed to keep it a secret. He never was good at keeping anything from me." She leaned her head back and her lips curved upwards, coaxed by memories of him.

Sophie rifled through the pages. "It's in a month from now!"

Em sighed. "I guess I'll have to figure out how to cancel everything."

Her sister was silent for a few moments. "Hang on a minute. What if you go anyway?"

Em's laugh was not one that held any mirth. "Go on a honeymoon without a husband?"

Sophie leaned forward again, earnest to make her point heard. "Not a honeymoon. Just a trip, already paid for and planned out. It's Ireland, Em! Ireland. The place where Mom was born. Like you said, you've been talking about going for years."

"I've always wanted to go... with Pete." There was a dull bitterness to her voice.

"I know. I know. Just think about it, okay? It was a big dream of his, too, you know that. Deep down he knew that you've always had a strong desire to know more about our mother's upbringing. I really think he'd want you to go."

Em nodded, mostly so they could stop talking about it. "I'm going to take Butter for a walk. Be back in time for dinner."

Sophie watched her go and sent up a prayer, to Pete, to God, to whomever would listen.

The more Em thought about it, the more confused she became. One day she thought Sophie was right, she should go, and the next day she thought the whole idea was completely insane. She did the one thing she knew how to do. She decided to ask Pete. That night before bed, she sat on the porch after dark, the lamp beside her giving just enough light for her pen to find its way across the page.

Dear Pete,

Do you remember when... ha ha here I go again. Do you remember when we used to write letters to each other when we were first dating? It was so silly in a way because we only lived 30 minutes apart, and yet I cherished those letters so much. We wrote the things that were hard to say to one another in the immaturity of youth. The yucky love feelings. I haven't had the courage to look at them again but one day I will.

You know why I'm writing you all these letters right? Just in case you haven't figured it out, it's because I want to connect with you, wherever you are now. I want to hear from you, Pete. I've been trying to remember my dreams because what I've been reading says that dreams are often when people who've crossed over connect back with the ones they love here on Earth. I even drink a lot of water just before bed so I have to wake up a lot. I keep a notebook by my bedside, just to record any messages or dreams you might send my way. Pretty pathetic pastime, eh?

Because you see, Pete, I've been trying to pick up the pieces and go on, but I can't be happy anymore without you or at least without being able to talk to you, to know you are alright, that you made it to wherever it is you've gone. I want to tell you one more time how much I love you, how deeply you are a part of me. I want to ask how to go on without you, how to be happy, how to feel anything anymore. Because I don't, you see. All I feel is numb inside, like a hollow bone.

Anyway, here it is, almost eight months later, and you still haven't contacted me—not a dream or message or anything. I don't know, maybe you're busy getting used to things where you are. I read about that too. But even if you aren't going to talk to me, I'm going to keep talking to you, whether you like it or not, Mister!

At this point, Em stopped writing and half laughed, half cried for a few minutes. How crazy was she anyway? She was sitting here telling off her dead husband.

Oh Pete, you know I'm not cross with you for not talking to me. I just wish we'd had more time together. And I wish you hadn't gone so suddenly without any warning. We were cheated out of our goodbye; we were cheated out of so much. I was angry with you for a while for dying on me but I realize now it wasn't your fault.

So the question right now, besides all of that, is this trip to Ireland that you planned! I am so confused. One part of me thinks I should go out of respect to the memories of us and another part of me thinks it's the worst idea ever, taking a second honeymoon without my husband. Any advice would be appreciated.

For now, for always, forever
Your Em

She put down her pen, turned out the light, and went to sleep almost immediately.

$$\sim 9 \sim$$

October 2005

*E*m and Pete were out on the Neuse River in a sailboat. Pete knew boats as well as anyone and he always wanted to take Em sailing, but Em never wanted to go. She liked their safe little lake and kayaking across it. She didn't like big ocean waves and knew nothing about sailing, though she'd watched Pete do it many times before.

"Em, I don't get it. You climb on those horses all the time and they can be so unpredictable. At least with a boat you're in control of what's happening." As he spoke, a gust of wind blew the boat sharply to one side. Once Pete got it back into balance, Em gave him a withering look.

"In control huh? Pete, we are on the ocean. The ocean is in control! That's the part I don't like!"

"We aren't on the ocean, we are on the river."

"But the river is connected to the ocean."

"Just sit down over there, Em. I have everything under control.

And remember you have a life jacket on, rather tightly too I see."

"I do, but I'd still prefer not to end up in the water. You know I'm afraid of the ocean."

"Yes, ma'am." Pete grinned then and she could never resist that grin, part boy and part man. She forgot her fears and relaxed into the beauty of being on the water and the safety of being with Pete.

They enjoyed a few hours sailing time on the river and just as they were starting to head back towards the shore, some weather kicked up and the water got really rough. The boat started to swing wildly from one side to the other. Pete motioned to Em to go below and he started to take the sails down.

As he was doing so, a huge gust came at him and he was nearly blown off the deck. Em watched in horror from the window below and started to yell Pete's name.

Just when she was ready to run up onto the deck to help him, she saw he'd grabbed onto the rail of the sailboat and righted himself. He quickly tied off the sail then and came below with her.

She clutched him tightly to her and found they were both shaking, he with the cold and she with fright. Fortunately, they always kept extra clothes on board and soon he'd changed his wet clothes for a soft flannel shirt and dry blue jeans. She grabbed him and pulled him towards the small table where they sat huddled together inside and waited out the storm.

It was over almost before it started and when they reached the shore safely, Em was still feeling shaken, so they sat in Pete's truck for a while before making the drive home. They ate the sandwiches they'd brought and just sat in silence.

"I'm sorry, baby. I should have come back to the dock sooner. I

thought we'd be back before the storm kicked in but I miscalculated." She could tell that Pete felt awful about everything so she tried to make light of it. But inside all she could think of was what would happen to her if she lost Pete.

It wasn't until a few days later that she brought up the subject with him. They'd had a great day at their house swimming in the lake and now were sitting on the dock, drying off.

"Pete, I want to ask you something."

"Anything babe, you know that. Just ask." Pete was in a really good mood.

"You know what happened the other day..."

"Ah, Em, I told you..."

"Shhhh." She put a finger to his lips and smiled sweetly. "It's okay, really it is. But it got me thinking. If something would happen to you, if you would leave me before your time..."

Pete's jaw set into a tight line and his eyes bore into hers. "Em, that's not going to happen! I promise you. I'm not going anywhere without you! Why do you think such things?"

"Just hear me out. If something were to happen to one of us, I just want to know that we have a plan."

"Well you know I have the life insurance policy to pay off the house for both of us."

"I don't mean that, Pete. I mean a plan for us to connect with one another."

"There's a plan for that?"

"I mean it, Pete. I know in my heart that we can never be really separated even by death. But I want us to let each other know, right now, how we will communicate with the other person after we die."

Pete was too busy living life to the fullest to think about such things. He lived in the moment. He was young, active, and healthy. But when he looked in those emerald green eyes he loved so much, he could see what this meant to her. He could never refuse her anything. "Ok, so what's the plan?"

"Well, I will appear to you whenever you are near water, for obvious reasons," gesturing at the lake before them.

"Are you wearing something see through?"

"Pete!" She punched his arm playfully.

"Ow!" He flinched as if she'd hurt him and she frowned. "Ok, ok. So you appear near water. What else? How will I know it's you?"

"You'll feel my touch or hear my voice." She was making things up as she went along. She really didn't know how it all worked. But she knew what was in her heart. "But you'll know I'm there, believe me, I'll make sure you do." Her voice became low and trembled for no reason. "I don't want to ever be without you, even after I die."

He kissed her on the forehead and stroked her hair. "I still think a see-through white gown would be special."

She just gave him a look. "So, what about you?"

"What?"

"How will you come to me if you go first?"

"I haven't really thought about it."

"Pete!"

"Ok, ok... I'll think about it. But first I need to cool off. Thinking about you in that gown is making me hot!" With that, Pete stood up, reached down, picked up Em in his arms, and jumped into the lake.

The moment Em opened her eyes early the next morning, she started laughing out loud. She couldn't believe it... she just couldn't believe it.

Just then there was a knock on her door that brought her out of her reverie.

Sophie peeked her head around the corner of the door. "Em? Are you okay? I heard some noise and wasn't sure if you were laughing or crying!"

Em jumped out of bed and flew across the room to hug her half-asleep sister. "I dreamt about him, Sophie! I finally dreamt about him!"

Sophie rubbed at her eyes. "Dreamt about who? Do you realize it's only 5 a.m.?" But then she saw the sparkle in her sister's eyes.

"C'mon let's have some tea and I'll tell you every detail!"

"Ok." Sophie tried to stifle a yawn but couldn't help smiling. She hadn't seen her sister this excited about anything in months.

They sat together at the big island in the kitchen, sipping their tea. Sophie rubbed at her eyes, willing herself to fully awaken. "So you had a dream, a pretty great one from the look on your face."

Em let out a happy sigh. "Great doesn't begin to cover it, Soph. All these months and nothing, despite all the letters I've been writing to Pete and all the books I've read, and nothing, until now."

"Tell me."

"It was about a time we went sailing and afterward I had a talk with him about how we would connect if one of us died."

"No way."

"Yes way. I'd forgotten all about that conversation. And now I know for sure."

"You know what?"

"That he wants me to go to Ireland."

"You do?" Sophie was clearly confused.

"He came to me, don't you see? I wrote to him just before I went to sleep and asked him what to do about Ireland and then he came to me in a dream."

"Huh. Wow."

Em laughed and rubbed her sister's head. "You are full of three letters words this morning!"

"You know I'm not a morning person. But I'm really truly happy for you. I've thought all along that you should go. And you know you don't have to worry about anything here. We will all be just fine, right, Butter?" She was tossing occasional Cheerios at Butter's mouth and Butter hadn't missed one yet.

"Don't keep feeding her those!"

"Ok, ok. It's great news, sis. Really. But if you don't mind, I'm going back to bed now." Sophie blew a kiss at Em and waved sleepily as she trailed off towards the hallway, Butter following closely at her heels.

As for Em, sleep was the last thing on her mind. She felt more energy coursing through her body than she knew what to do with. There was a lot of planning to do and no time to waste.

$$\multimap \text{IO} \multimap$$

Em still found it worrisome to think about actually leaving for two weeks, despite her absolute conviction about the rightness of her decision. She'd gone to see her dad that day, hoping she'd be able to make him understand that she was going away.

"Dad?" Her dad was in his room staring out the window at the gardeners, who were mowing the front lawn of the care home.

"Your mother and I have flowers just like that on the side of our house. I better remind her to water them later. It looks like it's going to be hot today." He turned to look at Em. "Will you let her know about the flowers?"

Oh boy, thought Em. *This wasn't going to be easy.* She didn't even know if she should tell him she was going away. "Dad, Mom's..." She started to remind him that her mother was dead, had been for many years, but she suddenly thought better of it.

"Of course, Dad, I'll tell her." She reached over and took her dad's hands in hers. "I have to tell you something, Dad."

He looked at her as if seeing her for the first time. "You

look a lot like her you know. Except for the red hair. Your mother doesn't have red hair."

Em had to swallow the sob that welled up in her throat. "No, Dad, she was, I mean is, dark Irish as you always said. But listen, Dad. I need you to know I'm not going to be able to visit you for a few weeks. I'm going away. I'm going to Ireland, Dad."

Her dad looked at her as though what she just said was the most natural thing in the world. "Good for you. Ireland is a nice place. Will you see Eva's sister there? Horrid woman."

She couldn't keep herself from laughing then. Maybe this wouldn't be as bad as she thought. "Yes, Dad, I will see Aunt Brigid. And I won't tell her you think she's horrid."

"Doesn't matter. She knows already anyhow. Horrid woman. Cold as ice."

Em patted his hand then. "Dad, listen to me. Sophie is going to be here to visit you a lot while I'm gone. She loves you so much, Dad."

"Sophie?"

"Yes, Dad. Sophie, your other daughter, remember?"

"Sophie. She's just a child. Not sure I can bounce her on my knee anymore. My knees are pretty sore you know." He looked down at his legs then, taking one of his hands from Em and rubbing his knee.

"Dad, Sophie is grown up now. And Dad, look at me a minute."

He looked up at her. "Mom is gone now. She died remember? She died a long time ago, when I was in high school."

Her father thought about this for a long moment and she could almost see him searching what was left of his memory. Slowly he nodded. "Yes, she's gone now and it's just you and me."

"And Sophie. The one who is going to visit you."

"Sophie."

"Yes, Dad, Sophie. She'll take care of you while I'm in Ireland and the people here will too, okay?" Em reached over to hug him, placing a gentle kiss on his cheek. He reached up and patted her arm.

"You always were a good girl."

"Sophie will come and visit you in a couple days."

"Tell her to bring me more peanut butter cups. Don't have any more."

"Okay, Dad, I'll tell her. I love you."

Her dad merely patted her arm absently, turning his attention back towards the window, where he'd been watching the gardeners.

As Em walked out the doors into the bright North Carolina sunshine, she thought to herself that she must remember to tell Sophie about the peanut butter cups.

Leaving her dad was bad enough, but leaving Butter and Fudge was possibly the worst part of all. Even having to say goodbye to her sister Sophie wasn't as bad. She and her sister were used to saying goodbye and hello and goodbye again. That's just how their relationship went. No matter where each of them were, near or far, there was always that invisible thread that could never be broken. And of course she knew that she and her animals were connected that way too, but she couldn't talk to them when she wasn't here, or cuddle with them.

As if to confirm her feelings, she looked down at Butter's face while she was packing. Her dog knew exactly what was happening. She laid on the floor with her head between her paws, looking up at Em, her eyes not leaving her for an instant. Fudge, who was sleeping in the empty suitcase on the floor, knew too. They would be like this up until the moment she left, faithfully reminding her that they knew she was up to something.

"But listen, guys, I'm leaving you in the care of the most loving Auntie ever! She will spoil you rotten, you know that, and you'll probably get way more treats than you do when I'm here! You won't even miss me." As she said that, Butter gave her a look that clearly denied the truth of her statement. Em went over to sit with her on the floor for a few minutes. Her packing could wait.

Her four-legged friend reached up and licked her face as she petted her. Suddenly a box under the bed caught her eye. She pulled it out slowly and blew a thick layer of dust off the top. It was a red box trimmed in gold with a gold latch on it. She'd acquired possession of the box and its contents when they cleared out her dad's place, and clearly she'd forgotten all about it till now. She remembered asking him about it during the moving process. He'd become very lucid for a moment, looking directly into her eyes to get her full attention.

"When you go to Ireland, read the journals in this box first. Promise me you will."

When you go to Ireland. Her father had said when, not if, and at the time, she just thought he was confused, but now... she wondered if her father knew about the trip that Pete had planned for them. Was it possible?

She'd forgotten all about the box with the trauma of moving him and his illness. Now she opened it and took out four journals. When she peeked inside one to look at the first page, she recognized her father's large scrawling script. Although his instructions were to read them "first," before she went, Em didn't think she was up for it at the moment, as just seeing his handwriting brought up emotions around his failing health. Instead, she decided tuck them into her carry-on along with her essentials, leaving her clothing for her larger suitcase. She would read them when she got to Ireland. She felt assured that whatever she needed to know, she would find out then instead.

She stayed on the floor with Butter a while longer, talking softly to her, telling her and Fudge where she was going and how long she'd be gone and just how much she loved them.

Fudge kept on snoozing but Butter looked as if she understood, resting her head in Em's lap. Aside from Pete, Butter understood her better than anyone.

Once on the plane and settled in, she got out her own diary

journal to write but instead found herself just sitting and staring out the window, fascinated by watching an evening sky that grew lighter instead of darker as they traveled east. It seemed to take a long time to sink into night. She thought about all the events of the last few weeks. Finding the papers with the arrangements for the trip to Ireland. The dream. Sophie being there, willing and able to take care of the house and the animals and look after their dad. Her sister had insisted that she would go with her the next time Em visited Ireland. "Besides, someone has to hold down the fort here!" Sophie had proclaimed, overriding all of Em's last-minute objections.

Then there was the ease with which her employer gave her the time off from the vet hospital, not to mention her father's journals and the memory of him urging her to read them. So here she was heading "across the pond" for the first time in her life. To Ireland. To feel what it was like to have her feet on the same soil where her mother once walked. To come face to face with the intimidating Aunt Brigid, a woman she barely knew.

Her stomach twisted in a knot of fear mixed with excitement. She'd never traveled anywhere without Pete. Why was she doing this anyway? But as the plane started its descent and the famous Emerald Isle came into view, she knew, despite the large lump in her throat, that there was no turning back now.

You know I'm doing this for you, Pete. It's all for you. I hope I don't regret it. But inwardly she knew this adventure was about so much more. For the first time in a very long while, she allowed herself to think about the few sweet memories she had of her mother as a young girl. Memories of a beautiful dark-haired woman singing her to sleep.

PART TWO

"Ireland—the one place on earth that heaven has kissed with melody and mirth and meadow and mist."

Irish saying

∞ II ∞

E m was bleary-eyed from a night of little sleep on the plane, though the bus ride to the Southwest coast of Ireland had been nonetheless enchanting in every way. Once away from the city of Dublin, the land rolled out before her from the big windows of the bus. A landscape of green fields dotted by small villages that lined either side of the often narrow roads—all was exactly as she'd pictured it, and more. She fought to stay awake, dozing here and there, and each time she opened her eyes it was to even more beauty. By the time she stepped off the final bus, she felt like she'd been born here.

She knew her aunt's driver was to pick her up at the station and she wondered if he would be holding up a sign or something with her name on it so she would know how to find him. She giggled at herself then, as it was just her and two others who got off at the small bus station in the center of the village of Leap in West Cork.

She smiled broadly then as she took her bag from the driver and, looking around, saw a man standing a few feet away, his hand to his Irish cap, giving her a nod and walking her way.

"You must be Miss Emerald," he said with a brogue and a smile. Instantly she felt his warmth and the sudden urge to hug him, but instead she shook the warm hand he offered and nodded. "I'm Jack. Jack O'Reilly. I work for Miss Brigid, your aunt. I'm here to collect you."

"Very nice to meet you, Jack. Thank you for coming to get me."

"Not at all, Miss Emerald, not at all. May I?" He reached for her bags and she nodded. Part of the famous Irish hospitality, she smiled to herself. It'd already begun.

Jack was a man possibly in his late sixties or early seventies even... it was hard to tell, but his agility as he threw the bags into the trunk belied his age.

"How are you findin' Ireland so far?"

"Well, to be honest, I've been napping most of the bus ride here, although what I have seen is beyond lovely. I've never seen so much green and I'm from North Carolina! But I guess you hear that all the time."

"Aye, that I do, but all the same, hearin' it never gets old. She's a beautiful land, that she is."

Jack got her bags sorted and her settled into the back seat, where he insisted she should sit so she could have a view from both sides of the car.

"How far is it to my Aunt Brigid's place?"

"Oh, now, not so far, it's just over the wee hill there. You could walk it if you wanted, either along the road or on the footpath through Brigid's woods."

Brigid's woods! She'd expected a small holding. "How much land does my aunt own?"

"She owns a fair piece around the main house, the cottage where you'll be stayin' and the horse pastures as well as a bit o' the woods."

"Horse pastures?"

She supposed he could read the excitement in her voice because he chuckled then. "Aye, we've a number of horses on the land. Your Aunt Brigid used to be quite the rider in her day, but then so did all the O'Shea's, right on down to your mother. I hear from your aunt that you're a bit of the horsewoman yourself."

"Yes, I guess you could say that. I work at a large animal hospital as a vet technician. I used to have my own horse named Magpie, but she died of a bad colic. I teach lessons part-time at a stable nearby but don't get much time to ride myself. You said you knew my mother?" Em was far more interested in talking about her mother.

Jack laughed. "Everyone knew Eva. It was hard not to know her."

"What was she like then?" Em felt herself holding her breath, waiting for his answer.

Jack didn't say anything for a long moment, as if he was remembering. "Eva was like sunshine on a dark day and Lord knows, we get plenty of those. She had a glow about her, even as a wee girl. She seemed almost from another world, as though at any minute she could just melt into the landscape. You would almost think she was Faerie folk. She was part of everythin' and it part of her." Jack cleared his throat. "But you should be talkin' to your aunt about all of this I imagine, when she's feelin' herself again that is."

His last words about her aunt didn't even register as she'd been suddenly caught up in a vision of her mother as a girl, one that didn't quite match her memory of her as an adult. She felt a tingle go through her. Pete always called them her "knowings." Whenever she got a tingle like that, it usually meant something significant was about to happen. She shook herself, coming back to the present moment. "I'm sorry, what did you say about my aunt?"

"I'm to let you know she's a bit under the weather. Nothin' too serious, mind you, just an ill wind blowin' through her, but she hopes to be feelin' right as rain by tomorrow and she passes along her regrets about not seein' you today. She'll be restin' up at the main house where she lives. She said to tell you that she hopes you have a good first day here gettin' settled in the cottage where your mother spent a good bit of her time." Brigid hadn't actually said all of that, but Jack felt he had to put a good face on things for the young woman's sake.

Em, posed to ask a million more questions about her mother, stopped herself at this turn of events. "Oh, dear, well I do hope she'll be alright!" She didn't know exactly how old her aunt was, only that she was several years older than her mother, so possibly in her early seventies by now.

"I imagine she will be, Miss Emerald, or should I call you by your married name?"

"I prefer just Em if you please."

"Ah, well then *just* Em," Jack smiled at her through the rearview mirror, his eyes twinkling, "since you've just arrived and won't be spendin' any time with your aunt this evenin' I'd hoped you might go to the local pub with me and my nephew Conor for a meal and a bit of craic?"

"A bit of craic?"

He gave a hearty laugh. "It means havin' a good time, sharin' stories, playin' music."

Part of her wanted to say no because she hadn't been social in months, ever since Pete's death. Then she remembered what her sister said to her when she dropped her off at the airport. "Have some fun! Experience life to the fullest in Ireland. Do it for me!!!"

Despite her misgivings, she heard herself say, "Yes, thank you. A bit of craic sounds great."

Jack laughed again. She noticed he laughed a lot and it felt good to be in the company of his laughter. "Grand. We'll come by for you at seven then. And the pub will have food on as well and it'll be my treat, just so you know."

"Oh, that's very kind of you but not necessary!"

"But it is! You're a guest in our country and besides, your aunt would have me head if I let you go hungry on your first night here."

Em couldn't help smiling as she gazed out at the stunning countryside. She felt as though she'd landed in a soft place indeed.

"Oh and once you get settled and rested, you should go and visit the horses. They're right in the field next to the cottage. Get an eye for one that you like for when we go ridin'."

Riding in the Irish countryside? This was getting better by the minute. "You take care of the horses and exercise them too?"

Jack chuckled. "I reckon Conor and I take care of most things these days, and yes, I've been known to sit a horse or two in my day. But there's always loads to do runnin' the place, so if there's one that strikes your fancy, you can ride as much as you want and you'd be doin' me a favor."

Been known to sit a horse or two? She guessed that Jack O'Reilly was being modest and would not be at all surprised if he wasn't some kind of Irish horse whisperer. She could see she'd have plenty to entice her on this journey—the horses, the breathtaking countryside, the warm hospitality, and she was already learning things about her mother. It erased any lingering doubts that she'd had about leaving home.

She wondered briefly if somehow Pete knew that she would be taking this trip solo. But there was no way he could have known... could he? She'd read that people have a choice about when they die and that often they get a feeling about it ahead of time. She wondered if he knew somehow and that's why he worked so hard to arrange this trip, get everything in order, just in case he couldn't go with her. She knew he would want her to feel whole again.

The irony of that thought struck her heart with a tangible force. It was Pete who'd made her feel whole in the first place, after her mother's death. Since then, feeling whole was something elusive, always just out of her reach. And just as that thought was coursing through her mind, she heard Jack say, "Here we are then!" as he pulled up in front of a little cottage hugged by oceans of emerald-green grass. She gazed upon the horses grazing in the field behind the cottage and felt another tingle coursing through her body—and she wondered if Ireland could change all that.

❧ 12 ❧

Em was eager to explore every inch of the cottage. It was an authentic Irish one but unusual in that it had two stories. Jack had told her that the second story was added on some years before when a family who worked for Brigid's father needed a place to live. "The family has long since moved on and Brigid has made sure ever since that the cottage is kept clean and in good repair." Jack's words rang in Em's head as she took in the tidy surroundings.

It held low ceilings on the first floor, a cozy living area complete with wood stove and a small kitchen at the back. Upstairs was a bath and two more rooms—one, a small library of sorts, filled with books and graced with a desk by a window that looked out over the horse fields. A perfect room for writing letters to Pete. Wandering into the other slightly larger room, she was delighted to find a bed situated just under a skylight for viewing the stars at night. No closet, she noticed, but a rack on wheels that would suit, along with a generous dresser with a large mirror.

Its simplicity and lack of clutter gave her a sense of clarity and rightness. She felt at home straight away. Looking at the rows of books, she wondered if they might be her mother's. She liked the idea of her mother being here, in this place that felt so comfortable to her.

The sun was shining through the windows, and even though she should be exhausted after the overnight flight and the long bus ride, she felt exhilarated by being here at long last. She was in Ireland. Ireland! She realized that she hadn't eaten much for hours now, but at that moment, even the thought of food didn't interest her. There was only one thing on her mind. She grabbed her jeans out of her suitcase, changed quickly and ran down the stairs. She found a pair of green wellies conveniently left by the back door and headed outside.

Being a horsewoman all of her life had always left Em more comfortable outside than in. If she didn't spend a good amount of time in the fresh air every day, she just didn't feel like herself. She walked along now to the field behind the cottage, feet sloshing in the soft mud, thinking of the words Jack had spoken about her mother. "Eva was part of the landscape," he had said. "Almost not of this world." The Eva he described did not match her own memories of her mother. Surely something must have happened to change her so drastically from the girl he described as glowing to her memory of the sad woman with the vacant look in her eyes.

All at once her thoughts evaporated as she saw the compact black horse in the field. "Hey beautiful." It was love at first sight as this gorgeous creature with her long feathered legs approached her readily, as if they'd known each other forever. The magic of a horse was something she would never get over and this one looked straight into Em's eyes and the rest of the world faded away under that soulful gaze. Em noticed that the horse was a mare, a very friendly one at that. She touched her velvety nose to Em's outstretched hand and blew on it softly, chewing and licking, a sign that she was conversing with Em, totally relaxed. "I choose you, Princess. I shall ask Jack if I can see the Irish countryside upon your back, okay?" The horse bounced her head up and down then and Em laughed aloud. She stood there for a long time in the shade of the tree behind her, talking to her, telling the mare what brought her there in the first place. The horse was quite a good listener though she half closed her eyes now and then in response to Em's soft stroking of her neck, head, and ears.

"Yes, I see. I'm feeling rather nappish myself. Maybe I'll just sit under this tree for a while and we can be together, okay?"

Em stepped back and found a soft grassy spot under the unusual looking tree, resting her head against it. The tree seemed to make a space for her body, almost molding itself around her. The little mare continued to stand by the fence with her head hanging over the rail, facing Em, cocking a hind leg, and moving into sleep as she stood, content to just be. For a moment, Em wished she had her journal with her so she could write to Pete in that perfect moment, but then she just gave in to the stillness. It seemed so long since she'd just been still at all, really still. She looked out at the green fields and hills beyond in one direction and, glancing to her left, she could see the blue Atlantic churning up waves. She loved their home in North Carolina, but this was undoubtedly the most beautiful place she'd ever been.

After a long while, her tummy started rumbling quite loudly. Even the horse picked her head up at the sound. Em stood up and moved to where she stood, giving her a hug over the fence, with a promise to return soon.

Once back inside the cozy cottage, she thought that before she did anything else, she should let her sister know she'd arrived safely. She filled Sophie in on her journey so far, describing how beautiful Ireland was and began sharing the details of the cottage when Sophie interrupted her.

"Em, it all sounds amazing. But what about Aunt Brigid? Have you met our formidable auntie yet?"

"Well, it turns out she is feeling unwell and won't be seeing me today. But I met Jack and he's a darling guy, you would love him."

"Who's Jack?" Sophie was trying to catch up.

"Jack is Aunt Brigid's driver and takes care of her horses and I'm not sure what else. He picked me up at the bus station today and drove me here to the cottage. And he knew our mother!"

Sophie was silent on the other end of the phone. Even though she'd wanted her sister to take this trip, she realized just now that she wasn't as excited as Em to find out more about their mother. She didn't know why, but she had a feeling that digging up the past, especially her mother's past, might not be such a good idea after all. She hoped she was wrong.

"Did you hear me, Soph?"

"Yes I heard you. I was just... thinking."

"Thinking about what?"

"Nothing important, Sis. Really, I'm happy for you."

Em hesitated for a moment, considering whether or not to push her sister for the truth, but she thought better of it. She knew full well that Sophie's relationship with their mother had been very different from her own. "Anyway, I'm going to the pub tonight for dinner with Jack and his nephew Conor."

Sophie laughed then, practically snorting into the phone. "Woah, going to the pub already! With not one man but two! Fast work!"

"Stop. It's just dinner. Jack is old enough to be my father, maybe even my grandfather. And his nephew is probably married or something."

"Or maybe he's a young single hottie."

"Come on, Sophie, will you be serious? I'm definitely not looking for anything like that! I don't even feel ready to go out, but I couldn't say no. Besides, I think it's what Pete would want me to do."

"It's exactly what Pete would want. You know that. And I'm sorry for teasing you. I'm just excited that you're there, having an adventure."

"Yes I guess I am too. And I do feel... lighter here than I have in months."

"Then enjoy yourself, Em. Stop with the guilt, okay?"

"Ok, I'll try. I wish you were here with me." Em and Sophie

were not only like twins in many ways, but they also took turns being a mother to one another. These past months it'd been Sophie's turn to mother Em and for that she was very grateful. She didn't know what she'd do without her sister.

"I'd love to be there, but this is your trip. Besides, someone has to take dad his peanut butter cups, not to mention cuddle with the two most adorable animals on the planet! Speaking of which, Butter is anxious for her walk. It is only eight a.m. here."

"Right... of course. Give them both a kiss from me. I miss everyone!"

"Stop thinking about us, we're fine! Go have fun! I can't wait to hear all the juicy details!"

13

Em felt a sense of relief having let her sister know she'd arrived safely, and suddenly she could no longer wait to fix some food for herself. She was delighted to find the tiny kitchen well supplied with fresh bread for toast and farm eggs on the counter, along with plenty of tea. The refrigerator was stocked with milk, cheese, butter, and some fresh greens. Though it was just after one in the afternoon by now, she made herself a full breakfast and a pot of Irish tea, and as she sat at the wooden table enjoying every delicious morsel—the eggs yolks orange and rich, the bread homemade and mouthwatering, the tea strong and flavorful—she marveled at how much she loved everything about Ireland already.

When she'd finished her meal and cleaned up, she did exactly what she'd been diligently doing for nine months now. She dug out her journal from her suitcase and sat for a moment, stroking the red leather cover before beginning the next letter to Pete.

Dear Pete,
Well you certainly called this one right. I've only been in Ireland

half a day and already I'm in love with this land. There's something about it, you know? Something that feels like belonging. I've always loved our home in NC and the house where I grew up but they never felt exactly like this does. It's almost a deja vu of my soul. Aunt Brigid has horses, Pete! But you probably already knew that.

I met Jack today, Aunt Brigid's driver. It seems he does a lot more around the place... he takes care of the horses among other things. Tonight I'm going to the pub with him and his nephew. I'll be trying not to picture how it could have been if you were here with me like you should be. I know, I know, there are no shoulds. We always said that didn't we. Live life forward, don't look back too much, or at least not with regret. I want you to know I'm giving it my best shot. And by the way anytime you want to connect with me here, that would be... well... amazing, Pete. See you in my dreams.

Love,

Your Em

When she finished the letter to Pete, she closed the journal and wiped her eyes. She realized all of a sudden that she was really tired.

Em knew nothing more from the moment her head hit the pillow. When she awoke it was getting dark outside. She looked at the clock by her bedside and saw that it was six. One hour until Jack would arrive. She dragged herself out of bed, and, shivering a little, started a bath, quickly opening her suitcases to find something clean to wear. There would be plenty of time for proper unpacking later.

Jack and Conor arrived a few minutes after seven. When she and Conor greeted one another, Em thought about her sister's remark earlier that he might be a young hottie. Young he was, younger than she, she guessed, and handsome in his own way. She smiled to herself, thinking about what kind of spin her sister would put on this one.

"Do you fancy stretchin' your legs a bit? The pub is just down the hill a ways," Jack smiled as he spoke.

"Yes, a walk sounds good." A walk was just what she needed after the long flight and bus ride.

As the three of them started off on foot to "the" pub, Jack explained on the way that even though there were several pubs in the tiny village, O'Flaherty's, situated smack in the center, was the only game in town.

"And it has the some of the finest music in all of southwest Ireland," claimed Conor as they walked companionably in a row of three across the dark road, Jack shining a flashlight to light their way. There was no such thing as street lamps here but the stars were out in abundance on what Em was to discover was an unusually clear and warm night. Em felt comforted by the presence of these two men flanking each side of her, the night sky blanketing them, and the ease of walking down the middle of a road at night without too much worry of a car coming along; come they might but they wouldn't be hell-bent like someone on a highway in North Carolina. Though it was still early days, she thought that she could get used to the pace of life here quite easily.

Conor was friendly, had a good sense of humor like Jack,

and she sensed an openness about him that made her feel instantly comfortable. She guessed him to be about 35.

"Do you have other family here, Conor?"

He shook his head, and she saw a shadow pass over his easy expression. "Just Uncle Jack. My two brothers live in Galway."

"That's why I'm always tellin' him he should find himself a wife and have some wee ones. A bachelor in his thirties has to be thinkin' about it now, eh?" Jack was now walking beside Conor and cuffed his neck in affection as he spoke. Conor's face reddened and he looked upset but was silent. Jack lowered his voice. "It's time, lad. Time to leave the past behind. There's someone out there for you, the right one this time, one who will stay."

"Uncle Jack, please! Enough said." Conor pulled away. Though Em was surprised at Jack speaking so frankly in front of her, she couldn't help wondering about the someone who'd gotten away. Yet she also felt as though she were eavesdropping on a conversation she wasn't meant to hear, so she tried to lighten the mood.

"Is that the village over there?" She pointed to their right. "It looks so alive with all its twinkling lights and so beautiful sitting right up against the sea!" Conor looked over at her, seeing her pure delight, and cracked a smile then, his shoulders dropping visibly and his arms swinging easily once more.

Before they even entered the pub, the music came wafting out into the street. The sounds of fiddle and drum accompanied by a woman's high-pitched voice made her want to start dancing right then and there. Strange, because she didn't see herself as spontaneous in that way, but the music—it held her, it seemed to dig right into her pores like it was part of her DNA, which, in fact, it was. When they walked through the door and saw everyone tapping or bobbing to the music, pints in hand, she felt an overwhelming sense of being exactly where she needed to be.

Conor leaned over to speak in her ear. "What sort of drink would you be having?" She looked up at him, unable not to notice wide eyes that sparkled like two sapphires. "Beer?"

"What kind?"

"Whatever you're having."

When Conor smiled, his whole face followed suit, and as he turned to walk up towards the bar, she felt the wave of attraction that his smile left behind. It disturbed her greatly. She watched as he stood up at the bar and a gorgeous young woman walked over to hug him enthusiastically. They laughed together and the woman placed her hand possessively on Conor's arm. Besides the fact that she was still grieving her husband and had no business feeling attracted to a young Irishman, he probably had a string of girlfriends his own age. She suddenly felt foolish. She shook herself, trying to shake off her feelings like a dog shakes water off his fur, and followed Jack to a table near the band.

They had a great view of the musicians and from the moment she sat down and Conor put a glass in her hands, she felt no need for conversation. Listening to the music was timeless-- the high soprano of the female singer, who reminded her of a bird lighting up a forest with her sound, along with the fiddle player, whose flair provided a framework that held everything together and at the same time infiltrated the group with his own unbounded style. He seemed to coax sounds out of that instrument that were beyond the ability of what it was designed to do. The drummer played a bodhran with a hand that moved in ways she'd never seen before, as if the sound itself had washed across this land for centuries. It was all so familiar and yet so new. She was brought out of her reverie only when Conor asked what she wanted to eat.

Jack looked across at her and smiled and nodded. He could see in her eyes that she had a natural kinship with the music of the land that held her roots. After Conor placed their orders, they sat for a long while, just listening, Jack and Conor conversing now and then but she staying wrapped in the music and filled with the feeling of sheer camaraderie amongst the people in the pub. She nibbled at her fish and chips, which were out of this world, and sipped her pint very slowly, but it was as if she didn't need anything at all. She realized a sense of peace, of being in the present moment, not grieving the past or worrying about the future, and it was a strange and powerful feeling indeed.

Then, in an instant, her mind caught up with her when she looked across the room and saw a couple about the same age as she and Pete locked in an embrace, the man stroking the woman's hair and gently kissing her forehead. In that moment, the feeling of loss came rushing back and it was like a knife to her heart. Silent tears started running down her face and sliding off her jaw. Conor and Jack were deep in conversation and didn't notice at first but then she felt Jack's eyes on her and Conor, who was sitting next to her, leaned in close.

"Is something wrong?" Embarrassed and unable to speak,

she grabbed a napkin from the table, shook her head, and made a dash for the ladies room.

Thankfully no one was in there as she shut herself in one of the stalls and sat down on the toilet, gasping for breath now. She felt as though her heart was going to burst, it hurt so much, and she couldn't breathe properly. She felt so scared and so alone. Then out of the fog that was her brain, she heard the music.

She got up and came out to the sink to quickly splash her face and dry it. She grabbed the door and flung it open to confirm what she thought she had heard a moment ago. It was true, they were playing *When Irish Eyes Are Smiling*. It was the song she and Pete picked to be played at their wedding, in honor of her mother and her own Irish roots. She walked over to the bar so that she could see the musicians. She felt glued to the floor, not moving a muscle. She couldn't risk missing a single beat.

The words washed over her. It felt like someone rubbing a salve on her aching heart, making her want to laugh and cry, shake and shout all at the same time, but instead she just stood there, transfixed. She was dimly aware that her heart pain was easing and her breath was slowing down.

"Pete, did you do this?" She didn't realize she was talking out loud until the man sitting at the bar next to where she was standing turned around.

"What's that you say? Would you like a pint, Miss? Are you alright?"

She looked at him as if in a dream state, nodding her head yes. "What kind would you like?"

"No, no, I don't want a pint thank you. I just meant yes I'm alright." Upon hearing herself say those words, she thought that if this music was Pete's way of connecting with her, she would be alright. But she didn't know for sure. Then, suddenly, she heard a verse of the song that was new to her.

"There's a tear in your eye and I'm wondering why that it ever should be there at all. With such power in your smile sure a stone you'd beguile and there's never a teardrop should fall. When your sweet lilting laughter's like some faerie song and your eyes sparkle bright as can be, oh then laugh all the while and all other times smile and then smile a smile for me."

Em walked back to the table in a daze, not even knowing how she got there. Jack was watching her carefully. Conor was at the bar ordering another round, and the same young woman was laughing by his side.

"Jack, I'm going to walk back now if you don't mind? I think I need some sleep."

"Not at all. I'll walk with you. I've had a long day myself." She just nodded and turned to go, not even aware of Conor's eyes following her out. The walk home was in silence and Jack thankfully knew not to break it with idle chatter.

As soon as she was back in the cottage, there was just one thing on her mind. She got into her pajamas, made a cup of tea, and sat in her bed to write to Pete again.

Pete,

I need to know. Was it you? Were you there tonight and somehow made them play that song just when I needed to remember? I mean, look, I know it's a very popular Irish song so it could have been a coincidence, right? But I've never ever heard that verse before. It was as though you were speaking to me, Pete, directly to my heart. I don't know what to make of it, but I do know one thing. Hearing those words, feeling the feelings of our wedding day again, the mere possibility of connecting with you makes me want it even more, to see you, to hear your voice. I just don't know if I can make it happen by wishing it, but I'm not going to stop wishing. If it was you tonight, thank you. Thank you so much.

Love,

Your Em

As she scribed the last words onto the page, the excitement wore off and she felt weary to the bone. She turned off the light and snuggled in, Irish Eyes still playing in her head and a soft smile on her lips.

✺ 14 ✺

Brigid was awake much of the night with dreams of her sister Eva. Just knowing that the girl Emerald was in the cottage down the road brought up so many memories. She'd finally dozed off after 5 a.m. and was sound asleep when there was a knock on her door. It was too early for anyone to be here. Rosaleen, her housekeeper and devoted friend, didn't usually show up till after 10 a.m. and Jack would be in the stables.

"Who is it?"

"It's Jack. Can I come in, Biddy?"

He was the only one she allowed to call her that. "Just a minute, Jack, I'll be right there."

She didn't want him to see her in bed looking like such a fright. She got up and quickly put on one of her nicer dressing gowns, ran a brush through her hair, and dabbed on a bit of color to her cheeks. Brigid was not a vain woman, but when it came to Jack, well, that was different.

She opened the door and there he stood, full of fresh sea air and cheeks rosy from the early morning chill. For a man in his mid-seventies, he was still quite handsome, at least she thought so. *Brigid*, she thought to herself, *you are such a silly old girl sometimes.* Imagine still having feelings for Jack O'Reilly after all these years! She would never have believed it if she weren't the one living it and even then she still didn't believe it sometimes.

Jack walked in and held out his arms and she didn't resist. He hugged her for a long moment and gently placed a kiss on her cheek. "How are you feelin'?'

He could always coax her into showing her vulnerable side and she hated that sometimes, so she did what she always did. She put up a wall, moving away quickly, and sat down in one of two comfortable leather chairs facing the large windows. Her room was spacious and bright. "Fine. I'm feeling fine, just a little tired." She was, in fact, a lot tired but she wasn't going to let him know that.

Jack smiled and sat down on the other chair, gazing at the morning sun as it streamed in over her bed.

"Did I get you up?" He gestured towards the bed. "It's a shame I knocked; I might have been able to catch you under the covers. Now that would be a good way to start the mornin'."

"You wicked man. Mind your tongue!" Brigid sounded like she was annoyed with him but he saw the faint smile tugging at her lips. "Besides I told you it just isn't proper. You are my employee after all."

"As you've said many times before, my love. But it doesn't change the way I feel, Biddy. And it doesn't change the way you feel either."

"What the devil you see in a cross old woman like me I'll

never know."

"I couldn't agree more."

"How rude!"

He smiled then in a way that he reserved only for her. "You know I'm teasin', Biddy. I like gettin' you riled up and puttin' the red in your cheeks."

"You're an ornery old Scotsman and full of the devil you are!"

"Only half Scottish and you know it! Me da was of pure Irish descent, born not far from this very farm."

Brigid was starting to feel very warm underneath her dressing gown and she felt it wise to change the subject. "Surely you didn't come by this early just to ruffle my feathers?"

Jack laughed heartily. "No but it's fun anyhow. I came about the girl Emerald, or Em as she calls herself." Brigid harumphed at that. "She's all settled in the cottage and Conor and I took her out for a meal last night."

"How was it?"

"I can't quite figure the girl out. Although technically speakin', you know she's not really a girl, she being close to 40."

"Get on with you now."

"Well, one minute she seemed excited to be in Ireland and the next she had tears streamin' down her face."

Brigid stilled herself for a long moment, as if lost in memories. "Grief can do that to you. She did lose her husband not so long ago."

"Of course. Well I think she's brave to come all this way on her own, after losin' him and all. And I can tell you, Biddy, she's anxious to find out more about her mother. That's where you come in. You can't keep pretendin' to be sick, you know."

"Aha! You *did* know I wasn't really sick!" She sighed. "There's no use trying to fool you."

"And?"

"And what? Now don't go giving me that look. Yes, I know, I know. Today is the day. I can't put it off any longer. It would be bad manners."

"Well you are the one who invited her to stay here!"

"Yes but that was two years ago and, well, I couldn't turn down her husband when he asked me. I mean it was to be a second honeymoon, after all, and we Irish are known for the romantic side of ourselves, aren't we? It wouldn't be right. Not to mention there is the matter of the cottage. And, truth be told, when I'd heard he'd died, I never thought she would still come. It's all just a bit awkward. So much history and so many emotions. You know I'm rubbish with that kind of thing, Jack."

"I've never known you to run from anythin' Biddy. Why start now?"

"I just don't want to dredge up the past, like some muddy river. Sometimes it's just better to let nature take its course and clear things up on her own."

"Nature has been takin' her sweet time doing that. The past still looks pretty muddy to me. It's been 20 odd years since Eva passed, Biddy. Don't you think it's time to get things out in the open once and for all?"

"I'm not sure as I can."

"We live in a small village and people talk, you know?" Jack pressed, placing a warm hand over hers. "If you don't tell her, someone else is bound to say somethin' sooner or later. Besides, where did hidin' the truth ever get anyone? Where did it get us? Just a lot of wasted years, I'll tell you."

Brigid took a deep breath. "We can't change the past so there's no use in looking back." Her words were harsh and clipped.

"Sometimes you can't move forward without lookin' back first and makin' the way straight."

"Ah go on with you, Jack. I'm getting a headache just thinking of it."

But when he started to withdraw his hand from hers to get up, she put her other hand over his and clenched his tight. They sat like that for a long time, his hand over hers, hers over his, both of them looking out at the sea and the sky. As always, Jack's loving presence, his warm touch, and the sight of her beautiful sea calmed her, easing away the pain of past memories and moving into the beauty of the land she loved so much and of this man beside her.

"Will you go by the cottage and leave her a note that I'd like to invite her for tea at 4 p.m. today?"

Jack got up then, smiling down at her and bent to kiss the top of her head. "Of course. I'll do it straightaway."

Brigid couldn't sit still any longer, knowing that Emerald would be there that afternoon. Memories of her sister Eva were too insistent in her mind. She decided to take a walk to visit their special place.

"Rosaleen? Have you seen my walking stick?"

"I have, Miss Brigid. It's on the back porch. I'll get it. But are you sure you're up for a walk? You spent a lot of time in your room yesterday and barely ate a thing for dinner."

She couldn't get anything past Rosaleen. They'd known each other since they were girls. "I just had a bit of sour stomach, that's all. But I'm fine now and I'm going for a walk. Now would you pleeeze get me that stick?"

Rosaleen shook her head and muttered softly to herself as she walked out of the room, coming back quickly with a wooden walking stick.

Out in the brisk morning air, Brigid began to feel so much better. She was strong and extremely agile for 70, but she'd started using a walking stick after the fall she'd had last winter. It wasn't a bad fall, but Jack continued to hound her ever since to use the stick when she went about the hills. She hated to admit that it did make her feel a bit steadier now and again, and she knew she would need it on the eighty step climb to the place where the ringfort stood.

She could already smell the scent of the sea wafting up over the hillside. She hadn't traveled much in her life—a few times to Europe and once to America after Eva died. America had seemed such a strange place to her, all those shopping centers and cars and houses that all looked the same. She'd been glad to return to her own country and had never felt the need to go there again, even though her nieces were there.

Brigid stopped to catch her breath several times, inhaling deeply the smell of the salty air and the richness of nature, willing herself into the present moment. Yet her mind kept churning over that visit to America so long ago, seeing the sad face of Emerald and the confused one of little Sophie at their mother's funeral. She herself could barely make sense of it all then, nor even now, after all this time. There wasn't a day that went by that she didn't feel Eva in her heart or see her dancing on the waves in her mind.

"I'm sorry, Eva," she said aloud to the wind's ears. "I'm sorry I haven't been there for them all these years. It was just too hard after you were gone. Somehow it felt easier to… I don't know, turn a blind eye and let their father raise them. I hope somehow you understand. I know I've told you this many times before. I thought I'd finally let it all go till now, till she decided to come. How will I face her knowing what I know and knowing what I did?" Brigid had carried on this conversation with her dead sister for years now, always the same, and always without an answer.

When she reached the top, she marveled as she did every time at the sight of the fort itself, the vast ocean to the west of it and miles of open green fields in every other direction, as far as the eye could see. Further away on one side was a forest containing a large number of hawthorn trees, well known as a home for Faerie folk. The ringfort itself was also a home for them and a place to be respected.

This spot was where Brigid came when she wanted to feel close to Eva. She walked carefully now around the outside of the large ringfort to stand near the edge of the cliff that overlooked the ocean. There stood two flat rocks good for sitting on, and Brigid sat on one of them now.

This was the spot where Eva used to go and speak to the dolphins. It was the place where Brigid always looked for her when she was just a young girl and late for supper.

∽ 15 ∾

The Ringfort, 1973

*"B*rige. BRIGE! Hurry! You'll miss it!"

"I'm coming, Eva. What is it?"

Eva was always faster than her. Faster. Brighter. Prettier. More full of life than her or anyone else in their village, maybe more than anyone else in all of Ireland, for that matter. Eva was pure Light.

"The dolphins, Brige!!! The dolphins are here!!!!!"

Brigid reached the top of the hill where the ringfort stood, where water, sky, and earth all came together. For Eva it was the most sacred spot of all and created by God in the heavens for her alone. She felt as though she and Brigid were the only ones who'd ever stood there. When they were growing up this was still part of their family's land, the O'Shea's land where they owned and raised sheep. This was the place Eva came to discuss everything with the sea, the dolphins, and the faeries.

"The dolphins have a message, Brige! Let's listen!"

Brigid sat down on "her" rock and Eva on hers. The view of the vast sea out in front of them extending to the wide cloudy sky... this belonged to them too. The view was their own. She looked at Eva, who jumped up suddenly, not wishing to be still, standing arms spread wide, eyes closed, raven hair blowing back in the breeze behind her, listening for a message from the dolphins who splashed and dived far below them. Eva could hear messages from all of nature. She had the gift.

"The dolphins are saying... EVA... AND BRIGID... will DO GREAT THINGS!!!!"

Eva turned then and shone her brilliant smile at Brigid. "What do you think, Brige? What will we do?"

"I know that as the oldest child, with no sons in the family, I am expected to take over the farm once I marry and..."

"BRIGE! The dolphins are saying we can do a-n-y-thing! Anything, not just what we think we should do, or are expected to do! What's in your heart, Brige? What's your grandest dream?"

Brigid sat for a moment in silence. "I haven't really thought about it. I just have always known what was meant for me to do."

"But what about imagination? Life isn't... well... LIFE without imagination!"

Brigid didn't think much about imagination. All her life she played the role of the steady rock to Eva's whimsical leaf-like nature. Just like now. She was even sitting solidly on a steady rock facing the ocean while Eva danced to and fro like a butterfly, waving her arms about like wings.

"Well, Eva, maybe you can teach me then. What does your imagination dream you into doing?"

"I want to see the world of course!!! Especially America! I want to see all the beautiful places that nature has made in this world."

"What about a husband?"

"Who needs a husband! I'm only 16. I mean I guess falling in love would be wonderful but not if it keeps me from my dreams!!!"

Brigid had a funny feeling go through her just then, a knowing that something was going to happen and it might not be good. What if Eva did leave Ireland? What if she never saw her again? Even though her gut denied it, she hoped against hope that Eva's fantasies were just in passing and that she and her sister would live a long life by each other's side.

✧ 16 ✧

E m had all day and she knew that she should take advantage of the sunshine as Jack had suggested. He had given her directions to the old ringfort that she could walk to from the cottage.

"It's a good distance if you aren't a walker, but you looked to be in pretty good step last night."

"Yes, but what is a ringfort? I mean I've read a bit about them but what are they really?"

Jack laughed at her then, but kindly. "Well, there are some things in Ireland you must just experience for yourself. Keep a sense about you for the unexpected. You never know what can happen here."

So here she was, on her way to see her first ringfort in Ireland. She thought it might be a good place to try and connect with Pete. She hoped so anyway.

She remembered Jack's words as she walked in its direction. "There will be a small sign on your left when the road bends back on itself. Look for the little sign then you'll know you're right." It was bright and refreshingly cool as she walked and the air was sweet smelling. It even smelled of magic. She breathed it all in deeply, so deeply then that she thought her heart would burst. She tried not to think about how this moment would be if... well, if Pete were there with her.

Em reached the part of the road where it "bent back on itself" as Jack described but she saw no sign. *Mmm,* she mused, *I wonder if the faeries hid it from me.* She smiled. Not in Ireland for two days and she was already talking faerie talk. She saw the remnants of an old stone building to her right just after she rounded the bend. Could this be it? Surely not. It didn't look like any kind of fort. Well fort maybe, but ringfort, certainly not, even though she didn't know what it would look like after all these many years. She'd read that ringforts in Ireland had been built almost 20,000 years ago, so it was hard to know what would be left of one now.

Just then, as she stood quietly on the dirt road looking first to her right at the decrepit building and then straight ahead of her down a path that seemed to lead nowhere, she heard a soft voice singing. She turned all around but could see no one and nothing, save the hill to her left, the road ahead, and fields to her right. Everything else around her was completely still, except for a soft breeze. The voice seemed to be carried on the breeze itself and it was beckoning her to follow the path before her.

Intrigued and not a little spooked, her arms suddenly covered in goosebumps, she followed the lilting voice down the path that seemingly led to nothing and nowhere. After a moment or two, the singing stopped but she carried on walking, convinced for no known reason why she should. A good stretch later, she saw a set of stone steps laid into the hillside on her left. Without hesitation, she turned and began to climb. About ten steps up stood a slate sign, showing a carving of the ringfort and telling a bit of its history and other details. Now she could see more steps ahead and a glimpse of something at the top.

As she got closer, the hair on the back of her neck stood on end and she felt chills going up and down her spine. Not only had she found the ringfort, but she felt something so familiar in climbing those stairs. Deja vu? A past life spent in this part of Ireland? Her sister Sophie was always talking about past lives and reincarnation. Em wasn't sure how she felt about it, but being in this timeless place of wonder began to open her mind to new possibilities.

Suddenly she stopped halfway up the steps as an image shot into her mind clear as day. It was of her mother putting her to sleep, tucking her in tightly and sitting on the edge of her bed.

"Tell me a story, Momma."

"Ah, darling it's late now. You should go to sleep."

"Tell me a story. Please. A story of Ireland."

"Alright then just a short one. When I was a young girl growing up on the farm, we had so much land, you see. We were richer than most, at least in the way of owning a lot of land, and some of the village folk didn't like us much because of it. But then your grandfather, he was a very smart man and he'd worked in his younger years in London as a bookkeeper, making a good salary and saving it all up so he could come back to this

country and buy back his father's land, land that had been taken away from the O'Shea family by the British. My father, your grandfather, always said to me, "I took their money from their country to get back what was rightfully ours. They don't know what a trick I played on them but I knew, lass, I knew."

Em, just nine years old at the time, moved around in her bed to get more comfortable but didn't take her eyes off her mother. "Then what, Momma? Do you go to the ringfort next?"

"Yes, yes I do. You see as much as we had everything and more, I still felt empty inside, unless I could be in nature. That was the only place in my world that understood me really. I was always different from the rest of my family. They were more concerned with money and farming and what the sheep were doing or not doing, but all I cared about was when I would get out of school and get back to being on the land. And I couldn't wait to go to my very favorite place of all."

"Your very favorite place." Em smiled up at her mother, repeating the words she knew so well.

"It was at the edge of our farm and it sat right up at the top of the world. I had so much fun leaping up those old stone stairs built into the hillside and when I reached the top, it was just me and stones and sea and sky. I would run and run around the stones in a circle, and then I'd go and watch the sea for my friends the dolphins and dream about visiting every beautiful place this world had made for itself."

"I like that place, Momma. It sounds so nice."

"Yes, it was nice. Very nice indeed. And now it's time for sleeping and dreaming. Good night, sweet Emerald of mine."

"Good night, Momma."

Em was breathless when she reached the top step but not from the climb. Her eyes were half closed but her ears, tuned into memory, were fully open and listening. She couldn't believe it had been so long since she'd thought of that story her mother had told her, so long that she'd forgotten all about the ringfort. And then her memory drifted forward to when the bad years came upon her mother, when she didn't talk about Ireland at all anymore. She hardly spoke about much of anything by then and her eyes had lost their glow.

These were the stones her mother ran around in a circle. This was indeed the place of Eva's dreams, the place where her fantasies played out in hopes of coming true. The circle of stones was very large. There was a low wall still intact made of the carefully stacked stones and she wondered if people lived there and if so, how many. In the center of the larger circle was a much smaller set of stones that formed a square, suggesting an ancient gathering place, perhaps where they had fires, cooked or prayed.

She stood for a long moment, trying to imagine its original look and the people gathered there. It was large enough to house several families, she thought, and there would have been many children as well.

Em was so entranced by the fort itself that at first she didn't see the woman sitting out by the edge of the cliff that overlooked the sea. The woman, who was facing away from her, didn't see her either until suddenly the yellow dog at her side barked at Em in greeting, wagging its tail.

The woman turned around and waved, beckoning Em to approach. As Em drew closer, she saw that the woman was dressed in loose layers of clothing that wrapped and swirled around her, seemingly without beginning or end. Her hair was braided and was a mixture of black streaked with white. It made its way clear down her back so she almost sat on it. As she turned her face up to Em in her approach, Em could see streaks of purple in her hair around her face and over the top of her crown, almost like God painted a wreath of purple pansies round her head. Em laughed for no good reason, except that she could. The woman laughed too and Em said, "Are you... my Aunt Brigid?"

The woman's gentle laugh turned into a great guffaw at her question. "Ah but I were, lass. No, I'm not Brigid, though I've known your family almost as long as the sea has taken breath. Brigid was here just a while ago, though. I'm surprised you didn't pass her along the way." The woman's energy was as full and fast moving as the clothes she wore, as if it traveled in every direction at once, whirling and swirling, as though the woman herself was a witch's cauldron and the steam rose off her head. Em felt a magnetic pull, like a force of nature as potent as the sea before her.

"It's wonderful to meet you at long last. You'd be Emerald then." She said it as a statement of truth and not a question.

"How do you know...?" Em shook herself. "Actually, I go by Em. Just Em."

"And who would have shortened such a magical name? Not your mother I know! You look... a lot like her. You have her gorgeous features but your hair is..." The woman stopped in mid-sentence, her voice trembling softly, and Em noticed a tear run down her left cheek.

"Red?" Em finished her sentence, wondering why the woman was so emotional upon meeting her, but equally excited by the fact that the woman knew her mother. Just then, the yellow dog came up and began bumping against her leg in a way that could not be ignored and Em, missing her Butter so very much, crouched down to greet him. As soon as she touched the dog, she felt such a feeling of having done so before that it almost knocked her off her feet. Somehow, in that moment, she felt that she'd known this woman before. But that was impossible. Then again, she'd learned long ago that nothing was impossible...

All of a sudden Em was 10 years old and her favorite word was Impossible. She used it as often as she could for about a month, feeling more powerful each time. She didn't know why but she loved the feeling.

Her dad, who was generally a man of few words when he was at home, which wasn't often, as his work as a family doctor kept them comfortable but him very busy, was sitting in his favorite chair that day, reading a medical journal.

Her mother had just asked her to clean up her room before she went out with her friend Marjorie to play. Em, testing her powers, stomped her foot lightly on the floor, looked at her mother, and said, "Impossible."

Her dad looked up from his reading and held Em's eyes for a moment. Then he spoke slowly as though to be sure he was heard and his deep voice rumbled across the room towards Em, coming to settle around her like a gentle hug, reassuring and wise.

"Or…" he said, "It's Possible." With that he pulled back his lips showing his straight white teeth, his left cheek creasing into the deep dimple where Em used to stick her little finger when she was small. She melted. She loved her father so much and would do anything to please him. In that moment, Em's world shifted from Impossible to It's Possible.

For all of the years since, whenever she faced a challenge, she heard herself repeating his words, seeing his smile, able to watch that moment in her mind like a favorite movie etched permanently in her head.

And now, standing between the ancient ringfort, where her mother wove her dreams, and the roaring sea some 200 feet below, she found herself gazing into the face of this woman who she could not remember ever having met before but still felt in every cell of her body that she knew. Impossible? No. *This time,* she thought to herself, *it's possible.*

Her voice was the one trembling now. "What's your name, please?" Em asked as she stood up, the yellow dog rubbing at her leg once more for attention.

The woman smiled then, her face revealing nothing and everything at the same time. She nodded towards the dog. "His name is Scout. I'm caring for him for a friend who's away to Dublin. As for me, some call me Muriel. But I've been called other names as well."

Muriel shrugged then as if she didn't care what people thought of her.

Em smiled. She couldn't help wondering what sort of names she'd been called but didn't dare ask. There was something about this woman that made you not want to ask too many questions, yet she was such a curiosity. Em decided to get to know her like she did a new horse. Gently, kindly, and with caution. She changed the subject instead.

"Do you come here often? It's so beautiful." Em looked out at the sea and then behind her at the open fields that framed the ringfort behind them.

"Yes, it is. Your mother loved it here."

"Did you know her well then?" Even though Em had spent almost 18 years with her mother, she still felt, in the ways that mattered most, she barely knew her. She nearly wept at the idea that this woman sitting before her might be able to help her understand Eva, the woman who was her mother.

"Indeed, I did... once upon a time." Muriel sighed deeply, her breath sounding as if it came from somewhere deep inside her very soul. "She was both a great treasure and a great sorrow, that one." Her voice shook and she tried to cover it up by quickly clearing her throat. Em looked into Muriel's eyes, and watched the older woman wipe away a tear. Just how close was this woman to her mother? Excitement tinged with fear rumbled its way through her again.

A part of her knew she'd come for this knowledge and yet suddenly she feared that she might not want to know everything. Even as a child, Em knew that her mother carried things inside her that neither she nor her father ever spoke about. Looking at Muriel and understanding how interconnected everyone was in the little village, she suspected that in some way everyone was part of Eva's past. Em was a problem solver and she usually loved a good mystery. Was this a mystery she was ready to solve? Her heart still felt so tender from losing Pete. Was she ready to open up yet another wound, one buried so long ago? Then again, wasn't that part of why she'd come?

They sat together in silence and Muriel said no more about her mother and Em didn't want to push. After all, they'd just met, despite Em's feelings of familiarity. Her mother was certainly right about the ringfort. It was indeed a magical place.

A little while later, Muriel stood. "I'm so sorry, but I must be going now, my dear. I've got to get home and put things right there. I very much hope to see more of you soon. It's been a pleasure, Emerald O'Shea." Muriel's eyes twinkled as she used her mother's family name—not Watts, the name she'd gotten from her father, nor McAllister, the one she'd taken on as Pete's wife—but Em didn't mind. It felt as though she were an O'Shea here. Muriel gestured to the rocks in the ringfort and the sea itself. "There's a lot to learn from the land here, Emerald. The land itself and the sea hold all the knowing. Listen to it. It will tell you things, things that the people may not wish to tell."

After saying goodbye to Muriel, Em watched her walk away, sure of step, her dress and scarves floating around her in the wind. She almost expected her to disappear into that wind, but instead, she saw her make her way lightly down the stairs as though she'd done it many times before.

She looked to the sea then, her mind brimming over with more questions than ever but her heart curiously at peace knowing she was in a place where her mother had stood and dreamt as a young girl. "What secrets do you have for me?" she asked the sea but the sea did not reply. She sat on the rock where Muriel had been and tried to imagine a young Eva O'Shea standing before her, talking to the dolphins. "If what they say is true, Momma, then I should be able to conjure messages from you as well as from Pete. Maybe you and he are together dancing among the waves."

E m was completely invigorated by her walk near the sea. She was beginning to understand how much she was like her mother in that way. She too had that same insatiable need to explore all of nature.

Her high energy turned into nervousness, however, as the time for tea with her aunt approached. She couldn't understand it. After all it was just tea, she reminded herself, as she put on and took off yet another top to wear. Normally she could care less what she looked like or who was going to be impressed by her. In her work at the vet hospital, it didn't much matter; the only ones she had to impress there were the horses she treated and they didn't give a whit whether she was wearing blue jeans or an evening gown—they slobbered on her just the same.

At home it was no different. Pete always thought she looked gorgeous and gave her a wolf whistle even when she got out of bed with puffy eyes and her hair resembling a rat's nest. Just thinking of him now made her heart hurt and she sat down on the bed, placing her hand on her chest, sensing the pain around it. The loss was just too much to take in moments like this, when it hit her all over again that he really wasn't ever going to hold her again, or whistle at her, or tell one of his corny jokes. She didn't know how people did this, how they got through it and continued to live.

Then, just as swiftly, her sadness turned into anger. Sometimes when she was upset about something else, she still felt angry with Pete for leaving her, and now she was angry with her aunt for causing her nervousness and indecision. She grabbed the closest thing to her on the bed, pulled it on, and stomped downstairs and out the door, almost running smack into a smiling Jack who was holding up one of his hands, about to knock.

"Woah, slow down there, Miss Em. This isn't the States, you know! We go a bit slower here most of the time, that is, unless, of course, we're runnin' late for Ms. Brigid." With that, he smiled but caught Em's scowl at the mention of Brigid's name.

"Is there somethin' on your mind then? You look like a storm a'brewin'."

Em took a deep breath and let it out slowly. She had to pull herself together but it took some effort. Not for the first time since she'd arrived did she realize how raw she still felt from losing Pete. Somehow being away from home brought up even more tender feelings than before. She looked into Jack's kind eyes. She really liked him. He felt like a kind of father figure she could still have a deep conversation with. She missed that with her own father. She sighed then and felt her shoulders drop about a foot, as though allowing herself to recognize that all she'd been carrying around was pretty heavy some days.

She looked at the scenery ahead of them as they walked companionably up the hill to Brigid's. She wanted to take his arm but felt too shy to do so. Just then, she stumbled on a rock and he took her elbow to steady her. After that, it felt like the most natural thing in the world to link her arm through his.

"It's just a lot of things, Jack, you know? Being here where my mother lived brings back so many feelings about her and so many questions. And I'm missing my husband Pete so terribly. Not to mention I'm about to have tea with my most formidable aunt." She sneaked a glance at him then and hoped she hadn't spoken out of turn.

"Well I can't say as I know exactly how you feel about all of it, but I do know it's always hard rememberin' those we've loved and lost. And the part about your aunt, well, just so you know she's not really as harsh as she might seem."

"No? She seemed pretty intimidating to me the one time that I met her. Although I can't say that I even know her. Maybe that's partly why I feel so intimidated. I'm carrying an old memory of her from a bad time in my life. My mother's funeral."

Jack nodded as though he knew about the funeral and Brigid being there. "I see, yes I see." He patted her arm that was still linked through his. "I've known Brigid nearly all my life and that's a long time." He smiled then and she smiled back, noticing the deep creases in his cheeks his smile created. His cheeks were ruddy and rough, and those creases made her want to hear every story that made him smile over the years. He was a straightforward man, and an easy one to love.

"So… what is she like?"

"Brigid? She's a hard one to peg. She'll do somethin' different than you expect her to every time. I think that's what I like best about her. She's never borin'." When he said the words, his eyes twinkled in a way that made Em pause before she spoke again. There was something there, she didn't know what, but there was something.

"Will you go in with me please?"

"Sure lass, sure I will, but then you and your aunt, you'll have some catchin' up to do on your own and I'll be tendin' the ponies."

"Thank you, Jack." She squeezed his arm, feeling such a comfort knowing that he would be beside her when she saw her aunt after all these years.

The slender woman who met them at the door ushered them in ceremoniously and reached for Em's jacket before she had a chance to take it off. "Rosaleen, this is Ms. Emerald, Brigid's niece."

Rosaleen smiled and nodded her hello. "Welcome, Ms. Emerald. Ms. Brigid will be waiting for you in the back. I'll just take you through."

The house was old and grand, especially for such a small village. The rooms were large and the ceilings high, unlike the cottage where Em was staying. The furniture was ornate and cold looking and Em was glad she was not staying in this big house.

They walked past a bright white kitchen that appeared to be much more inviting and Em hoped for a moment they would be having tea in there, but Rosaleen kept going—down a long hall and into a large room with floor-to-ceiling windows framing two sides of the room. A woman sat by the windows and rose, turning and walking towards them when they entered the room.

She was taller than Em remembered, her dark brown hair pulled up in a bun revealing the grey beneath; her clothes, covering a trim figure, were plain and unrevealing. She wore a beautiful cameo necklace, though, with matching earrings and yet it was her eyes that captured Em's attention the most. They were a fiery green flecked with grey and blazed out of a face that looked neither young nor old but rather had a timeless quality. Her mouth hovered somewhere between a smile and a frown. Her eyes took in Em's appearance without missing a thing and Em, suddenly feeling under scrutiny, was happy that, in her haste choosing something to wear, she'd decided on a pale blue sweater and black slacks that she'd brought along for a special occasion. This occasion was special, although not quite the one she'd imagined when she packed for this trip.

Brigid just stared for a moment without saying a word and Em finally broke the awkward silence. "Thank you for having me to tea, Aunt Brigid. It is nice to see you." Em heard her words come out of her mouth but they never reached her heart. They felt hollow and forced and then she felt Jack's hand at her back, encouraging her to move forward and sit.

"Well, Bid... I mean Ms. Brigid, this looks like a very nice table you've set. Why don't you sit down, Em, and make yourself comfortable." Jack scowled at Brigid behind Em's back as if to say, "Be nice!" Brigid scowled back at him and waved him away as Em moved towards one of the two chairs that faced each other by the tall windows, with a tea cart between them already fitted for tea.

"Well," Jack said and cleared his throat as Em hastily sat on one of the high back chairs, as if she wanted to get this tea over with as soon as possible. "I'll be goin' then."

Em turned to look at him with pleading eyes and Jack shrugged slightly and smiled at her. "Let me know if you need anythin' at all, Ms. Em." His voice was tender and encouraging and Em felt the message behind his words. He was telling her he was rooting for her and that everything was going to be alright.

"How do you take your tea?" The words came as a surprise to Em, who was nervously twisting her wedding ring around her finger, feeling foolish all the while. She wasn't usually so easily intimidated, but she kept remembering the last time she'd seen her aunt. The energy of that encounter was still a palpable thing, even after all this time.

"Milk, sugar?" Brigid prompted, bringing her back to the present moment.

"Uh, just milk, please."

Brigid poured some milk into the bottom of an empty cup and filled it to the brim with the steaming tea, handing it to Em. "There you are then."

Brigid sat back in her chair, sipped a little of her tea and set the cup down on the table between them. "I apologize for not being able to greet you yesterday."

"It was no bother, really. It gave me a chance to settle in and get my feet under me after the journey." Em was beginning to find her voice. After all, she reminded herself, she was used to soothing difficult horses, even when they were injured, so one outspoken aunt surely couldn't be too much to handle. "Thank you," she said then in a confident voice, "for allowing me to stay in your lovely cottage. It is just perfect."

Brigid looked nonplussed then. "My lovely cottage? Dear girl, do you mean your husband didn't tell you? That cottage doesn't belong to me. It was your mother's, left to her by our da, and it's yours now, yours and your sister's."

Em nearly spilled her tea all over her lap. "But... I didn't... when..." her confident voice of a moment ago leaving her in a rush. "No one told me."

"He knew. Your husband knew. I told him when he made the arrangements to bring you here."

"I don't understand. That can't be right. Pete would never keep anything that big from me. He would have told me!"

Brigid just shook her head. "That may be true but know it he did. We talked about it on the phone when we made the final arrangements. I was certain he would have wanted to tell you, but I suppose he decided to wait until you were here, the same as the will intended it to be. But then he... and it was... too late..." her voice drifted off, as if she was suddenly at a loss for words.

Too late. Those words echoed in Em's heart like a drum that got louder and louder as she sat. Her head began to pound with the words, too late, too late, over and over again until she felt she was going to be sick. It was too late. Suddenly she was back in the hospital waiting room, listening to the ER doctor.

We tried to resuscitate him, to restart his heart, but it was too late. I'm sorry, Mrs. McAllister. Em began to shake then, just like she had that night. She must be having a flashback. She knew about post-traumatic stress, but she never knew it could feel so real. She had to get out of there, and now.

"I'm sorry but I have to leave. I don't feel well." Em got up and half staggered towards the door. Brigid jumped up and followed her out to the hallway. "Rosaleen! Rosaleen!!"

"Yes, Ms. Brigid?" Rosaleen came out of the kitchen, wiping her wet hands on a dish cloth.

"Call Jack. Tell him to come and take Emerald back to the cottage. Now please!"

Rosaleen stepped back into the kitchen and picked up the wall phone. Em was walking toward the front door, slightly bent over with one hand on her stomach.

"I'm, well, I didn't mean to upset you." Brigid spoke as if she had something stuck in her throat. Apologies weren't exactly her forté. "Are you going to be alright?"

Em couldn't answer. She just yanked open the front door and miraculously, she saw both Conor and Jack rushing towards her. Before she knew what was happening, Conor was standing right in front of her and she nearly fell into his arms, He had no choice but to catch her where she stood.

"What in the devil happened, Biddy?" In the excitement, Jack forgot himself and called Brigid by the nickname usually reserved for their time alone.

"Conor, I think you need to take the girl back to the cottage and let her lie down for a bit." Brigid's voice was shaking, quite unlike her usual commanding air. Conor didn't hesitate. He picked Em up easily in his arms and carried her over to the car not ten feet away, gently sitting her down on the front seat. Brigid and Jack looked on as Conor took over the situation, rounding the car quickly and heading off down the road.

It was Brigid who then was near to collapsing in the aftermath, and Jack, quickly assessing this, led her inside and back to the room where teatime had begun and ended just as quickly. Rosaleen poured them both a whiskey and then she scurried out of the room. But they both let their drinks sit on the table as they sat side by side on the couch that also faced the large windows to one side of the sitting area, looking out over the ocean and fields surrounding Brigid's home. The sun would soon be setting as the days were growing shorter towards the longer nights now.

Jack had one hand on Brigid's back and he stroked it gently, over and over, not saying a word, just waiting for her to tell him what just happened.

"I don't understand anything, Jack. I don't understand the girl, nor her dead husband. She didn't know, Jack. She didn't know!"

"Know what, Biddy?"

"About the cottage being hers. He never told her! How was I supposed to know? I just thought..."

Brigid laid the side of her head down on Jack's waiting shoulder, a gesture that stirred his heart. He was sorry about what had happened between her and Em, but he relished the closeness he felt for his beloved Brigid in these moments. It wasn't often she let her guard down.

"It's not your fault. You didn't know. But I still don't quite understand. Is that why she charged out of here?"

Brigid lifted her head then, her eyes blazing. "You aren't the only one who doesn't understand! I tried to explain that I thought her husband Pete would have told her about the cottage and then all of a sudden, she got this glazed look in her eyes and seemed to go into a trance or something. Then she clutched her stomach and nearly ran from the room. I don't know what to think, Jack. I've spent two minutes with the girl and I'm already in over my head. Why did I agree to this visit?"

Jack took her hand and made eye contact with her, forcing her to focus on him with the intensity of his gaze. "Brigid O'Shea, you haven't done anythin' wrong. At least not yet." His attempt at humor hit its mark when the confused look on her face turned into one of annoyance, as if she wanted to swat him. Jack ignored her look, saying gently, "Give it some time, Biddy. Remember, the girl lost her husband less than one year ago. She is still sufferin' a powerful loss."

Brigid dropped her shoulders then and let out a breath, her scowl relaxing. "Yes, I suppose you're right, Mr. O'Reilly, even though you can be quite impertinent, you know!" Mr. O'Reilly was Brigid's affectionate name for Jack, one she called him both when she was teasing him and also when she was annoyed. It always made Jack smile to hear it, and although she'd never tell him so, his smile still made her heart flutter even after fifty years.

He was a rogue, that one. A genuine "half" Scottish rogue, as he was keen to remind her at any opportunity.

Suddenly they both shifted their thinking, speaking simultaneously.

"I wonder how she's…" spoke Brigid.

"I hope she's okay now…" said Jack.

They looked at each other and smiled, a smile born of two minds long intertwined. Their relationship was built not so much on words and actions but on those moments when it was confirmed how much they moved as one, no matter how different their day-to-day lives could be.

✧ 18 ✧

Conor helped Em out of the car when they reached the cottage. She seemed to be trying very hard to compose herself and at the door she started to say goodnight, but he insisted on coming in until he was sure she was alright.

Em felt like a shell of herself, as if she weren't real, as if none of this were real. She remembered reading a lot about trauma after Pete died and knew that this feeling was a kind of bodily dissociation that happens when someone has experienced a traumatic event and then relives it.

She sat in the tiny living room and watched abstractedly while Conor lit a small fire in the wood stove. It was a cool afternoon that was heading quickly toward evening now and the stove was the only source of heat in the cottage. Em knew how to use the stove but hadn't yet done so, and she watched the flames through the glass door, feeling comforted by them.

Conor slipped away into the kitchen and a few moments later, she heard the kettle boiling. When he brought her a steaming cup of tea, she sipped it gratefully, wondering at the taste. It was sweet but warming at the same time.

"I put a shot of Irish cream whiskey in it. Figured you could use it."

"Thank you." She glanced briefly at him and then stared back into the fire. "I'm afraid I'm not very good company right now." The words sounded hollow inside her head and she knew she was speaking perfunctorily for his sake. She still had the feeling that nothing going on was real, and at this particular moment she suddenly wished she could be with her sister, sitting on her couch with Butter beside her.

Instead she was sitting on a couch in a little cottage in Ireland, in *her* cottage it would seem, with her feet up, a blanket covering most of her while Conor sat across from her in a high back chair. And slowly, between sipping the hot tea laced with whiskey, watching the flames of the fire, and sensing Conor's easy presence, she started to feel more like herself again. She noticed that her breathing was slowing down and she could feel herself exhaling deeply again, just like she did in yoga practice. They didn't speak but the silence was rich and easy. She looked at him and could sense the kindness in him that seemed to radiate outward.

"Thank you. I mean really, thank you for this."

Conor smiled, shrugging his shoulders at the same time. "You had that same expression as you did the other night at the pub, only more intense this time." When she said nothing, he continued. "Sorry. I don't mean to get too personal."

Em sighed deeply. "No, it's okay. Talking about it helps sometimes. I guess maybe you know about my husband?"

Conor nodded. "Jack filled me in just so I would be aware, you know, and not say anything stupid. I'm very sorry to hear it."

She just nodded and didn't speak for a long moment. It still hurt when someone offered their condolences, well-meaning though they were. It made it feel more real. "I guess I think I'm alright, you know, but then sometimes it just hits me square between the eyes and the pain is almost too much to bear."

He looked down then, as if lost in a memory of his own. Then he spoke, the sound of his voice coming out as if from a deep place inside him. "Loss can be like that. It's a finicky thing."

She was pulled away from her own sorrow abruptly by the feelings his voice evoked. She couldn't stand to see anything or anyone in pain, no matter how she felt herself. "Did you, well, I don't mean to pry, but did you lose someone close to you?" She remembered what Jack had said that first night about Conor getting over someone.

He laughed then, a hollow sound and got up to stir the fire as if to soften his feelings around the conversation at hand. "My parents were killed in a car crash five years ago."

She wasn't expecting anything like that. "Oh, Conor, that's awful! I lost my own mother, as you probably know, Brigid's younger sister, a long time ago, but to lose both your parents so unexpectedly! That must have been just devastating."

Her reply was so full of feeling that it made him turn to look at her for a moment instead of staring into the fire. The compassion he saw in those green eyes just about floored him. Then, unexpectedly, he smiled. "I am supposed to be comforting you."

"I guess we are comforting each other." She found herself tentatively returning his smile. "You know, my sister Sophie says there's always a reason we meet people."

He simply nodded and they sat in companionable silence for what seemed like a long time, until Em began to yawn. "I'm feeling so much better now but I'm pretty tired all of a sudden. It must be the whiskey." She attempted a smile that didn't quite make it past her lips.

Conor stood up, giving her a small nod of understanding, and made his way towards the door.

"Of course. Well goodnight then and you have Jack's number if you need anything, right? And I think my number is there as well by the phone. And Ms. O'Shea's too."

Ms. O'Shea? Em was confused for a moment and then she realized he was talking about her Aunt Brigid. "Yes, yes of course. Thank you again for your kindness." She felt an unexpected heat rise in her cheeks as she said goodnight to a man who already felt like a new friend.

As Em lay in her bed that night, she held a book in her hands that she'd picked out from the little library room. The dedication inside said, *"To my Anam Cara, love always, S.* She'd heard these words before, somewhere, but didn't know what they meant so she looked it up. "Anam Cara" meant "soul friend" in Gaelic. Who was her soul friend? This was her mother's cottage and she presumed the books had belonged to her. Was it someone she loved? Yet another question. She already had so many.

When she closed her eyes, instead of seeing Pete's face or his smile as she usually did, willing herself to dream about him, it was Conor's face she saw instead. She'd only known him for a couple of days, but he already felt like he could be a good friend. Was he to be a soul friend too? Her mind wandered back to the book and she fell asleep wondering who was her mother's Anam Cara.

$$\sim 19 \sim$$

Em woke up late the next morning to the sound of rain on the roof and her first thought was "I own a cottage in Ireland! Sophie and I own a cottage in Ireland!" She still didn't understand why Pete hadn't told her about it and she was angry that her aunt had kept this from her, from all of them, for all these years, but she couldn't help feeling secretly thrilled at the same time.

She jumped out of bed and looked around her now with a sense of wonder. It was only 9:30 a.m., which meant 4:30 a.m. in North Carolina, still too early to call her sister. So instead, in order to burn off some energy, she began her morning routine of yoga and breathwork, followed by breakfast with the inevitable cup of black tea. Jack said he would take her riding today but she guessed that would be postponed. Still she couldn't help but be entranced by the way the rain made the green appear even more vibrant as she sat in the tidy kitchen, looking out the window while sipping her tea.

After breakfast, she unconsciously began to re-arrange little things in the cottage, placing a table just so, moving a vase from the living room table to the windowsill. She imagined bringing some of her belongings here, maybe a few of her favorite pieces of artwork for the walls or a piece of pottery or two—just to make it feel like her own, though the cottage was already perfect in its simplicity. The feeling of new ownership began to replace the anger she felt about being kept in the dark. The restorative effects of a long night's sleep had washed away any bad feelings around her flashback of the day before, and she felt surprisingly more whole than she had in a long time.

She thought of Conor then and the things she'd learned about him the night before. He was definitely a man with some complexity to him and she had to admit she was interested in getting to know him better. She felt there was more to his story that she hadn't yet learned. When she was a young girl, her dad always told her that she should be an investigative reporter as she had an insatiable curiosity about people. Her love for animals tugged her in a different direction when it came to her career, but he wasn't far from wrong. She definitely liked to learn what events shaped people to become who they were, which was probably why the gaps in her mother's history bugged her so much even after all this time.

After breakfast it was still raining and Jack had rung to say that they were going to wait for a better day for their ride. He mentioned that Conor might be stopping by to invite her to lunch and she felt a sense of sudden anticipation, followed by a strange nervous twinge. Did she want to spend time with him or not? When she hung up the phone, she caught her own expression in the mirror, as if it were mocking her. "Well I can't stay here all day, can I?" Then she burst out laughing at her own silliness.

Em decided to take this time to explore the cottage, looking in the cupboards and drawers. She felt as if she were snooping and yet if the place was truly hers, then she guessed everything in it was hers too. At least Brigid hadn't said otherwise.

She found more books stacked in one of the downstairs cupboards, mostly travel books, along with books about connecting with angels and spirits, and some faerie tales. Another memory buried long ago in the recesses of her mind came forward. These were exactly the kind of books her mother would always read to her—books about adventurous, mysterious, magical things happening to people. She sat there on the floor, remembering her mother's words and how she looked then, all young and beautiful.

"There's no point in reading a story that's just about ordinary things!" her mother would say to Em when they sat curled together in Em's bed at night. Sophie hadn't been born yet and Em had her mother all to herself. Even her dad hadn't taken much time away from the two of them. They were "thick like thieves" as her mother liked to say. It had been years since Em had thought about any of this. Maybe being in her mother's cottage, a place where she had spent time as a girl, was unlocking something in her.

Em sat on the floor in the low-ceilinged room for a long time, holding the books in her hands, letting the memories speak to her, thinking about her mother and those days when they were thick like thieves. What had happened to make her mother change so drastically?

She allowed herself to recall the painful memory of that day, the day when Em was about 12 years old, the day when it was as if a light had gone out inside the woman known as Eva. From that day on, Eva merely went through the motions of motherhood, leaving a lot of the care of Sophie to Em and her father. She wished her sister were here. She wanted to talk to someone about everything that was happening inside of her.

She looked impatiently at the clock, which stubbornly still said only 10. Sophie had told her to call anytime day or night but she didn't want to disturb her sleep so she sent her sister an email saying, "Call me when it's good for you."

Less than five minutes later, the cottage phone rang with an incoming call. Em grabbed it quickly, feeling suddenly a bit breathless. "Soph? Oh shoot did I wake you with my email?"

"No worries, Sis. I just got up to go to the bathroom and I saw your message. You know I am eager to talk to you anytime, day or night! How are things going there? I miss you! I know that sounds silly because we don't usually see one another that often but now that we are roommates it's different!"

Em laughed and let out a sigh. She sank into the feeling of safety that her sister's voice brought to her suddenly. "It's good to hear your voice too."

"Are you okay? Is Aunt Brigid being mean? What's going on there?"

"It's not so much about what's going on here, it's more about what's going on inside my head. I'm here, it's beyond beautiful and peaceful, the people are great, even Aunt Brigid is alright so far, at least the little I saw of her, but Pete is still gone and I'm still... remembering."

Sophie knew just what that meant. "What happened?"

"I had a... a moment... yesterday when I went for tea with Brigid."

"Oh boy. Did she set you off?" Sophie knew that Em was still deeply affected by the suddenness of Pete's death and she had helped her through several of her "moments," which she knew full well were PTSD episodes. Sophie had even worked with a therapist herself to learn how to help her through them, since Em refused to go see someone herself. She loved her sister more than anything and hated to see her suffer.

"You know, Sophie, it's not anything that anyone does; some days it's just everything. Like when I went to the pub the other night and I saw a couple kissing, it took me back to Pete and our early days, when passion drove us to be in each other's arms every moment. Or yesterday when Aunt Brigid said something that brought back the memory of that... day in the hospital, when the doctor told me he was gone." Em was surprised by how calm her voice sounded.

"But actually, I'm feeling better today, calmer than I could imagine, although it still is wonderful to hear a familiar voice, especially yours. And you'll never guess the news I got yesterday."

Em told Sophie the whole story of the cottage. "Are you kidding me? All these years and no one ever told you??? We OWN a cottage in Ireland? Mom's cottage???? Em, that's... wow... I don't even know what to say! I mean it's crazy!"

"I know, I know. It's really hard to believe but I'm actually already feeling as though it's right. There is a sense of Mom here somehow. It's hard to explain but now that I know it, I am going to explore every inch of this place, searching for clues of her. I'm actually really excited about it the more I get used to the idea."

"But all that time, Em? All that time!"

"Yeah, that part kind of freaks me out, not to mention I could have come here much sooner with Pete and with you too! But past is past, as Dad always says, and the important part is... we own a cottage in Ireland! Mom's cottage!!! Speaking of Dad, how is he?"

"He's okay, really. He's okay! I saw him yesterday and he is already out of peanut butter cups! I don't know if he's really eating them all or sharing them with the nurses, but the man can go through them. As soon as I walk in to see him, I always remind him who I am just so he doesn't have to think about it and then he smiles. He asks me every time where you are and I tell him that you are in Ireland and he smiles even broader. He likes it that you're there, you know? But that doesn't mean he remembers."

"Yeah, the short-term memory is out of the picture now entirely. I often wonder why that happens... like is it an intentional thing not to remember the world as it is, only the world as it was? I wonder a lot of things when it comes to Dad. Please give him a big hug from me, will you? I miss seeing him a lot."

"It must be hard I know! But he's in very good hands and I've been visiting him a lot. So don't worry."

"I'm not worried. You're amazing."

"I am, aren't I?" Sophie teased. "But now I wish I were there with you in our Irish cottage!"

"Sophie, you have no idea how much I wish you were here too! It's so ironic, the timing of all of this. But we will just have to make a plan to come back here together… soon."

Suddenly there was a knock on the cottage door. "Soph? Someone is here! Is it okay if I talk to you later?"

"Of course! Love you!"

"Love you too," Em said as she hung up and walked to the door of the cottage. She opened it to find Conor standing there with the hood pulled up on his raincoat, grinning through the raindrops.

"Good morning." Em gestured for him to come in and take a seat, but he just closed the door behind him, pulled back his hood, and stood on the mat just inside the front door. "Apologies for barging in but I wanted to see how you're doing today."

She smiled, feeling a rush of warmth all over. There was something about these O'Reilly men that made her feel at ease. "Better. Much better. I owe you a big thanks."

Conor broke into that wide grin that engulfed his whole face and leaned against the door jamb in an easy manner. "Just seeing your face is thanks enough." For some reason that made her blush. Noticing her unease at his remark, he quickly added, "I mean seeing you look so relaxed today is, well, great."

She couldn't deny she liked this man more each time she saw him. But it had been a very long time since she'd been alone with a man who wasn't Pete, at least a man who could make her blush. Truth be told, Pete was the only man who had ever made her blush, who had ever made her heart sing. He was her one and only.

Conor cleared his throat, bringing her out of her reverie. "I wondered since you don't have a car and it's going to rain all day, might you be interested in taking a wee drive and sharing a bite of lunch with me? See the sights a bit? I mean it's bucketing down out there now, but it should ease up soon. Anyhow, it beats being cooped up all day and it's my day off."

Em just looked at him but didn't immediately reply. Was this a date or just a casual thing? She didn't know the rules anymore.

He sensed her hesitation and spoke easily, as if he was used to asking women to spend the day with him. She remembered the pretty woman at the pub the other night. "I mean if it's no, it's no but just thought I'd offer." He said it as if he'd be pleased if she said yes, but his life didn't depend on it. Okay then, if it was casual she could deal with that. It was his air of quiet confidence that helped her to decide.

"Well yes, I'd enjoy that, thank you."

"Great. I'll be back to pick you up around noon?" Em nodded. "And there's someone I'd like you to meet, so I thought to ask her if she could join us for lunch. Would that be alright? If not, it's no bother."

Em looked curious but unperturbed. "Sure. That's fine."

"Right then, see you at noon." With a smile and a nod, Conor turned and opened the door, making a run for his car, deftly dodging the puddles that had formed on the walk. Em stood in the doorway, watching him go and wondering who it was that Conor wanted her to meet.

She could smell the sea even before they arrived. There was a knowing in her, a connection with something that felt so right, that was growing inside her every moment she was here in Ireland. It wasn't being with Conor, although that too felt perfectly natural. It was more about how she felt inside, as if something clicked inside her, fell into place in a way it hadn't for months. The people here moved more slowly and held a reverence for the ordinary things and ways. They lived life in the present moment, allowing nature to be their guide. Like just now. They were stopped along the road where they'd parked just to bask in the beauty of the stretch of beach known as the Strand. She and Conor sat in his Jeep listening to the rain and watching the waves roll onto the sand, which seemed to stretch on forever. There was an intimacy about being huddled in a warm car next to someone while the weather raged outside and she sensed that he felt it as well.

"This is one of my favorite places," he said leaning towards her and pointing over her shoulder to her left. "Back that way is an entire nature preserve with a castle on the grounds and walking trails through the woods." He smelled of wool and lemon as he leaned closer, trying to show her where the castle was, but it was hard to see it in the rain. "Ah, tis a shame about the weather," he said, his face so close to hers she could feel his breath on her cheek. She squirmed in her seat and he immediately sat back in his.

"I like the rain," she said resolutely, focusing her attention straight ahead at the beach. Just as the words were out of her mouth, it slowed to a drizzle and the sun peeked out.

Conor opened his car door, sticking out his hand to feel the air. "You know what they say—if you don't like the weather wait ten minutes! I think it's about over, at least for now. Shall we walk?"

She smiled and nodded, relieved to move about. In the back seat, Conor's terrier Ruffles thumped his tail against the door in full agreement.

∽ **20** ᷲ

Brigid and Jack were out for a drive. Brigid had been so upset after her brief encounter with Em, even the next day, that she felt raw with nerves and when Jack checked in on her after breakfast he could sense it right away, so he decided to make light of his own chores that morning. He had more important things to tend to, or rather, more important people.

"Come on, Biddy," he said pulling her into an embrace that she did not resist. "Let's go for a ride. I'll take you to the Strand and we can walk the beach and have lunch after." He knew that the Strand was far enough from the village that Biddy wouldn't worry about who would be seeing them together. Not that it really mattered anymore. Everyone knew about Jack and Biddy.

Though she and Jack never publicly proclaimed their involvement and didn't generally show affection away from the confines of her home, they managed to spend time together, though if you asked Jack it was not nearly enough time. If he had his way, he'd be in her bed for the rest of eternity, holding her whenever he wanted and not just the stolen moments that they shared.

As they drove along the winding road that led to the Strand, Jack thought about all the years they had loved one another, and about the family he always wanted to have with Brigid. But fate had dealt them a different hand, and, not being a man who believed in regrets or roads not taken, he let such thoughts pass on by and instead reached across the seat to take his beloved's hand. As he did so, a hare ran into the road and Jack swerved to avoid hitting him.

Brigid pulled her hand out from under his and spoke sharply. "Keep your mind on the road, Mr. O'Reilly." Jack knew it was not him she was cross with, but herself, so he let her remark go along with her hand and said nothing. That was the best part about their relationship. He let Brigid be Brigid and she mostly did the same for him.

Despite her jagged nerves, she was looking forward to walking on the beach. It was a place where she and Jack had spent a lot of time together in their younger years. In fact, it was where they had first met. After that, they shared many secret moments out from under the watchful eyes of her da, who did not and never would approve of her dating the man who was the son of his hired man, the same man who would take over as caretaker when Jack's own da got too old to keep up with the demands of the job.

She was grateful that somehow her da never found out about her and Jack, the way he'd found out about Eva and her love. The consequences of that discovery made her shudder even now, decades later. But their da was long gone from this world and Brigid had been in charge of the farm for many years. She took orders from no one, but as she looked across the seat at Jack, she admitted to herself that she depended greatly on him and couldn't have done it all these years without his guidance and support. She caressed his features now with her eyes; his calm expression, his reddish cheeks with their deeply carved lines, and his twinkly eyes, always ready to laugh. To her he never aged. He was as handsome as when she first came to know him, nearly five and a half decades ago.

The Strand, West Cork, Ireland, 1963

Brigid was walking the beach with their dog Angus and her sister Eva. Her da was in the seaside restaurant chatting with some of his mates and sipping on a pint. A little while before, he had twisted his lips over Eva's fidgeting, and, Brigid, sensing his disapproval, had suggested that she and Eva take their dog for a walk along the Strand.

Eva was throwing a stick into the ocean and Angus, a bronze Irish setter, was furiously chasing it, paddling and splashing about, obviously having as much fun as Eva.

"Eva! Don't throw it out so far! The tide is coming in!" Brigid shouted to her. She was so busy watching Eva and Angus that she tripped over a log straight in front of her and fell onto the sand.

"Are you alright then?" She heard a voice behind her that sounded slightly amused and she broiled.

"What kind of person...?" Brigid turned to look up into the eyes of a young man who looked and sounded a bit more Scottish than Irish,

but at the sight of his blue eyes twinkling at her, she was even more cross to feel her own heart miss a beat or two. She tore her gaze from him and spoke brusquely to cover up her confusion at this turn of events.

"What kind of manners have you been taught? Do you think it polite to laugh at someone when they have an accident?" She looked up, scowling at him while she continued to lie there, rubbing her right ankle, which was scraped from catching the side of the log.

"Ah... such a beautiful girl to have such a temper," he said, getting down on one knee to examine her ankle, touching it lightly with his finger. When he did so, Brigid felt a shiver go through her as his touch felt like an electric shock, and she pulled away quickly. No one had ever called her beautiful, not even her da.

"I didn't ask for your help nor your rudeness, thank you!" With that, she made a sloppy attempt to stand, but her ankle was a bit stiff from the fall so that she nearly fell again in the process. But the young man caught her arm easily and put his other hand around her waist.

"A bit cheeky, aren't you?" she asked breathlessly, her heart pounding furiously.

"Hi! I'm Eva!" Eva appeared at Brigid's other elbow and Brigid used the distraction to stand up to her full height of five foot ten inches and then, jerking away from his hold on her, brushed the sand from her trousers to hide her flushed cheeks.

"Hi Eva, I'm Jack. Jack O'Reilly's the name. Pleased to meet you." He smiled and nodded at Eva, temporarily ignoring Brigid, for which she was grateful. She was still trying to calm her racing heart. Where in the world had this Jack O'Reilly come from? She'd never seen him before and she knew everyone in these parts, even out here at the Strand.

"Nice to meet you, Jack O'Reilly. I see you've met my sister Brigid," Eva giggled, staying far enough out of her sister's reach that she couldn't swat her.

"Oh Brigid is it now? That's a good Irish name." Jack chuckled again in that infuriating way as though he found everything amusing and Brigid felt a rising irritation. Just then Angus showed up, fresh out of the sea, and shook his wet fur all over Jack's trousers. Brigid looked at him and it was her turn to laugh now.

"This is Angus," she said between peals of laughter. "I hope those weren't your good trousers."

"My only trousers," Jack said calmly, a smile still on his face. "But they'll dry." He bent down to pet Angus and the dog rubbed against him adoringly. Somehow Brigid found that even more irritating.

She looked at him then, wondering why he wasn't angry when his only pair of trousers was soaking wet, or if he was even telling the truth. But his calm demeanor unruffled Brigid's feathers faster than they could rise. She always had her back up about something, but for some reason, watching Jack O'Reilly, unknown stranger, petting their dog as if he had all day to do so, she couldn't think of anything to be vexed about.

"We must be getting back, Eva," she said, but it was Jack who looked up to hold her gaze. He watched her steadily without a sliver of self-consciousness, yet also with an equal amount of respect. His gaze made her feel as if he already knew everything about her and he approved. In all of her 17 years on the planet, no one had ever looked at her that way. Oh, the local boys ogled her sometimes though she pretended not to notice. Her da looked at her as if she were someone to watch over and protect from all harm, and *also to keep in line at all costs. That wasn't a problem as Brigid was always, first and foremost, respectful of her da and wished to please him, as unattainable as that seemed. Pleasing him did not come easily but she continued to try. It was a full-time job keeping him from being cross with her or suspicious that she was doing something she shouldn't, not to mention she'd taken on the role of looking after Eva since... well since she couldn't remember when.*

Their mother died a few months after Eva was born due to lingering complications during her pregnancy and delivery. As a young girl, Eva's long succession of nannies all left in short order when they tired of the Master of the household's short temper. Subsequently Brigid became Eva's constant companion and guide.

All of this ran through her mind in a few seconds while she watched Jack O'Reilly watching her. She didn't know who in the world this Jack O'Reilly was. He was annoying and ill-mannered and yet... she had to admit she felt something else as well. And then, as if reading her thoughts, he stood, touching the brim of his cap and nodding towards Brigid before turning to walk casually toward the sea, bending to pick up stones for skipping across the water. She watched him for a moment, wondering if she would ever see him again. And then she straightened her shoulders, turned back towards the restaurant, and took Eva's hand. "Come along, Eva. Da will be waiting for us."

As she did so, she couldn't help sneaking a glance over her shoulder and there he was, just a little ways down the beach, grinning at her. She turned away quickly, acting as if she didn't notice, but inside she felt a secret thrill.

Brigid was reliving every moment of that first meeting as she and Jack strode along their favorite slice of beach in Ireland, hand-in-hand. With each step, Brigid felt her cares and worries melt away—worries about Em and the past she was hiding from her, worries about all the things she wished she'd done and hadn't done in the years since Eva left Ireland. She remembered now only her Jack of those days, and the one beside her now too, the one with the strong step and the handsome profile, the one whose warm hand rested in hers. She was a doddering old fool and it was a good thing he couldn't read her thoughts—and at that precise moment, he looked at her and grinned, making her wonder if he could. Blast the man, she thought, but she smiled to herself anyway.

She was looking for shells and stones as they walked, reminiscing silently. She let go of Jack's hand when she saw one that she really liked. It was a small, light grey pebble in the shape of an L. She liked to find ones shaped like letters. Someday she'd have all the letters of the alphabet. As she picked up the stone, she heard Jack's voice and looked up.

"Well, well now, if this isn't a grand meet-up! What brings the pair of you here?"

Brigid looked up and saw, just ahead of them on the beach, Em and Conor walking together with Conor's dog Ruffles between them. Ruffles was frisky and full of life, even at 15 years of age. When he saw Jack, he ran up to a hand waiting to pet him. Jack knelt on one knee to receive Ruffles' kisses while Brigid stood straight up. She'd shrunk a little with age but was still quite tall. The height difference between her and Jack had never mattered to either of them, but just now, with him kneeling and her erect, it created a large gap between the two. Despite this, Em couldn't help but notice that they looked very comfortable together.

Though the two of them might look comfortable, Em definitely was not. Seeing her aunt so unexpectedly, especially after what happened yesterday, put her back up and made her feel immediately on edge. Then suddenly, she heard her father's strong voice in her head. "If the waters appear murky, best to hold your head high and plunge straight in. Don't let anyone know you're afraid."

"Hello, Aunt Brigid, Jack. How are you today?" Em asked, proudly pulling her own self up to her full five foot five.

Brigid was taken aback by Em's show of confidence. After yesterday's sudden departure and Em's breakdown, she expected a much more fragile niece, though she hadn't been expecting to see her so soon. "This is quite the coincidence!" As she said it, she caught a look out of the corner of her eye that passed between Jack and Conor. She cleared her throat loudly. "Don't you think so, Mr. O'Reilly, that this is quite the coincidence meeting Emerald and Conor here?" She gazed at him, her eyes squinting from the bright sunlight but penetrating nevertheless.

"Aye, Ms. Brigid, it is surely a funny thing at that. How are you today, Miss Em?" Jack quickly shifted his gaze away from Brigid's.

"I'm good thanks," Em replied, smiling broadly at the kind man's face. "Thanks to Conor here for taking such good care of me last night. A good night's sleep didn't hurt either." She refused to discuss what happened yesterday. It was time to move on.

"I'm pleased to hear it, that I am. Are the two of you by any chance considerin' a bit o' lunch at this fine establishment?" He pointed to the seaside restaurant behind them along the Strand.

Conor spoke up. "We were indeed. We were just taking Ruffles out for a bit of a stretch first."

"Do you fancy joinin' us then for a bite?" Jack said at the same exact moment Brigid blurted, "Oh well we weren't..." Brigid stopped in mid-sentence and closed her mouth in a straight line, shoving her hands in her pockets. Jack knew her body language meant that she wasn't happy but she wasn't going to fuss. There was rarely a time in their long history when Brigid closed her mouth on purpose. He knew he would hear it from her later, but he pushed on, knowing this needed to happen. These two women had to break the ice somehow and it was as thick as a glacier at the moment.

"That would be nice, thank you." The soft words, spoken

quietly by Em, surprised them all, including herself.

"I'll just put Ruffles in the car and meet you in there," Conor said, touching her elbow and nodding at her reassuringly. She smiled at him, realizing how glad she was that he was with her. There was an easy assurance about him that allowed her not to think so much at a time when she was still pretty mixed up.

Jack, Em, and Brigid turned and began to walk towards the cozy-looking restaurant at one end of the beach. Brigid lagged behind, picking up shells along the edge of the shore. Em thought she looked more like a girl just then instead of a woman in her seventies.

She and Jack strode comfortably in sync. "Jack?"

"What is it, lass?"

"What did you mean about Conor that night when you spoke about him finding the right one, the one who will stay? I don't mean to pry but..."

Jack sighed. "Yes, he tires of hearin' me on that subject and I shouldn't have spoken about it in front of you but it's out now I suppose."

"You don't have to tell me."

"Ah, well, you might as well know. Conor was madly in love a few years back. He absolutely adored the woman, but she turned out not to be true."

Em didn't press for details, but she couldn't help thinking about the woman at the pub. "But he's young. Surely he's started dating again?"

"Aye he dates, that he does, but casual like you know. His

heart is still locked up with the other and he won't let it go." Em looked at Jack but said not a word.

Suddenly Jack felt Brigid pinch him on his arm, letting him know she was there. He wondered if she was still cross with him for inviting Conor and Em to lunch, but when he looked at her she didn't look cross. Rather, the way her jaw was relaxed and her eyes soft, he thought he saw a slight sense of relief. So maybe he'd been right after all. It would be easier to be with the girl when everyone was together.

Conor met them at the door to the restaurant, and they sat at a round table in the main dining area. It was busy and filled with the sounds of families and friends eating and laughing. The whole atmosphere comforted Em and made her feel like she was part of something, instead of feeling all alone in the world, which she so often felt these days. At the same time, she'd almost forgotten what it felt like to be with other people and not feel afraid.

Brigid told Em the history of the restaurant on the Strand, and about the generations of the family who had owned it through the decades. "The fish gets caught and brought in daily here so you can never get a bad meal. And the owners, they're just like family to us, right, Jack?" In describing this place, which Brigid obviously loved dearly, she dropped her stiff attitude for a few moments and also forgot to cover up her deep affection for Jack. Em was intrigued and wanted to know more about their story. Somehow the idea that her Aunt Brigid might be in a romantic relationship, especially with a wonderful man like Jack, made her seem much more approachable. She couldn't wait to tell Sophie that it appeared their Aunt Brigid had a soft spot for a man named Jack O'Reilly.

Brigid herself felt a bit more relaxed seeing Em for the second time, here, with Jack at her side. Maybe this would be okay after all. Maybe she could have this time with her niece and manage not to tell her... well, everything. She put aside her guilt for the moment. "So how are you feeling today? I really didn't mean to upset you yesterday."

Em looked up from her menu, meeting Brigid's eyes square on. She did seem sincere, and Em didn't know why she was so surprised. Her image of her aunt, created long ago, had been stuck in her head for so long that it was difficult to separate it from the woman she saw before her now. The woman who was sitting rather close to her "employee" did not, at this moment, look at all like the intimidating aunt she remembered. Maybe there really was more to Brigid than some old memory she held of her. After all, a memory is just a memory but people can always change.

"Thank you, I'm fine today. I was just, well, taken aback by the news. But in the light of day, I'm thrilled that my mother left me the cottage. Left us the cottage, I mean, Sophie and me. I just wish we would have known about it sooner. I would have liked to bring my father here."

"Yes, of course." Brigid was clearly unseated by that statement and didn't know what to say. "How is your... how is Jonathan? Is he still with us then?"

"He's still here," Em replied. "But his mind is not. He's in an assisted care home. He has dementia." Em found it difficult to say those words aloud without crying but today she managed it somehow.

Conor placed his hand on top of hers briefly. "I'm so sorry." The touch of his hand was both comforting and familiar, almost too familiar. Brigid was happy the attention was diverted from her for a moment. When Em looked back at Brigid, both she and Jack were looking at the two of them with curiosity in their eyes. Em pulled her hand quickly into her lap.

"One thing I've been learning lately is that the present moment is all we can really count on." Em smiled and lifted her water glass. "Here's to a chance meet up and a great lunch!"

They all clinked glasses and Em saw Brigid visibly relax, her shoulders dropping and her face softening. She sensed that the older woman was holding on tightly to the past. She wondered if she would ever make any real headway there.

"Speakin' of lunch," Jack announced, "it's about time one of us went up to the bar and ordered some food don't you think?"

"I'll go," Conor obliged quickly. "Fish and chips all around? And beers?"

"Extra mushy peas for me, Conor." Brigid smiled at him and Em thought she looked at least ten years younger when she smiled.

"Yes, ma'am, extra peas. And sparkling water, no beer." Brigid smiled again and touched his arm. "You're a good lad."

"What about you, Ms. Emerald?" Conor said, with a twinkle in his eye as he used her full name on purpose.

"It's Em to you, not Emerald, and I'll go with you." She

poked him lightly as she stood. It felt easy to banter with him but painful too, because it reminded her of the constant banter she and Pete had shared so naturally that it had been like breathing. She missed that.

Over lunch, they spoke of light things only: the weather, the birds, Brigid's horses, what Em did back in North Carolina. Em didn't ask any questions about her mother and they didn't talk about Pete either. It was just casual conversation and Conor continued to tease her over lunch, poking fun at the way she ate her fish and chips, first peeling all the batter off and dipping the fish only into the tartar. One time she threw her napkin at him and saw Brigid raise an eyebrow in surprise.

After Em and Brigid decided to make another date to meet for tea, this time in the village, Em and Conor left first and they decided to take Ruffles for another short walk along the Strand before they left. She waited until they were out near the waves, walking along the sand. "Conor? Was Aunt Brigid the person you said you wanted me to meet today? Did you know she was going to be here?" It made her wonder if this was had been a setup and Conor had played a part in it.

"No, well, I kind of knew she was. Uncle Jack mentioned that he might be bringing her here but it wasn't for certain. The person I wanted you to meet was running late so I told her we would come by her home for tea after, if you want to that is." Again that openness, no strings attached kind of attitude that set her mind at ease.

Once again, she couldn't help herself from thinking about

how safe she felt with him. And they did have some things in common... they'd both lost parents and now, thanks to Jack, she was aware that Conor knew what it was like to lose someone you were deeply in love with. Impulsively she grabbed his elbow as they walked along. "Thanks, Conor."

"For what?"

"For... making me feel, I don't know, at ease here, I guess."

He laughed, almost snorting as he did so. "Am I that boring?"

"No silly, you're not boring at all. It's just, you know, I'm a long way from my home and I'm here on what was meant to be my... second honeymoon."

"Bloody hell," Conor swore under his breath. "I didn't know that. I'm, well, I'm sorry, Em."

She sighed. "Yeah, me too. Thank you for saying that. Anyway, I guess what I was trying to say is thank you for making me feel comfortable here. It means a lot."

"You're welcome. It's easy actually. I like being with you." When she looked up from the sand then and into his eyes, she found he was looking at her intently. Maybe too intently. Just then Ruffles came running up between them, shaking his wet fur all over them. They both laughed and it eased the tension of the moment.

"So this friend of yours that you want me to meet, who is it?"

"Just the most amazing person I know."

"Is that all you're going to tell me?"

"Yep. And that I really want you to meet her. And, I don't know, maybe she can help."

"Help?"

"Help you with whatever it is that you really came here for."

"How do you know I came here for anything other than a visit?" His words made her feel unreasonably defensive.

"Well... excuse me if I'm being blunt, but a woman who has lost her husband doesn't come on her second honeymoon by herself and leave her family behind just for a holiday. I mean there has to be a bigger reason. It just makes sense."

"Oh that's what you decided, is it?" For some reason she was unexpectedly angered by his words. "Well if you are so great at judging my situation, then tell me what use it was for me to sit at home feeling hollow all the time, waiting for the door to open and my husband to walk through, telling me it's all been a mistake? Does anything make sense after that?" She stopped walking and turned toward the ocean, trying not to cry. She felt him behind her, tentative hands lightly on her shoulders. They were warm and curiously comforting and her anger instantly started melting away.

"I'm sorry, Em, I didn't mean to upset you. It's just a feeling I had, that you probably were here for another reason. I mean you told me a little about your mother last night and I know you've never been back here."

"Back here? I've never been here at all." She turned curiously to face him then.

"They say in Ireland that if your roots are Irish you're from here, no matter if you've been here in body before or not. When you come back, it's as though you've come home." Her eyes filled with soft tears at his words and she reached out her arms impulsively, hugging him then. His arms came around her and she could feel the strength, the solidness, the warmth of him. It had been a very long time since she'd been this close to a man, and she stayed for a long moment in his embrace. He made no move to let her go.

She was the one who pulled away first, a little embarrassed, and, pasting a bright smile on her face, asked, "Maybe it's time we go?"

"Yes, I suspect my friend will have a pot of tea brewing already." He took her arm this time, guiding her in the direction of his car.

More tea, thought Em with a smile. But she didn't resist. At this very moment there was absolutely nothing about this place or this person that she wanted to resist. She let it all fall away, settling into the ease of just being, an ease that seemed second nature here, in this place that Conor said was already her home.

Conor drove up a long steep road that curved back on itself. It was only wide enough for one car, like many roads in these parts, and you couldn't see more than a few feet of road ahead of you, so naturally Em wondered if they would run smack into another car on the way. Just as she was certain they would, they turned left into a driveway that climbed even higher and pulled up alongside a grey cottage with wide windows facing the sea.

As soon as the door opened, there was a rush of wind that accompanied it and the woman's clothing swirled up around her face and ears. It was her! The mysterious woman named Muriel that she'd met at the ringfort yesterday. This was the amazing person that Conor knew? Somehow it all made perfect sense.

Once more, Em was overcome with that nagging feeling that she'd known Muriel before, somewhere, somehow. She thought to ask but held her tongue. Instead, she followed Conor and Muriel into the cozy living space. Tea was already set at a round table in the kitchen area while a fire crackled in the nearby sitting area. Ruffles had run ahead and settled himself by the fire as if he knew this place well.

The room was filled with colors, just like Muriel herself. Today, she had on a flowing lavender gown that matched the streaks in her hair. There were candles everywhere and a scent of some essential oil wafting through the air. Or was it the woman herself that smelled of it?

"I call it Happiness," Muriel said, answering her unasked question. "It's an essential oils blend of rose and lavender flowers." Muriel smiled sweetly. "I harvest the flowers, extract the oils, and mix my own concoctions. It brings the essence of healing flowers inside all year round." Em felt a familiar tingle go through her. She knew she was in no ordinary place and this was no ordinary woman. Surely this could be a place where she might connect with

Pete. She looked around as if he might be lurking in one of the corners, then smiled back at Muriel, feeling foolish all of a sudden.

"You know of essential oils, yes?"

"Oh yes, yes of course. I work with horses in a large animal practice back home. We use them as complementary therapy sometimes. Plus my sister Sophie often uses them."

"Sopheea, yes?" Em liked how Muriel said her name.

"Yes, Sophie is my sister."

"You girls and your nicknames."

"Actually, Sophie isn't a nickname, it's her real name."

"I see. I always thought... well, no matter." Muriel spoke as if she'd known all about her and her sister forever. It made her feel quite strange.

"How is it that you know my family again?" At that, Conor laughed. He couldn't help himself. Em raised her eyebrows and squinted. "What's so funny?"

"It's just that, in a town like this, you couldn't not know the O'Shea family. I mean everyone knows everyone else anyway, but the O'Shea's own more land than anyone else around here, so everyone knows them."

"They do?" Not being from Ireland, Em was quick to forget how poor a country Ireland had been and for how long. The fact that her mother's family owned much of the land around the village, not to mention several homes, would certainly set them apart from the rest of the folks.

Conor nodded. "Yep."

"Well then, Emerald," said Muriel, handing her a cup of

steaming tea and gesturing towards the milk and sugar on the table along with the biscuits, which Em refused politely, still full from their lunch, "how are you getting on so far?"

Em let out a breath that came from the depths of her being. "Good. I mean it's great here."

Muriel sensed an incompleteness in her statement. "But?" she prompted gently, pouring her tea.

Just then Ruffles head went up as he barked at something he heard outside. "I'm going to take Ruffles outside and have a quick look," Conor spoke, and he got up and strode out the door, Ruffles beside him.

Muriel sat patiently and waited for Em's answer to her query.

"It's just that I have certain plans and hopes for being here and I don't know if I'm going to accomplish any of them."

The older woman smiled with a knowing expression. "Progress is a funny thing, my dear. Sometimes we think our feet are stuck in the mud when in fact we are moving along quite swiftly. Look at you for example. You've lost a husband, yes?" Em nodded, gulping. Everyone did know everything around here! "And you've pulled yourself together enough to travel across the ocean to a place you've never been before. You've left your home, your family, everything you know to come here. You've met people and from the looks of it, you're making friends fast."

Em couldn't deny any of what Muriel was saying, but how did she know all of that?

As if reading her thoughts once more, "I know Brigid very

well you see and she's been keeping me up to date on your whereabouts. I can feel your uneasiness and I understand. I also sense you want answers to things you don't even know the questions to yet."

Em nodded silently, her eyes glued to Muriel's dark ones. She felt the answers to all the questions of all time lay in those eyes. Again, as with Conor, she had that same sense of instant trust, though she didn't know why. She'd never known anyone like Muriel. Once more she felt the tingle along with goosebumps going up her arms. Another knowing, Pete would say. Definitely a knowing.

"I think I can help." Muriel reached out her hand to lay it gently on Em's arm. Her hand felt very hot. "Would you like to come by and see me again? Just you on your own?" Em nodded, feeling Muriel's words hit home on a completely different level than was intended. Just her on her own. Yes, that's who she was now.

Her thoughts were broken when Conor walked back in with Ruffles. "It was just a fox, nothing to worry about." Conor half winked at Em and sat down to his tea, Ruffles snuggling in once more by the fire.

The rest of their visit was lighthearted and fun. Conor and Muriel shared an easy camaraderie and Em joined in wholeheartedly. As they stood up to leave, Muriel leaned over and said to Em, "I'll be seeing you."

⌒ **22** ⌒

Em arrived at Muriel's house two days later, breathless and excited. It was only just down the road from the cottage—she couldn't very well call it Aunt Brigid's cottage anymore but nor could she quite call it her own yet. The wind was blowing in from the ocean quite strongly the whole way, taking her breath and making her cheeks burn. Jack had offered to pick her up later if it rained again or if she did not feel like walking home.

"I just know that after a long visit with Muriel, your Aunt Brigid usually has a lie down, no matter the time of day. Or a good long sit with a cuppa in front of her favorite view." Em wondered at Jack's comment. First off, why would she need to lie down after visiting Muriel, and secondly, which was her aunt's favorite view? She guessed it was the large room with the floor to ceiling windows where she'd had her first meeting with Brigid—the same room where she'd first learned about the cottage.

When Muriel opened the front door, heavy and creaking under its weight, the warm flicker of many candles created a glow that framed her laughing face.

"Come in, come in, my ginger-haired girl. You're lovelier every time I see you. I think Ireland agrees with you," she said with a wink.

She gestured Em toward the same chair that she herself had occupied for their last tea. As Muriel moved about the kitchen, Em settled in at the table, feeling perfectly content. She turned her gaze to look around the open living space more closely than last time, noticing things she hadn't on that first visit. It held a nice-sized cooking area with an island. To the right of the table where she now sat was the fireplace flanked by two cozy armchairs with tiny end tables. On the opposite wall were two doorways. One led into what looked like Muriel's bedroom and the other door, partially closed, emanated a soft light from within it.

She must have had a look of curiosity on her face because she heard Muriel say, "That's my healing room. Would you like to see it?" As she spoke she glided across the room, again making no sound save her skirt and the gentle click of the bangle bracelets stacked on her right arm. She opened the door and Em saw that the room was lit with the soft light of two Himalayan salt lamps. "Have a look around while I get us some tea ready. After all, we'll be in here today so I want you to feel comfortable with the space."

"We'll be in here today?" Em turned to ask Muriel, but the woman had already left the room. *"Be in here doing what?"* she wondered. She forgot her own question as her eyes began to take in all the beautiful photos, paintings, and statues carefully placed about the room. They were all of women and Em recognized a few of them—Kwan Yin, Mother Mary, and one in the corner, a painting under a gold light. She didn't recognize the woman in the painting but felt the sheer strength in her face and the spirit in her eyes. It almost made Em quiver.

Em had never felt that she was as tuned into energy as her sister Sophie was, yet all the same, it felt very powerful in this room. Center stage was a massage table covered with beautiful gold and purple silks. Directly above it hung a large clear crystal that caught the sunlight streaming in the window, transmuting it into rainbows of color all across the room, hitting the table and the walls with prisms of light. On the other side of the room, she saw shelves filled with instruments... drums, rattles, chimes, bells, and what she knew to be singing bowls. The entire space felt much like Muriel herself—loving and nurturing and with a high degree of energy.

Em left the room to find that Muriel was now seated in one of the cozy chairs in front of the fire, where she'd laid out their tea and biscuits on the tiny tables. As she sat across from her, Em asked, "Why all the women?"

"Why not? Women have been the healers, the nurturers, the givers of life, not to mention the warrior queens... did you see the statue in there of Matilda of Tuscany?"

"Is that the one of the woman holding a sword on horseback?"

Muriel's smile spread across her face, showing pronounced dimples and laugh lines that made her look very much alive. "The very one! She was something alright! I have a book for you if you're interested in learning about her."

Em nodded. Reading about great women in history was always high on her list.

"Who is the woman in the portrait?"

"That's Brigid of course!"

Em looked confused. "Brigid?"

"Brigid, Goddess and Saint of Ireland. Brigid of the Holy Wells. Brigid of Kildare. If you don't know about Brigid, you must learn if you are going to spend any time here. She is one of our most revered female figures!"

"Are a lot of women named after her?"

Muriel chuckled. "I suppose you're referring to your Aunt Brigid. Yes, Brigid is a common Irish name and believe me, even underneath that... ahem... crusty exterior, your aunt is a very strong woman, not unlike St. Brigid in that respect."

They continued to talk about these women while they "tucked in" as Muriel put it, to their tea and biscuits. "I always felt as if your mother had the potential to be one of those women. But she never got the chance."

"Why? What do you mean?"

"Ah, well, that's a story for another day, dear." She looked kindly at Em. "In the meantime, are you ready to do what you came here for?"

"What's that?" Suddenly Em felt her heart beating rapidly in her chest. She wasn't scared but she had no idea what to expect. And she couldn't stop thinking about what Muriel had just said about her mother.

As if reading her thoughts, Muriel spoke. "You came to Ireland to learn more about your mother, Eva, yes?"

Em nodded. "Yes, and I have learned a bit more about her already. But I get the strong feeling that there are secrets involving my mother's past. Things that others know but I don't. You yourself alluded to it just now."

"You're not far wrong. There are things to be shared, things to be told. But, for now, those things are meant for your Aunt Brigid to share with you. After all, she was her sister and she will know the stories better than anyone. My advice is to give it a bit of time. You've only been here a few days."

"I suppose." Em was not convinced but willing to listen. She knew Muriel was trying to help.

"You also came here to heal your heart, yes?"

Em's eyes filled with tears at her words. "I guess I was hoping coming here could help me make this pain go away, the pain of losing my husband. And that I might be able to connect with him, know if he's alright. I've been trying for months, hoping to get a sign from him of some kind. The other night in the pub... well, it doesn't matter, it probably was just made up in my head."

Muriel let out a sigh, soft as a feather falling to Earth. "Sometimes we want things so badly that we push for them, we insist that they happen the way we choose them to, on our timetable. But, as I'm sure you know, life isn't like that. Grieving doesn't have a timetable. Neither do those who have moved on. In that part of our existence, there is the deeper understanding that there is no time or space and all things happen at once. Whereas, in our earthly perception of time, they happen when we let go—when we are truly ready to receive them."

Em let the words sink in, waiting for that now familiar sense of despair, that feeling of being transported back to the day of Pete's death, just as she had at Brigid's the day they first met. But it never came. She didn't know who this Muriel was but somehow in the gentle but powerful energy of her presence, she allowed herself to stay in the moment, the place where Pete no longer existed, at least not in a body. Tears rolled silently down her cheeks but she held steady to her heart.

"Emerald, your heart is wounded and you are looking for information because you believe it will make you feel better. That's quite natural, anyone would. But what you haven't realized yet is that you have to learn to transmute your grief in order to connect."

"How?" Em's voice was but a whisper.

"By allowing yourself to find the place inside of you where your own wholeness lies. You're still whole in and of yourself, whether with your husband or just you on your own. When you begin to fill yourself up again, you'll connect with him easily, from a place of love, not of grief or longing. I might be able to help you with that. I'd love to try... if you'll let me."

"Yes please." Em's voice was still soft and her eyes glazed with tears, but she smiled.

Muriel smiled back, her eyes twinkling like two dark stars in the sky. "Sometimes we have to move in the dark without understanding everything in order to find the light." The older woman held out her hand and Em took it. "Come with me to my healing space and we'll figure it out together, shall we?"

Together they walked to Muriel's healing room and as Em passed through the doorway she felt an indescribable shift.

❦ **23** ❦

Em's time spent with Muriel had left her wanting nothing but to rest. Jack had been right and that evening her mind was quiet. She went to bed early and fell into a deep sleep. In the morning, she couldn't even remember her dreams, which disappointed her because that was the place she felt was most likely for Pete to show up again. But then she remembered what Muriel had told her about letting go and focusing on love instead of longing. As she showered and dressed for the day, she knew that she had much to process from her time with Muriel. For now, though, the sun was shining through the bedroom skylight and she felt good. The healing session had left her feeling light and energized.

As she was contemplating what she would do that day, she heard a knock at the door.

She ran down the stairs and swung the door wide to find a smiling Jack O'Reilly, asking her to go riding and she said yes immediately. Em decided that being free up on a horse's back was just the thing she needed. Merely thinking of it gave her a sense of herself as truly whole for one solid moment and it was wonderful.

"How soon can you be dressed and ready to ride? Half an hour?" He smiled again and she watched the corners of his eyes curve upward.

Em nodded enthusiastically. "I'll be there!"

"Grand. Just walk up behind the horse pasture and you'll see the stables."

"Got it!"

He stood there for a moment as if waiting to take his leave and Em couldn't wipe the smile from her face no matter how hard she tried. The man was just so endearing. "Go on, then, you, and let me get ready!" She giggled and Jack waved his hand and turned to walk away.

When she got to the stable, Conor was tacking up the beautiful horse Em had fallen in love with the first day. For a moment, Em's heart fell. "Are you riding her?"

Conor laughed. "No, silly. You are. My horse is already tacked up and in his stall." He pointed to a large chestnut gelding in the corner stall.

Em couldn't hide her excitement over riding the horse Conor said they called Beatrice. She was already so connected to her. She walked up and stroked the mare's forehead, whispering, "We are really going to get to know each other today."

She could tell by the way Conor moved around the mare and spoke to her that the method of horse handling he'd been taught was similar to her own back home. Natural horsemanship had taken hold in North Carolina, especially with the arrival of her teacher, the famous Lou Lynn. Em had been lucky enough to take some classes with Lou, and her teachings aligned with everything she herself had ever been taught about horses. It pleased her very much to see how Conor handled Beatrice, as horses were such a big part of her life and the way a person related to a horse told you a great deal about them. It was easy to see that Conor too worked with a horse as a partner, not something to be broken or dominated.

As soon as she eased into the saddle and picked up the reins to ride out on Beatrice, following behind Jack and Conor down the driveway, Em felt like she had ridden her all her life.

The Irish Cob, as she had learned Beatrice was, felt solid, strong, and sure-footed, and Em's legs wrapped around her like a pair of well-fitting jeans. The more she rode her, feeling her easily negotiate her way over rocky hills and on slick roads wet with rain from the previous day, the more Em felt the power and agility of the mare. Beatrice might be small by nature of her size, but her strength and agility made her a giant in anyone's book. Em's trust was immediate and the feeling felt mutual, although she imagined that Beatrice, or Bea as she already thought of her, had carried a number of other riders just as safely. The horse clearly knew her business and all Em had to do was listen and follow her lead.

After riding the hills and fields around the village, they finally reached a stretch of beach. In order to get onto the beach, however, they had to jump a low gate that separated the road from the beach. Jack stood by, looking at her from his horse, nodding that it was okay to jog over the gate from the road. Em hesitated for a moment, because there were only a few feet between the horse and the gate and all of her experience with jumping in an arena had never prepared her to just pop over a gate from a near standstill. She looked at the low gate and then back at Jack, who said, "She's done this many a time. Just point her, she'll take care of you." Em pointed the mare towards the gate, not quite closing her eyes but moving into a place of total trust, clucking gently to her to break into a few steps of trot on the approach. She felt Bea's legs leaving the ground, her head and neck tucking forward and down as her body rounded over the gate, neatly and cleanly, her own body folding naturally to meet the horse's uprising one and they landed in the soft sand on the other side, two as one. Em was elated and rubbed the horse's neck over and over, talking to her gently. "What a good girl you are!"

The three of them, Jack, Em, and Conor, walked along the beach on their horses in companionable silence, watching the waves, the horses dipping their feet in now and again. Ruffles, who'd come along for the ride, barked at the waves as they came in gently around them. Em noticed how easily Conor sat a horse, and when she looked at Jack, you could not tell where the horse stopped and he began. She let out a long sigh, feeling a deep sense of ease come over her.

Conor turned to her then. "Would you like to race?" he asked, his face creased in a mischievous grin.

"Race?"

"Yes, a race along the beach. Sometimes it's nice for the ponies to stretch their legs a bit and just run. Beatrice loves it."

She looked down at Bea. "Is that true, girl? Do you like to race?" Bea seemed to bob her head as if in response. Em had always ridden in a very strict environment at home. Ring riding, lessons, training. None of it had involved all-out racing on a beach. She felt a little intimidated, but game to try.

"Sure!"

Conor looked pleased. "Ok, then, we'll go down the beach a ways and then race back towards Jack, who will wait here for us. Just a short sprint."

Before they turned to ride down along the beach to where the start of the race would be, Jack rode up to Em and leaned towards her, speaking quietly.

"Mind yourself, lass, as Beatrice here has a very fast start. Conor's horse can beat you on a long stretch but if you can get a head start you can outride him easily in a sprint this length."

Em nodded. They reached a point about 100 yards down the beach and turned to get ready. They watched Jack as he raised his arm to signal the start of the race. When he lowered his arm like a flag a moment later and whistled at the same time, Beatrice bolted forward, taking Em off guard. Em had been perched forward in racing position, but her stirrups were too long and when her horse took off like a shot, her seat plopped backwards, hitting the saddle momentarily and causing her to pull up on the reins automatically, slowing Beatrice down just enough so that Conor easily moved ahead of her. Even though Em recovered quickly and let the mare have her head, she couldn't come close to catching him. When they reached Jack, he was chuckling. "I told you she had a fast start."

"You weren't kidding. I just wasn't ready. Next time I'll be ready!" Though she'd lost the race, Em was glowing with pleasure, her cheeks flushed. Just as suddenly, she felt tears spring to her eyes as she imagined this same scene if Pete were here sharing this moment with her. How different it would be. Then she wanted to laugh through her tears, thinking of Pete riding a horse. He always said it was her thing and he was okay with that. As she wiped at her cheeks with the back of her hand, she couldn't understand how she could feel so happy and so sad at the same time. Conor appeared beside her on his horse and saw the tears on her face, his own smile evaporating.

"Are you alright, Em? Are you hurt?"

She attempted a smile through her tears. "No, I didn't get hurt just now. The hurting happened a while ago. It's just still kind of sore around my heart." She knew she was letting her guard down and showing her vulnerability, and when she looked at him, she caught something different in his eyes. Something that was compassion mixed with desire, as though he wanted to wash all of her sorrows away. Even though she'd only known Conor for a few days now, she felt that he truly saw her, the woman behind the grief and the sorrow. The feeling it gave her reminded her of when she had met Pete, and was grieving the loss of her mother, but this was different because instead of being a young innocent girl, she was now a woman. Conor's look made her feel both comforted and uncomfortable at the same time and so she looked away, silently riding along beside him

Something about the feeling of him next to her on his horse, Jack quietly trailing behind them, and that moment of deep connection they'd just shared felt familiar, too familiar for the short time they'd known each other. Their horses were walking so close to one another that Em and Conor's legs bumped now and again, and it held an intimacy that added to Em's unease.

Just as she thought she couldn't stand it another moment, Ruffles came running from the waves where he'd been chasing a seagull and began jumping around enthusiastically but alarmingly close to her horse's legs. Bea was ever so mindful of him—though her ears did take a turn for a moment—until Conor called Ruffles forward to walk nicely next to him, moving away from her as he did so, breaking the tension that she had felt building within her.

Jack quietly rode up beside her and began telling her stories about the land itself in his singsong voice. Em sighed, grateful for his presence, suddenly looking forward to being back at the cottage and writing to Pete.

24

E m was relieved that Brigid had suggested for them to meet in the village this time for morning tea. The thought of repeating their first tea experience was none too desirable for either of them, so this change of location was definitely the order of the day.

Glebe, the small café and tea shop where they were to meet, was quickly becoming a regular stop for Em. The bright-eyed Fionnuala smiled and greeted her immediately upon her arrival. She noticed that her aunt was already seated at a table by the windows, a cup in front of her.

As Em sat down across from her, Fionnuala came over straight away. "Morning, Em. What can I be getting for you then?"

"Hi Fionnuala. How are you today? I'd love a cup of your chai tea, please, and a blueberry scone with butter?"

"I'm good, thanks for asking. You'll be having your almond milk on the side then?" Fionnuala smiled as Em nodded and smiled back.

"It would seem that you're quite the native already." When Em looked at her aunt's expression, trying to judge if she was being critical, Brigid seemed to sense her nervousness. "That's good. That's a good thing. Your mother had the same outgoing way about her as well."

"My mother?" Well, well, this was a switch. Brigid was actually mentioning her mother without her asking. Maybe this would be easier than she thought.

"Yes, your mother." Brigid tried to sound casual but had to clear her throat, as if brushing away some long-held cobweb that had been stuck there. "Eva was the friendliest person in the village. Everyone knew her and everyone loved her." There was something in Brigid's voice that made her words sound like a rebuke.

Em decided something right then and there. She was finished being intimidated by her aunt's brusque manner. Instead she would try to see Brigid's perspective. "That must have been difficult for you."

"Whatever do you mean?" Brigid said curtly.

"Well, my sister Sophie is a bit like that. You know, very outgoing, always the life of every party. Everyone loves Sophie. And I love Sophie too, I do, it's just, sometimes, it can be a bit tiring trying not to compare myself."

Brigid scowled at her for a moment, annoyed at being observed this way by her niece, and then, surprisingly, she laughed. Em realized that it was the first time she'd seen Brigid laugh! It changed her whole appearance and energy. "Forgive me, but what did I say that was funny?"

The older woman stopped laughing but her face still held

a smile. "Me trying to compare myself with Eva! That's what's so funny. You couldn't compare yourself to Eva O'Shea any more than you'd compare yourself to a Michelangelo or a skyrocket. Eva was not like anyone else in the world. There was no comparing yourself to her."

Hearing Brigid, her mother's sister, talk about her mother Eva so openly brought her emotions right to the surface. She placed her hand over her heart without thinking about it. During their session together, Muriel had coached her to breathe into her heart, placing her hand there. Except that this time was different. When Brigid said those words about her mother, Em was sure her heart had stopped for a moment. She just sat there, dumbfounded and silent.

"On no, please don't tell me I've done it again! We haven't even been here 10 minutes! What? What did I say this time?"

Em didn't answer for a long moment, a moment in which she began to feel the reassuring beat of her heart once more. Yes, yes it was still there, still working. She looked at Brigid. "I'd just forgotten that's all."

"What? Forgotten what? Don't speak in riddles, girl."

"I'd forgotten... who she was before... everything changed." Em sat up straighter and held Brigid's eyes as she spoke. "And I'm no girl, Aunt Brigid, I'm a grown woman, a woman who has been kept in the dark for too long. I want to learn about her past, who she was growing up, why she left Ireland, all of it. No one has ever told me those things. Not her, not my father. All of these years I've just accepted it but now, since Pete is... gone, I've realized that it's time for me to know." Em was shaking now but she didn't care. Fionnuala approached their table, then seeing their tense faces, disappeared just as quickly.

It was Brigid's turn to be silent. When she spoke, her voice was harsh. "The past is the past. It never does anyone any good to drag it back up."

"But some of us don't know that past. Some of us need to understand it. Some of us have a right to know. I have a right to know. I want to know my mother. What you said just now about her, it made me remember. I'd forgotten how wonderful she was. In all the pain of losing her, those years of not having a mother around, I'd forgotten who she was to me. I need to know her again, Brigid." She used her aunt's first name, wanting desperately to reach her. "I need to know who she was and why she was so... so lost in the end."

"And what makes you think I have the answers? What makes you think I know what happened to her? I didn't see her for years!" Brigid spoke emphatically, but she didn't meet Em's eyes.

Just then Fionnuala came swiftly to their table, bringing Em her tea and scone. "Would you like a refill?" she asked Brigid, who shook her head no and looked out the window. She slipped away just as quickly, leaving the two women alone.

After that, they just sat without talking, for what felt to Em like forever. Finally, Brigid spoke. "I don't know if I can go back. I just don't know if I can do it. It was all so long ago now and there are things that... shouldn't have happened. Things that should have been different. But they weren't." She said the last three words as if trying to convince herself of it. "You're asking a lot of me."

Two pairs of green eyes, one emerald and the other dark green laced with grey, met and held for a timeless moment. Em's voice softened. "I can imagine that this must be really hard and I apologize if I sounded pushy about it, but I do really want to know these things. Can we just give it some time and you can think about it? It would mean so much to me." With that, she lightly touched the older woman's hand across the table. Brigid tensed, looking at the hand touching hers, but she did not pull away.

"Your hands."

"What about my hands?"

"You have your mother's hands. She had the most beautiful hands, not big and rough like mine."

Em knew that to overreact would scare her aunt away, so, even though she felt like crying, happy crying this time, she smiled instead. "Thank you, Aunt Brigid."

Brigid pulled her hand away then, busying herself with her tea and clearing her throat. "So... I hear you've been riding my Bea."

"You call her Bea too? It suits her, don't you think?" Em smiled sweetly and began to tell Brigid how much she loved her horse and about the race on the beach.

"And when Jack waved his arm, Bea took off so fast that I..." Brigid was smiling now too. This was something she and Em apparently shared—a great affection for horses, especially one Irish Cob named Bea. If an outsider walked past the shop just then and looked at the two of them, they would have thought they were good friends. Or better yet, family having a day out.

～ 25 ～

Em could hear Muriel's words from her healing session echoing in her mind as she made herself a late lunch in the cottage after her tea with her aunt. "You have to release some of the grief around your heart, Emerald, if you truly want to connect to Pete." She decided that this afternoon, she would try writing to her mother instead of to Pete. What the older woman had said really made sense. Her emotions were still so raw and close to the surface, made evident by the number of times she'd been brought to tears since her arrival. At home, in her routine, she'd thought she was getting a handle on things. Being away from her home and family make her realize even more what it meant to be a single woman for the first time in her adult life. Maybe she had to give it a rest, this constant search for connection with him. Besides, the discoveries about her mother, however small, were a growing seed of yearning inside her. She still wanted very much to connect with Pete, but maybe there was a bigger purpose for her being here.

In all the years since her mother had passed, Em couldn't

remember a time when she'd simply connected with her in a space of love, something that Muriel had suggested was the most important element of after-death communication. But the pain of losing her when she was 17, just on the brink of starting her adult life, precluded her from doing so, and instead had created a wall between herself and her feelings for her mother.

Her love had turned into a feeling of loss instead. When it was time for her to marry Pete, her mother should have been there and she wasn't. When she'd lost her babies due to miscarriages, it was her mother who would have been of great comfort to her, but she had been gone. Losing her mother had been like losing a part of herself, a part that she'd had to pretend she just hadn't needed anymore. She'd just carried on as if it hadn't happened.

Until now... because here, in this place, sleeping in the cottage where she imagined her mother had slept, standing on the edge of the ocean where Eva had stood and dreamt and spread magic all around her, she knew that the time had come to remember she'd had a mother. She wondered if her healing session with Muriel had loosened the tight grip on her forgetting. She knew that the grief of Pete's death was intertwined with that of her mother's. Maybe unpacking this older wound from the depths of her being would somehow lead her to Pete.

She looked outside her window and decided that since it was a nice afternoon and she hadn't anything else to do, she would take her journal and go sit next to the field where Beatrice would be grazing. She always found it much easier to open her heart in the company of animals because they loved so unconditionally.

Em made herself comfortable under the hawthorn tree where she'd begun to sit frequently when she wanted to journal. She'd found out since from Conor that these were trees much revered in Ireland and were very connected to the otherworld. She closed her eyes and leaned back, her shoulders touching the soft moss around the base of the trunk and brought to mind the exercise that Muriel had shared with her yesterday about opening her heart. She was familiar with similar practices from all of her years of yoga, but she knew from experience that there are those times when we need to be reminded of what we think we already know.

Reverently, she laid the journal, with its red leather cover, in her lap, laying her blue pen on top and placing her hands over her heart. Breathing in and out of her heart, she tried to connect to a feeling of love... but she didn't feel anything. So, in her mind, she brought up the image of the photo that was on the nightstand by her bed in the cottage—Eva as a young girl standing by the ocean at the ringfort, her raven hair blowing wildly behind her, her arms spread wide. She'd been looking at it every day, several times a day, and she could see it clearly now—every detail—the red of her jacket, the spread of her dark hair against the pale sky, the deep blue waves tipped with frothy white behind her. Eva as a young woman with all of her life in front of her. "What happened to you, Momma?" she spoke out loud to the hawthorn tree.

As she continued to hold the image, resting her back against the hawthorn tree, embraced by the stillness around her, she began to connect with a feeling of pure love, pure caring for the woman who had brought her into this world forty years before. She expanded that feeling of love and focused on it, still breathing in and out of her heart and keeping her hands there.

She moved into a timeless realm, so aware of the beating of her heart and her breath that she began to feel as though her physical heart was actually expanding along with a tingling feeling, as though someone was tickling her, moving up and down her spine. But no one was touching her, at least no one in the physical world.

She felt tears spring to her eyes. "Is that you, Momma? Is that you?" Her tears were happy tears. Then suddenly she heard a snort and the tingling feeling immediately stopped. She opened her eyes and saw Beatrice standing at the fence line, staring straight above Em's head and blowing loudly through her nostrils. Em turned and looked up at the tree but saw nothing.

"What is it, Bea? Do you see something I don't?" Suddenly Em had a crazy thought. What if? What if the horse could see or sense her mother? What if she were really here? She looked at Bea, who looked back at her. "I'd like to know what you know, girl."

But the mare revealed nothing, just hung her head over the fence and half closed her eyes. That was one of the things that Em loved best about horses. They could be on high alert one minute and totally relaxed the next. If only people could do that, there wouldn't be so much stress in the world.

She decided that if her mother's essence was lingering around somewhere, now would be as good a time as any to write to her.

Dear Eva,

It seems right to call you Eva here, instead of mother, because here, you were still just Eva. You weren't a mother yet, just a girl with hopes and dreams. From what I've been told about you so far, you were quite a bright light in this little village. I can see that in the photo of you standing by the ocean at the ringfort. Your eyes are full of stars. I have the photo by my bedside now, right next to the photo I brought of Pete, so I can look at you both the last thing before I go to bed and the first thing when I wake up.

I guess I feel like I owe you an apology, because to be honest, until Pete died, I never really thought much about trying to contact you. I was too busy feeling sorry for myself by the loss of not having a mother around. Too busy to feel anything, first because of helping Dad look after Sophie and then trying to be a good wife to Pete. And, well, I guess you know about the miscarriages and my inability to have a child of my own.

But it was a great loss, the loss of you in my life. So many times, I felt I just needed someone to talk to who really knew me and I guess you would have been that person. I never understood why you just gave up and stopped wanting to live, or why you would want to leave us.

I mean I know you died, at least your human body died, but why so soon? You seemed really healthy even though you were sad those last few years. I didn't really believe it when Dad said you were sick. I mean I always thought you would just get better, you know? You were younger than I am now and you had a good life. At least I think you did. I mean Dad doesn't have a mean bone in his body but I don't know what kind of husband he was. When I think back on it, I never saw the two of you kissing or hugging much, so, maybe, I don't know. There's so much I don't know about you. I never got to know you as an adult.

I have so many questions. Like why did you leave Ireland when you loved it so much? Why didn't you talk to me about Brigid or my grandfather or this place? Except for the story about the ringfort, you never told me anything about Ireland.

Despite all of my questions, I want you to know that, deep down, I still really love you and I'd love to know more about you. In fact, it's one of the reasons I'm here in Ireland, although I haven't found out very much yet. I wish Aunt Brigid would open up to me, but I don't know if she will or not. She's the only one, now that Dad has lost most of his memory, who could tell me anything. I mean I guess Jack could too but he's too loyal to Brigid so I don't want to involve him in this. And it seems that Muriel knew you pretty well, though I'm not sure how or why, but I don't know how much she will tell me either.

I guess, too, I'd like to connect with you as well, maybe just a sign from you that you're here, that you've been here. I haven't felt you around. I haven't felt anything of you for so long now, Mom.

Muriel says that the signs can come in all kinds of ways, big and small and I have to learn to quiet my mind and pay attention. And I want you to know I'll try. I really will. Okay, well that's all for now I guess.

All my Love,
Your daughter, Emerald O'Shea

❧ 26 ❧

That evening Em popped around to see Muriel after dinner. She fidgeted in her chair waiting for Muriel to finish reading the letter. Finally, she could wait no longer. "Well? What do you think?"

"I think it is wonderful that you're trying to connect with your mother."

"I hear a big BUT in that statement."

Muriel's lips curved into a gentle smile, and her eyes made Em feel as if she were being held in a warm embrace. "No 'but' exactly—just a question. Have you ever tried to connect with your mother in the same way you are trying to connect with Pete? Perhaps long ago?"

Em looked down at her tea cup, sitting untouched on the round kitchen table. "Honestly, no. I remember having a few dreams that I thought were about her, but it's so long ago that I can't remember now."

"Well then, there you are! You were connecting then, even if you didn't recognize it! Good for you! Still, it's been a long while, as you just said, and even though there's no time where she is, it's still a lot of questions to put forward at once. Does that make some sense? You might want to simplify things a bit."

"I understand what you are saying, except that the questions have just begun pouring out of me. It's as if I'm finding the courage at last to allow light into a space that was in complete darkness for a long while and everything is rising up to meet that light and expand it." As Em spoke the words, she knew that the same words spoken to anyone else might fall on deaf ears. Yet she also knew, in this very moment, that this woman understood her inner workings completely and was here in her life to help her know herself better.

"Yes, of course. You're moving very quickly through new stages of healing and awareness, Em, and it's a wonderful thing to witness." Muriel paused. "And yet— these things take their own time. You've opened up the door and let in the light, as you so beautifully expressed it, and yet it might behoove you to go gently at first, to get very clear on your intentions in this process of self-discovery and connection with all that is."

Em nodded in agreement. "What do you suggest?"

"For starters, who is it you most wish to connect with? Pete or your mother? It would be good to choose one at a time to make it easier for you to receive and understand the messages when they come."

"Well, I thought it was Pete but since I've arrived I've begun to see how much grief is still around my heart." Em spoke slowly and thoughtfully. "You said that it's more difficult to connect when you're grieving so I just decided to focus on my mother instead. I thought that if I worked with that older wound of losing her, it might open me up to connecting with Pete."

"You're learning to trust your inner wisdom and that's a very big step indeed. Yet I don't believe we can heal our wounds like checking off a checklist. The best advice I can give you is to be gentle with yourself and with the process. I can understand completely that it must be difficult to be patient when you've come here for a few short weeks and are hoping to unpack decades of memories. It might be helpful to remember that others in this story of yours, like your Aunt Brigid, have also been holding onto things for a very long time."

Em gave a rueful laugh. "And holding on very tightly too! But I do hear what you are saying, although it doesn't make me feel any less frustrated."

"Why don't we go to the healing room now, then talk about this more afterward."

Pete had always told her that patience was not one of her virtues, and at this very moment she was feeling fed up with the whole thing. But something in the wisdom emanating from Muriel's eyes gave her pause. She remembered how peaceful she had felt after their last healing session and she knew, despite what her ego was telling her, she needed to let it all go for now.

Muriel got Em settled and comfortable on her table and for the first few moments Muriel used her crystal singing bowls over her chakras and Em felt herself breathing deeply and starting to relax. The room grew quiet and Em felt soft warm hands resting gently on the sides of her head. Pretty soon, Em forgot the questions, the answers, and even their conversation. She heard her own voice as if it were coming from far away, deep and resonant, asking, "Is this Reiki that you do, Muriel?"

"I've been trained in a number of holistic healing practices and Reiki is one of them." Even before she finished her sentence, Em drifted easily back into the same dreamlike state and time ceased to exist. At one point her stomach vibrated with energy from the crystal bowl that Muriel was using over her, the waves of sound flowing over and over in her ears and through her body along with a soft chant emanating from Muriel's throat. And then she knew nothing until Muriel touched her shoulder.

"Just lie there for a bit and I'll be in the kitchen whenever you are ready." Em did that for a few long moments, at last starting to come back, reluctantly, to an awareness of her body and the room she was in.

Once back at the kitchen table again, she asked Muriel about the feeling in her stomach. "Yes, that was your solar plexus and I was using the crystal bowl that is attuned with that area. You may have heard the sound of my voice also?"

"Yes, yes I did."

"That was the sound of the musical note E that reverberates with the solar plexus energy. The vibration of sound helps to re-align areas of the body, particularly the chakras that are out of balance. You've mentioned to me that you've done a lot of yoga and you know about Reiki, so you must be familiar with chakras or energy centers, yes?" Em nodded.

"Well as you may already know, the solar plexus chakra, or

energy center as I have come to know it, is where we hold our personal power. It's also about what we do and do not cooperate with. The more we are working with the energies around us, the better we are able to learn and grow. Energy centers like to be in balance, both with themselves and with each another. Think about this in relation to what you wish to achieve here. You might try sitting with your hands on that area of your body and asking what it needs to stay in balance, how you can cooperate with it."

She sat quietly after that, thinking over Muriel's words. "No one has ever explained chakras, I mean energy centers, to me that way before. It makes so much sense. So, if I'm pushing my personal power up against my aunt's without regard to keeping my balance, then it upsets me, her, and the balance between us. Is that what you're saying?"

"Exactly. It results in her pushing back even harder, instead of cooperating with you. The energy you get is the energy you give. I suggest that you tread softly with Brigid and stay aware of your own place in this, your own feelings and reaction. She may come around or she may not, but ultimately you will come away better for it."

"I really like that, Muriel. Thank you. If I might ask, do you have any more suggestions for connecting with my beloved Pete?"

"Keep doing what you are doing. Journaling and paying attention. Practicing opening your heart and most of all, believing it's possible. Belief is everything in after-death communication. And don't forget to go have some fun! You're in Ireland, the land of beauty, poetry, song, inspiration! Go with abandon and practice being like a child again! Let the answers find you… if they can catch you!" And with that, Muriel raised her tea cup to clink against Em's in a traditional Irish toast. "Sláinte," she said. "It means to your health."

"Sláinte," replied Em.

Go with abandon and practice being like a child. As she walked downhill to the cottage that afternoon, she realized that those words were ones she could do something about.

The next afternoon, Em thought of Muriel's words and prepared to do just that—have some fun. As her steps brought her closer to the barn where she was headed to see if Conor was around, she started to second guess herself. Conor seemed so completely at ease around her, while she, on the other hand, had begun to feel less at ease the more comfortable he became. She guessed it was easier for him. He wasn't getting over someone. Or was he? She remembered Jack's words to Conor that first evening she was here about finding the "right one" the next time around. If he was getting over someone, he didn't act like it, at least not around her. And as for her, what right did she have to feel good about spending time with another man—a good-looking Irishman at that—when she was still grieving her husband? She was still wearing her wedding ring, for God sakes! Instead of turning around, she just walked faster in the direction of the stables, repeating to herself, *Live with abandon and practice being like a child. Have fun.* She was breathless by the time she reached the stables and when she walked through the doors she found Conor there, whistling while he swept the aisle of the barn. When he looked up at her, she felt her heart flip flop for a moment and she almost turned around and ran. Almost. And then he spoke.

"Hey."

"Hey yourself. How's your day going?"

He nodded. "Better now," he said with a slow smile.

She decided to ignore his remark and its implication and rushed on to say what she'd come to say. "Okay, well, I was wondering what you're doing later, I mean, after work and everything." God... she sounded like she was 16 again.

"That depends. What do you have in mind?" His voice was deliberately teasing and Em nearly lost her nerve.

"I thought maybe a bite to eat and take in some music at the pub—a bit of craic as you'd call it?"

That slow grin spread across his cheeks, his eyes, even his forehead. You couldn't keep from smiling back at that face. "That would be grand. Wednesday's special is usually cod. Fresh caught."

She felt herself smiling back, and then it hit her square on—had she just asked a man out on a date? Suddenly she wanted to get out of there as quickly as she could. "Ok then. See you at my place at 6?" Her place. Those words sounded so surreal coming out of her mouth but it was her place! Hers and Sophie's.

He nodded and resumed sweeping, whistling once more. As Em turned and headed back towards the cottage, she wondered if this was what it felt like to go with abandon. It had been such a long time since she felt anything close to abandon that she wasn't really sure.

Near the end of the day, Conor, freshly washed and dressed for the evening, began walking to the cottage to meet Em for their date--was it a date? He knew that Em needed a friend right now and that she was still hurting a lot, and he wanted to be that friend. But he was feeling so much more. If he was honest with himself, his own heart had been crushed not so long ago, and he vowed not to fall for anyone for a long time. But then Em walked into his life, and in the space of a week, she was quickly becoming the only thing he thought about, the person he most wanted to see every day. Damn it, she was just too beautiful, fun, and, even when she was sad, nearly perfect. He didn't want to fall for her, and yet— he couldn't help himself.

So that was it, he decided. He would stay open, continue to be there for her, and enjoy every moment he was able to spend with her. After all, she was only here for a little over a week yet and that wasn't very much time at all.

∽ 28 ∾

Em dried herself after a leisurely bath that evening and pulled on a simple cotton dress with leggings. Nice but not too fancy. It was just a night out at the pub, no big deal, she told herself. The phone rang and she jumped on it.

"Hello?" Her voice came out sounding expectant, thinking it would be Conor. Maybe he was cancelling their plans.

"What's up, Sis? You sound a bit on edge." It was Sophie.

There wasn't a single emotion she could hide from her sister even if she tried. "I was just thinking it was Conor. We're... going to the pub for a quick bite to eat and to enjoy some music."

"You have a date with your hunky hunk Irish guy?"

Sophie's remark struck a chord in Em and she snapped at her sister in response. "It's not a date and he's not my hunky hunk Irish guy!"

"Ok sorry! I was just teasing. But it seems like a date. And he sounds pretty dreamy to me."

"Like I said before, it isn't a date and he's just... Conor. He's become a friend I like spending time with, ok? I'm just practicing living with abandon and having fun. Muriel suggested it would be a good way for me to, you know, relax and let my answers come to me."

"Uh-huh. Well just how much abandonment are you planning?"

"What do you mean, goof?" Em put the phone on speaker, throwing it on the bed. She pulled the dress over her head, changing into a lavender sweater and jeans instead. It was not a date.

"I mean is it going to involve you getting naked later?"

"Sophie!!!!!! Absolutely not! Do I have to remind you that I lost my husband just nine months ago?" She sat down on the bed now, her eyes unexpectedly filling with tears. "Oh, man, what am I doing anyway? I can't go."

"Hey, Sis, I'm sorry, I was just having some fun. Of course you should go. Pete would want you to go."

"Do you really think so, Sophie? I mean I think it's too soon to..."

"To what? To want to have fun? To have a date with a hunky hunk Irishman?"

"Will you quit calling him that!"

"It's not too soon, Em."

"He hasn't even been gone a year!"

"Yes, but you're still young, and you're in Ireland, for God's sakes! You have a life to live! Besides, spending time with someone else can be healing."

"Here we go, talking about healing again."

"What do you mean?"

"I mean it seems like that's what this trip is all about for me."

"And that's a bad thing? Listen, healing aside, go have some fun and stop worrying so much! Just go! I need to live vicariously through you right now!"

"Oh so it's really all about you then!"

"Well, of course. Isn't it always?" The sisters laughed and then Em heard a knock at the cottage door.

"Shoot! He's here! I have to go!"

"Go, go with abandon, live a little. And maybe keep your clothes on.... for now."

Em couldn't help but laugh. "You're impossible."

"And... that's why you love me."

The knock came again.

"I really have to go!"

"Love you! Have fun!"

It was fun, every bit of it. From the walk down the road in the dark, sharing lighthearted stories with Conor about their lives, the Irish music that fed her soul, the wonderful food, and the people who now recognized her as one of them. She even danced a bit when encouraged to do so by an older man who pulled her to her feet. Conor sat watching her, an amused smile on his face.

That night as they walked home, she was a wee bit tipsy and she bumped into him a couple times until he took hold of her hand. That made her feel really strange and she wanted to pull away. She looked at him and he said, "Is this alright?"

After a long moment, she realized it was alright. His hand felt warm and strong and it tingled where it met hers. She nodded and decided to ask him the thing she'd been wondering about.

"What happened, Conor?"

"What do you mean?"

"Jack told me about... about the woman you planned to marry. What happened?" She squeezed his hand gently then.

She felt his whole arm stiffen up and she thought he would let go of her hand, but instead he held it more firmly as he spoke. "I met her in Galway at an art show four years ago. She was the most exquisite thing I'd ever laid eyes on and when she looked at me, she made me feel like I was the greatest person on earth."

He stopped talking and she squeezed his hand again gently, encouragingly. "Go on. I'd really like to know, if you want to tell me that is." He looked over at her, and seeing her face lit with compassion, he continued.

"She was an artist and a great one at that. Funny because art isn't really my thing, but my crony's girlfriend wanted us to see this art show one night before dinner. Who knew that night would change my life forever."

Em knew that feeling; it was the same one she'd had the night she met Pete at the bowling alley.

"We fell fast in love, lust, I don't know, all of it, or at least I did and she made a good show of it. I don't know, maybe she did really love me, at least she made me feel that way. I proposed after four months and she said yes. But then one day about a month later, I was out with my brothers in Galway and I saw her, sitting at the end of the bar. She was wearing a low-cut black dress and the silver hoops I'd given her for her birthday. I still remember exactly how she looked sitting there, one gorgeous slim leg crossed over the other, one black high heel swinging gently back and forth. And I watched her lean in against the big man next to her, laughing at something he said, and then..." Conor's voice caught for a moment, "kissing him on the mouth as if no one else in the world existed. I knew too well how she could kiss like that, how she kissed me that way, somehow making me feel invincible."

Em stopped walking and looked at him, forcing him to stop also if he didn't want to let go of her hand, which it seemed he did not. "That's just awful! How could she? Oh, Conor. What did you do?"

Conor had a faraway look in his eyes, eyes that stared straight ahead, glinting with the hint of tears. "It was so weird, Em. I think after what you described to me about what happened to you at the pub the other night, I realize now that I must have left my body for a moment because it felt as if I were watching my heart literally shatter into a million pieces and then fall to the floor. At first, I felt nothing. And then the rage hit me hard. I wanted to kill him, I wanted to yell at her, to make her feel as badly as I felt in that moment. I've never felt that kind of anger towards anyone. Luckily my brothers hauled my butt out of there and took me someplace else to get really drunk and then they put me to bed."

She could feel his pain like a palpable thing. She continued watching him as he refused to look at her, eyes glued to the road ahead of them, her thumb now gently brushing the back of his hand. "I can say that I know what it feels like to lose someone you love more than anything, but to lose someone like that must be so very hard."

He closed his eyes, squeezing them tight as if to shut out

the memory. "Yeah it was, but I'm doing my best to put it behind me."

"Have you found anyone else since?" She couldn't help herself. She was thinking of the woman at the pub that night.

"I date some, yeah. But nothing serious. Too risky." He laughed then, but his smile seemed forced. He looked over at her for the first time. "So now you know." He let go of her hand and gestured for them to continue walking.

"Thank you for telling me. Really. It helps."

"How does it help?"

"My dad used to say that you never know what another person has experienced in their life and until you do, you can't know who they are. And I like to know about the people I spend time with."

Conor nodded. "Yeah, I see that. I guess we've both had our share of sad times... and happy ones too."

They walked on in silence, stopping from time to time to admire the clear night sky filled with stars. A feeling of peace came over them both. When they reached the door of the cottage, Conor stood there expectantly. She didn't want to ask him in just then, it felt too intimate to do so, and yet she didn't know how to say goodnight. Impulsively, she moved forward and kissed his cheek. "Thank you for everything, Conor. I had a really good time tonight."

"Thanks for listening. I don't think I've ever talked about it to anyone before, not in detail like that."

His close proximity to her, combined with the sweetness

of his nature, almost made her change her mind and invite him in. But she just couldn't. It was too soon. She knew it would be no small fling. "I appreciate your honesty and, well, I'll be saying goodnight." Though her words sounded composed, she was feeling quite the opposite. She turned away from him, throwing open the door and scurrying inside so quickly she almost tripped over the landing. She didn't stop to turn around and see those blue eyes again. What was it they said about two broken hearts?

As she climbed into bed, she had an overwhelming urge to talk to Pete. Sighing, she pulled out her journal to write. It wasn't as good as having him there in person to talk to, not nearly as good, but it was something. And somehow using one of the special journals he had given her made her feel a tiny bit closer to him. She wrote exactly the way she always spoke to him in life, telling him her every thought, uncensored, hoping he would be listening somehow.

Sweet Pete,

Do you remember when I used to call you that when we were first dating and you hated it? Just because you were young and still had the swagger of your youth about you. Thank goodness not so much swagger that you completely scared me away, not like the other boys I knew in school...

Em paused for a long moment, lost in memories of their early life together.

You always said we had the best of the best because we had found each other and we both knew exactly what we had. We were so very lucky, Pete, at least up until recently that is. But I am trying to move forward, truly I am.

This new friend of mine, Muriel, says that you can see and know everything from where you are now. If that's true then you know who Conor is too. He's really nice, I mean he's been really nice to me. I feel really comfortable with him and, to be honest, I think he's attracted to me and I'm so confused, Pete, because I feel kind of attracted to him too. But I can't, I just can't, you know, because my heart is so full of love for you. Wow, this is really weird writing a letter to your dead husband telling him you might be attracted to another man. I'm sorry, Pete, I hope that wherever you are, if you are listening, this doesn't hurt you in any way. I mean it hurts me a little even at the same time that it makes me feel, I don't know, something a little like hope. Hope that one day I'll actually be happy again, really happy.

Anyway, you'd like him I think. He's easy to be around, like you, only different in other ways too. Younger, more innocent, but wise at the same time if that makes any sense. And he's lost someone too, so we have that in common. Don't get me wrong, the memory of you is still so strong, but there is something comforting about spending time with him and I'm supposed to be gentle with myself right now, take care of myself just like you always took care of me. Like the incredible partner that you were and always will be. My hero and my best friend. The one I will always love.

Night for now. See you in my dreams?

Love always,

Your Em

⌎ 29 ⌏

E m sat on her little patio the morning after her dinner at the pub with Conor, feeling the warmth of the sun and the soft breeze that kept blowing strands of her hair in her face as she watched the horses and talked to Sophie. It was late morning in Ireland and there was always so much to catch up on.

"Come on now. Tell me more about your date with hunky hunk."

"It's Conor, and I told you it's not like that!" Em spoke firmly even though she knew she wasn't being totally honest with Sophie. She just wasn't ready to talk about what Conor was to her, especially when she was still unsure herself. Shifting the conversation in a slightly different direction, she blurted out, "Besides he's closer to your age. If you were here, he might give you something else to think about instead of..."

"Oh believe me, I have plenty to think about!"

"You do?"

"Well, there is this cute guy I see every day when I am out walking Butter. I haven't actually had a conversation with him, but he has the nicest smile. And then there's the male nurse of Dad's.

Wow he's delicious and funny too."

"Really, do tell." Em twisted a lock of her curls and sat back in her chair, silently praying that her sister had learned something from her relationship with Myles.

"Oh, there's nothing to tell. He's got a wedding ring on but I was thinking of asking him if he has a brother. Dad asks about you every day."

Em swallowed hard. "How is he?"

"He's great, he's really great, Em. I'm keeping him well supplied with his favorite snacks and the weather's been nice so we go outside almost every time I see him, which has been about four times a week."

"Wow! He's going to be spoiled when I get home." Em smiled then, able to let go of that particular worry. She knew her dad would be in good hands with Sophie from the start, but she was so used to being the one to care for him. "I don't even see him that often!"

"Yeah, I know but I'm not you, and I'm no replacement for you, Em, let's face it. And I figure if I see him more often he won't be wondering where you are. Funny about that because I think he does wonder and then he forgets what he's wondering about."

"That *is* the blessing and the curse of his disease," Em sighed. "And how are the four-leggeds?"

"Butter and Fudge are fine and more spoiled than ever. Butter is warming my feet and Fudgie is in my lap right now!"

"That's weird—Fudgie never sits on anyone's lap but mine!"

"I must smell like you or something."

"Are you saying I smell?"

"Funny."

"Hey, I have a question, Soph. You know those journals of Dad's? The ones we found when we cleaned out his place?"

"You mean the ones Dad left for you to read before you visited Ireland? Sure, I remember."

"To tell the truth, I'd forgotten all about them myself until I was packing and found them under the bed. And, well, I know it sounds weird but I felt Butter guiding me to take them with me. At first, I thought I'd read them on the plane, but I didn't, and once I got here, I sat them on the desk and haven't touched them since."

"Any idea why?'

"I'm not sure... maybe I'm scared. You know I've always thought there was more going on in our house than anyone ever talked about. I guess I'm afraid I might find out more than I really want to know."

"Yeah I get that. But isn't there... maybe a part of you that does want to know?"

Em let out a heavy sigh. "Yes, there is a part of me that wants to know. At least the adult me has been telling everyone that. But somehow, deep down, there's a scared little girl who isn't sure she is ready to find out the answers at the same time she's asking the questions. Does that make sense?"

"Yes of course it does, Em. It makes total sense. It must feel scary. On a personal level, it's harder for me to relate because your perspective on our childhood is much different than mine. As for me, I don't particularly care to look back but I respect you for wanting to do so, although I can imagine it feels conflicting."

Em felt as though her sister was not as detached from their family history as she let on, but she didn't say anything. Sophie was much younger when things changed at their house and both Em and her father had tried their best to normalize life for her, to shield her.

"I know how important this is for you, Sis, and I'm sure you'll read them when the time is right. And I'll be here for you when you do, just a phone call away."

"Do you think it's okay I haven't read them yet?"

"Definitely. And even though I said I'm not that interested in digging up the past, I must admit I am curious, so you better be prepared to share what you learn when you DO read them."

"Of course. That goes without saying."

"Miss you." Sophie giggled then. "Butter just took Fudgie's spot on the couch and she's licking my face. I think that she's saying hello to you."

"Hey, Butter," Em said into the phone. "I miss all of you too, but I know it's important that I'm here right now."

"Agreed. Well, you better get ready for whatever it is you are going to do today."

"I'm going riding with Conor."

"Conor again? Mmm... so how is that childlike abandon working out for ya?" Sophie teased.

"Will you stop already? We just have fun together and he keeps me company. He's the only person around this place that's even close to my age and he loves to ride like I do. Since they start so early in the morning, he gets a break midday and that's when we go riding. Today he's going to take me to see a faerie tree."

"Huh. It's a good thing you're in Ireland because if you said stuff like that here, people would think you were losing it."

"No worries in that regard. I think I lost it a long time ago."

"Have you seen scary Aunt Brigid again?"

"Yes, we've had a few meals together but she doesn't say much about the past. Every time I try to talk about Mom, she changes the subject and draws her mouth together like she's sucking a lemon. But maybe it's just as well. I am supposed to be living in the moment, according to Muriel."

"This Muriel sounds pretty wise."

"Yeah. I know it seems strange when I say it out loud but I do trust her, Sophie. I can't explain why. Maybe it's because Mom has been gone for so long, but she feels so maternal to me. It just feels right to spend time with her."

"I'm happy you are spending time with good people, Em."

I can't wait for you to meet her when you come to see OUR cottage! I'm sorry I couldn't bring you along this time, Sophie, especially in light of the cottage and all."

"It's ok, Em. Truthfully, all kidding about other men aside, it feels good to be alone right now. I'm realizing that I too have a lot of healing to do."

Em's heart swelled with love for the little sister she had mothered for so long and who now returned that mothering in equal measure. "That's great, Sophie." They sat in silence for a few moments.

"Well, I'd better get ready to go. Conor will be here soon."

"Can you send me a picture of this Conor? I want to see this Irish hunky hunk and put a face to my fantasy."

"And say what to him? Can I take your picture because my sister wants to see what you look like? No way!"

"You're no fun."

"Ok, ok, if the opportunity arises, I'll see what I can do."

"Like I said, I am living vicariously through you right now."

"What about the male nurse?"

"Ah he's just a bit of eye candy, but, to tell the truth, the idea of you hooking up with an Irish guy is much more exciting."

"I don't know how many times I have to say it. I'm not hooking up!"

"Sure, sure. Well, speaking of dates I have one with Butter just now for a walk. I can see it in her eyes and, besides," Sophie giggled, "she won't stop licking me! But here's my two cents, for what it's worth. You need to relax about spending time with hunky Irish. It's okay! Even if you did hook up, which I fully expect you to tell me about, you'll be back here before you know it, so it can't be anything too serious."

Her sister's words reminded her of what Conor had said the other day when she asked him if he was dating. "Nothing serious. Too risky." She certainly agreed with him about that.

She and Conor had begun to establish an easy way with

one another. It felt comfortable being together, comfortable with a tinge of something else mixed in. But she didn't think either one of them was spending too much time thinking about the something else. All least she wasn't, especially since he'd told her he wasn't interested in a real relationship with anyone. For all she knew he could be seeing lots of women. The thought of that, while a little disturbing, was somehow reassuring too. She didn't have to worry about him wanting to get too close. Being with him helped her get out of her own head around all the reasons she thought she had come here and all that she'd left behind.

That morning, for their ride together, she'd dressed in dark blue jeans and a traditional pure wool creamy white Aran sweater she'd bought in the village, which the shopkeeper had called a "jumper." Her hair was pulled up in a bun, a few of her curly locks escaping down her back. When she met him at the barn, she'd noticed that he looked at her with a heavy measure of approval he no longer tried to hide. While his attention made her slightly uncomfortable, it also made her feel more alive. He teased her a lot and she liked that. But what she needed most, and received from Conor, was his easy companionship. For all of her adult life, she'd had a partner, someone to come home to, to share things with, to help shoulder the burdens that came along. And as much as she appreciated her sister, it felt challenging at times going through life without that person.

"Race?" Connor broke into her deep musings, bringing her back to the present moment with a jolt.

"Are you kidding? After the last time?" She'd beaten him

by two lengths on little Beatrice the last time they'd raced. She'd become one with her Irish Cob in the week since she'd arrived. She couldn't believe it was already more than a week. It was one of those times when it feels you've lived a lifetime inside of a day and yet, when you stepped back to look, time was passing by in a blink.

"I'm not afraid to lose. But the question is, are you?" With that, he cracked on with his tall chestnut gelding, leaving Em laughing her head off when Bea took up the race and she nearly fell off. She quickly grabbed the mare's mane and got up out of the saddle, laughing the whole way down the stretch of beach.

"The winner!!" Conor trotted in a circle, standing in his stirrups, his right arm above his head in a show of victory.

"Cheater you mean! That was definitely not a win!" She couldn't stop laughing.

"Depends on your definition of winning. I got you laughing, didn't I?"

"You nearly killed me in the process." She pretended to sound indignant but she was smiling widely at him now, breathing hard and holding her stomach with one hand.

They walked their horses out, allowing everyone to catch their breath. "I haven't laughed that hard in... well I can't remember when." She gave Conor an appreciative look.

He just smiled back, saying nothing at all.

"Well, what's next mister?"

"The faerie tree I expect?" he answered.

She nodded. As they left the beach and rode down the lane

towards the woods once more, she realized that when she was with Conor it was becoming very easy to open her heart.

It took them over a half hour's ride along the narrow country roads to reach the lake where the faerie tree lived. Just as the lake came into view before them, a breathtaking sight in the afternoon sun, Conor turned off into the woods and soon dismounted. "The trees here are very thick so it's best if we walk the horses the rest of the way. It isn't far."

As soon as Em's feet hit the ground, she felt it. "What is that, Conor?"

"What is what?"

"I don't know, it feels different here somehow. It's as though the energy is coming up through my feet, like a subtle earthquake."

Conor looked back at her and smiled as he led his horse along a path that took them deeper into the woods. "I'd say it was the faeries welcoming you. Has Muriel told you about the fey?"

"The fey? Is that another name for them?" Em felt tiny shivers all over now.

"Yes, they are often called the fey. You should ask Muriel about it because she knows more about it than I do, but I do know that their energy makes itself known to people who are open and who welcome them."

She hadn't been aware that she had welcomed the fey but

she did so now, silently saying hello, just in case.

She could see the tree before they arrived, and, as they approached, Conor took the reins of her horse as well so she could take a closer look. "They say it's right to ask if you can move into the energy of the tree," he said gently.

Em stopped her movement and asked, not questioning this ritual. She felt that the tree was welcoming her and so she moved closer and sat on a flat rock just in front of it. She grew still and felt the sensation of being bathed in a soft energy that seemed to float all around her. She wasn't afraid of it—in fact, it felt familiar and safe.

There were many things placed in front of the tree and on its branches—small rocks, ribbons, tiny statues, crystals, notes wedged inside of things. She knew, without being told, that these were offerings to the fey, representing people's prayers, wishes, or hopes. The tree itself she recognized as a hawthorn just like the one she'd sat under near the cottage. She felt connected to this one as well, and it to her. She closed her eyes, breathing deeply. The soft airy energy continued to flow around her and she forgot where she was, she forgot about time. In this space, in this moment, everything was... one. It was a feeling she wanted to sink more deeply into, possibly stay in forever, but just then she heard one of the horses snort and she came out of her reverie, remembering suddenly where she was and who she was with. It felt so surreal to return from the place she was just a moment ago. She turned her head to look behind her where Conor stood with the horses.

As usual, Conor was smiling at her. "Just a small branch

falling on Scully's head," he said, pointing to the chestnut he rode. "Take your time, we're good here."

She wanted to leave something at the tree, something of Pete. She had a bracelet that she wore constantly, a charm bracelet that Pete had given her many years ago and each year he'd added something new. One year, when they'd spoken often of going across the sea to Ireland, just before it became obvious that her dad was losing his memory, he had given her a tiny ship for her bracelet. Now, she took the bracelet off and managed to unhook the ship. Standing and putting it into a small opening in the tree, she then placed her hand reverently on the tree's trunk. "Please bring him to me. A sign from him is all I ask, to let me know he's still with me," she whispered.

She walked back to where Conor stood, patiently minding the horses. "Thank you so much for bringing me here."

Conor just nodded and handed her Bea's reins. "Would you like a leg up?"

"Yes please." He took hold of her calf as she raised it and lifted her easily into the saddle, as though she weighed nothing at all. His hand lingered on her calf and she felt that now familiar spark of connection, and in that moment, still feeling full of the love she'd received, sitting by the faerie tree, she did not want to shy away from that spark. Instead, she smiled down at him and said the only words she could think of at that moment. "You're real!"

Conor laughed. "I think that's true enough."

She felt her cheeks grow warm. "I mean... it's just... I guess

I've just been affected by the faerie tree." She was full of feelings at the moment, ones that words could not describe.

"It can have a way of doing that." He smiled and her eyes soaked up the deep dimple in his left cheek, and eyes that matched the sky. She felt... she felt... and then he let go of her leg and turned away, gracefully mounting Scully. She didn't know whether to feel rejected or relieved.

As they rode back through the woods towards the lake, Em realized that not only was she affected by the faerie tree, but somehow, in the midst of her grief and longing for Pete, she was also affected by Conor. They rode home blanketed by a rich silence, Em feeling so very present and filled with gratitude.

∽ 30 ∾

Em took the opportunity the next day to get to know the village on her own. She'd had lunch at one of the "other" pubs in town and poked around in the charity shop, chatting to the friendly people she met everywhere. She knew that she was avoiding reading the journals, even though she'd moved them downstairs to a prominent spot in the living room to remind herself to read them. But every time she was in the cottage they seemed to be staring at her. Now back in the cottage, she stood still, looking at them for a long moment, debating with herself, but also noticing the afternoon sun shining brightly through the window. She heard Jack's voice in her head. "Make no mistake about it—when you're livin' here, lass, and the sun is out, you're to be out with it."

Em decided to heed his advice and sit outside under the hawthorn tree and write. Her time with Conor the other day had stirred up a lot of emotions, leaving her feeling the absence of Pete even more strongly. She felt that writing to him now might bring some clarity. Besides, Muriel had told her to write and write until her words flowed without thought, assuring her that doing so would help her to connect with him.

Darling,

The time is going so quickly here. The other day, I saw a faerie tree. Oh Pete, you would have laughed at me because I loved it so much! It was a hawthorn tree, just like the one I sit under now as I write to you. Beatrice is here now too, keeping me company, though she looks like she is napping. Jack told me she has some age on her, but when I'm on her she feels ageless! Maybe I shouldn't be racing her on the beach, but she loves it so much!

Conor tricked me when we raced, and I almost fell off!

Suddenly it just felt wrong to be writing to Pete about Conor. She sat with her eyes closed tightly, trying to feel Pete around her. She wanted him back so badly, wanted to feel his strong arms around her again, his hands holding hers. Instead, she felt nothing but an empty heart and when she looked down, empty hands. She had to keep trying. She wouldn't give up... she simply couldn't. She wanted to write until her head stopped thinking but her mind was whirling and she was too confused about everything. She breathed in and out of her heart, like Muriel had shown her last week, and she tried to believe. She wanted to believe that she could really communicate with Pete. She heard Muriel's words as if the woman was standing over her. "Get out of your grief. You must be in a place of peace before you will truly see the signs."

She wiped the tears from her cheeks. She made herself sit with her eyes closed... until, at last, she felt a peace come over her. It was a beautiful peace that seemed to come from all around her and inside her at the same time. It didn't feel as though it were hers alone but that it belonged to everyone and everything. For a moment, she put aside her doubt, her grief and her anxiety, and just melted into the feeling. She didn't know what it was and she didn't care.

When she opened her eyes, she saw it... a rock that was no more than ten feet away from where she sat. It was a smooth rock, like many here in Ireland, and it seemed to have some writing on it. She got up and walked over to look at it. As she peered down, her heart began to beat wildly and she could feel her pulse quickening. The message, painted in small black letters, was "HELLO." This was the fifth or sixth time she'd sat writing right here under this hawthorn tree, facing the field where Beatrice grazed, and she'd never seen this rock before today. She was sure of it. HELLO.

Time stood still and she almost laughed out loud. It was happening, it was really truly happening. The song in the pub, the dream she had, and now this. She could no longer deny with any part of herself that Pete was connecting with her.

"Pete! It is you, I know it is!" Tears, happy tears, streamed down her face and Beatrice woke up and started bobbing her head up and down as if she too was excited by the event. Em walked over to the animal she now thought of as 'her' horse, who stood very close to where the rock was, and wrapped her arms around her neck. "It's true, my beautiful horse! It's really true! He does still exist. He is around! You knew before I did, didn't you? Beautiful, beautiful girl." She stroked the mare's neck and scratched under her chin and the horse responded by laying her head over Em's left shoulder. They stayed there like that, in a happy caress, for some time.

Suddenly Em pulled back to look Bea in the eye. "I have to go see Muriel!" She kissed the horse on the nose and skipped off towards the cottage, filled with renewed vigor and hope. She just wanted Muriel to confirm what happened. She needed to believe it was real.

It turned out that Muriel was away in Dublin and wouldn't be back until tomorrow. While Em was anxious to share this exciting moment with her, she also felt fueled by that Hello. She felt like an entirely different person, like someone whose eyes had just been opened for the first time. She moved through the day paying attention to every detail of everything she did or saw. She looked for signs everywhere and waited impatiently for Muriel's return. She understood now that the time she was spending with Muriel was an apprenticeship of sorts.

The next day, when she was sure that Muriel had returned and was settled, Em popped in for a visit.

"Wait a minute. Does that mean that the dream I had telling me to come here to Ireland and the song they played at the pub that night..."

"They were all signs from your beloved, yes."

"But why didn't you tell me that before, Muriel?"

"Because you had to learn to believe for yourself first. I could have told you but you had to feel it in your own heart."

"You did help me though. I know that everything we've been doing together has helped. Oh Muriel, I just feel so happy, like a weight is lifted. It doesn't change the fact that Pete isn't here in the flesh, but it brings me such joy to know he is still around! He hears me. He sees me."

"And he wants to help, Em. This much I know."

"Help with what?"

"With all the other questions you came here to have answered. You can know now, without a doubt, that Pete will be a guide for you going forward. You still have much to discover."

"How do you know what you know?"

Muriel just smiled and sipped her tea. "I've been blessed to be able to spend a lot of time learning to listen, really listen. And you? You do the same, far more than you know. You are so much like her."

"Like Eva?"

"Yes, like Eva. You're a dreamer just like her, though a part of you had forgotten how to do that. You have her magic."

Em felt a strange sense of excitement at Muriel's words. "I've never allowed myself to think about her. It just hurt too much and then after a while, I couldn't remember anymore. But I feel like her when I'm up at the ringfort. I see her face in the photo I have in the cottage when she was a girl and can imagine how she felt being in such a glorious place. But I don't know if I'm like her or not. I guess I've always been kind of practical, like my dad."

"Maybe you just needed to come here to bring out the playful side of you again." The older woman's eyes held deep knowing.

"Lately, when I'm there at the ringfort, I've been thinking about when I was little, trying to remember what she was like then, but it seems that my heart has been closed for so long I only get bits and pieces. I can see the face of my dad, his eyes sparkling like two bits of glass whenever he looked at her. What I mostly remember are the later years, though, when everything was different. I'm not sure when it changed and I never understood why."

"Your dad, have you ever talked to him about it?"

"No, I mean, I tried a few times after she died, but he was so closed off. He didn't want to talk about anything to do with her. So, I just stuffed it down deep and carried on. It wasn't long after that I met Pete and my whole life changed."

"And now? Could you ask him now?"

Em looked down at the floor and didn't speak for a long moment or two. "Now my dad has no memory anymore. He lives in a world all his own."

"I'm so sorry. Dementia?"

"Yes," she nodded. Clarity struck Em like a sudden blow. "The journals. It's all in the journals. That's why he was so insistent. It all makes sense now."

"The journals?"

Em told Muriel about her father's journals. "Even though he wanted me to read them before I came here, I didn't, but I did bring them with me. I wonder if he wrote down the things that were too painful to tell Sophie and me, things he could no longer express."

"It sounds as though you may have brought some of your answers along with you."

Em nodded. "I have to go now, Muriel. Thank you so much for the tea and for... everything."

∾ 31 ∾

E m walked to the ringfort the next day. Though she'd told Muriel that it was time to read the journals, still she resisted, living instead in the present moment. More than reading about the past, she wanted to feel it for herself, to connect more fully to her own memories of her mother—the ones she kept locked inside.

She found herself talking to Pete on the way up the steps.

"I think of you every single day here, Pete, many times a day in fact. Every step I take on this Irish soil just reminds me more deeply of how I'd love to be sharing this with you. But maybe in a way I am?" She thought, smiling, of the rock and the wealth of other little signs she'd been flooded with since then that Pete was with her. A penny she'd found in the woods. A wind that would wrap itself around her when she was thinking of him. And last night she'd dreamt of him again. She felt the urge to send him love and realized it was a love that didn't contain quite as much grief or longing as before. It felt lighter the more she connected with him. Looking for signs was quickly becoming second nature to her and it felt intrinsically right.

She was dancing across the ridge at the edge of the sea,

singing an Irish tune that Conor taught her the day before called *The Boys from County Cork.*

"You have made yourself at home here, I see." The voice startled her, coming from behind. She turned and saw her aunt approaching, a cane in her right hand. Though Em hadn't spent much time with her aunt, she'd never noticed her using a cane before.

"I have?" Even though she was working hard to be at ease with her aunt, she still couldn't help feeling defensive over everything she said. What did she mean? Wasn't she supposed to be feeling at home here?

Brigid cleared her throat and sat on the flat rock near the edge of the cliff leading to the sea. She sighed heavily as if the walk had tired her. "Yes. It's good."

Somehow the words didn't seem to reach her heart and though Em still felt uncomfortable she tried to recognize what her aunt might be feeling. "It must be difficult for you to have me here, after such a long time."

"What is it that you do? Are you a counselor or something?"

"No. I work with horses for a living. Why do you ask?"

"Because I feel as though you are always analyzing me, how I feel, what I'm thinking, and I don't much like it."

Brigid hadn't slept well and had woken with a stiff neck. She felt cross today and she'd come to the ringfort to lift her spirits. It was disappointing not to be alone here and worse, to have to deal with more questions from this niece of hers. She could almost hear Jack's voice, saying, "Be nice, Biddy." But today, she just didn't feel like being nice. Today she just wanted to be alone.

Em bit back the words of retaliation that rose in her throat. She knew it would only make things worse. "I'm just trying to get to know you."

"Why?" Brigid couldn't help herself... she just felt combative.

"Because... because I crossed an ocean to see you, to be near my mother's birthplace, to find out..."

"Yes, yes to find out the answers to your questions! Always questions, always demands. I told you. The past is in the past and it is better left alone. You're not here to get to know me. You're just here for your own reasons."

Em grew silent for a long moment. There was some truth in what she said. She did have an agenda for being here, at least when she first arrived. But now that she'd begun to experience the beauty and the magic that this land held for her, and she'd connected with Pete, those reasons didn't seem quite as important as they had in the beginning.

She picked up a stick, tracing circles in the dirt. "You're right, Aunt Brigid. I did come here with a specific purpose in mind. But you're wrong about me not wanting to get to know you. I've done nothing but try to know you since I've arrived. And my mother's history *is* my business. She carried me inside her body, she raised me until I was 17!! Of course I want to know her better. I *need* to know her better. I lost my husband and I feel as though I can't move forward until I make peace with what's past. Can you understand that?" Em could feel her face flush with emotion.

This time Brigid was the one who was silent. She stared straight ahead and when she did speak it was as though she were stuck inside another time. "Carry you inside her she did, against all odds of it working out. She was so brave... my little sister... despite everything that happened to her, despite watching all of her childhood dreams disappear into thin air. She was always the brave one. I was just the stubborn one. And look where my stubbornness has gotten me. I'm old and alone." Em wanted to say, "But you have Jack!" but stilled her mouth into silence.

Em didn't understand much of what her aunt had just said but at least she was talking. What did she mean when she said against all odds of it working out? Tentatively, she asked, "What were her dreams?"

Brigid smiled then and Em relaxed. "She used to come here all the time and dance and sing to the fey and to the dolphins and the sea birds. It was the place where she came to dream of living a grand life, traveling the world, creating beauty and magic wherever she went." She looked at Em then, as if she just remembered Em was there and not her sister. "She did create beauty and magic. She may not have gotten 'round to seeing all the world, but she did know how to create magic."

Brigid's words must have called forth the magic of her mother Eva because they hit her chest and she felt an opening where previously there was none, like a flower bursting open in the spring air. All of a sudden, it was as though not only the memories, but her mother's love could be felt once more inside her own heart. She felt overcome by the sensations, the sounds, and the feelings of her mother again, after all these years. She could remember being a little girl and seeing her mother's face over hers as she tucked her into bed at night, and there were always colors around her, beautiful colors.

She sat down on the grass opposite where her aunt perched on the rock, smiling into the sea with her eyes closed. "She did, didn't she?" she whispered. "I don't remember the details but I do remember the feeling. Tell me, Aunt Brigid."

"Tell you what?"

"How? How did she create magic?"

Brigid softened as if she too could feel the magic of her sister there with them and for once she chose to remember her without the pain. "She had a light about her. Everywhere she went, people felt it. Everyone wanted to be with Eva. The shopkeepers would smile when they saw her and they gave her things, without her even asking."

"What kinds of things?"

"Food, supplies, you name it. They knew that my sister was a person who lived for others. She looked after the poor and the needy because we were so well off you see. And Eva felt as though she had to give back. Our da would never give away his riches so Eva went 'round the village collecting things and taking them to the poorer folks. And then there were the animals too."

"The animals?" Em turned to face Brigid now, her arms hugging her knees, her eyes wide.

"Animals seemed drawn to her, all living creatures, even the dolphins, spoke to Eva. The village people always said she was part fey. She was so full of fun and laughter. Pure joy that one."

Em felt a kinship with her aunt in those moments when they sat together, lost in memories of Eva, one who meant a lot to them both. Em looked up and thought she detected a few tears brimming from the corner of Brigid's eyes, but the woman swabbed at her face with her fists and stood up abruptly, breaking their momentary connection. "I better be getting on. Looks like rain. Mind you don't stay too long, you don't want to get caught out." She turned to walk away without another word.

"Brigid?"

The woman turned back. "What is it?"

"Thank you. Thank you for telling me those things."

Brigid gave a curt nod, cleared her throat, then turning her back to the sea once more, moved steadily away, her cane sounding her departure as she engaged it firmly with each stride. Em turned her face back towards the ocean and continued to sit there for a long time, feeling into all the beautiful memories of a mother who had left this world long ago.

❧ 32 ☙

Em woke up in the cottage the next day and immediately noticed how still everything seemed. There was an overwhelming sense to her that she wasn't alone, as though a very peaceful presence was there. She grabbed her notebook off the nightstand and started to do some writing.

Pete, I feel a presence here. Is it you I feel?

After that, Em sat still and waited for her pen to move across the page. And move it did within a few moments. But the writing wasn't about Pete, it was about her mother. Suddenly memories of her mother were showing up on the page, one after another. She wrote and wrote until her hand was cramping and she had to shake the pain out and yet she still wrote some more. "Just continue to move your hand across the page and don't stop to correct anything or to think." She remembered the words of her writing teacher from years ago and kept on writing.

She felt as though the words were coming through her, not from her, as if it were her mother writing them. They were words describing happy times full of laughter and love, times they'd spent together reading and walking in the woods and making up faerie tales. She wrote about the time when they decorated the forest with paper faeries and unicorns. They hung them in the trees and then they danced among them and sang to them. She remembered feeling as though her mother was the most incredible person in the world. Em didn't stop to think, she just wrote, but she knew that these memories were precious and she hadn't thought of them in such a long time. It seemed as though the bad years with her mother had erased the other times.

When she finished, she just sat and stared, listening to the silence. She felt the air around her and it was different, as though the presence was no longer there and yet the stillness remained.

"You'll know you're starting to settle when you begin to listen to the silence. Ireland, she has a way about her. She has a way of slowing you down and helping you to hear what needs to be heard." Muriel had told her this on their last visit together.

Em knew a lot about fight or flight, something horses did by instinct and something people did far too often in this fast-paced world of cell phones and to-do lists a hundred miles long. Horses reacted to a danger or threat quickly, easing back into a calm and steady state just as quickly when the danger passed. But for Em, ever since the day the water flooded under the bathroom door in her home in North Carolina, she was on high alert and never truly relaxed, even in sleep. Often, she would wake up as stiff as a corpse, her neck and shoulders tight as if she'd been holding on all night, holding on for dear life.

But here, in the stillness of the morning, in the aftermath of her writing and the love those memories evoked, she began to feel exactly what Muriel was talking about. She felt she could just exist in this place—for the first time in a long time, she could let down her guard and just feel safe to simply be. Was Pete bringing her this sense of safety and stillness? He always did that in life, why not now too? Could it be that his death was now here to inform her life? She sat with that thought until the morning light came peeking through the skylight and her tummy started to growl. Then, taking a long slow stretch, she rose from her bed, putting on her green robe and matching slippers, and padding downstairs to the kitchen for a cup of morning tea.

The day quickly turned cold and wet, the rain relentless on the roof of the cottage and Em had no mind to do anything. She stayed in her robe, made a second pot of tea, and warmed the leftover scones she'd brought home from Glebe Gardens. Day-old scones were probably not the thing to do, but today they were her thing.

She huddled close to the fire, wishing Butter was beside her. It was in those quiet moments, like when she was in bed writing to Pete or sitting here now with nothing to do, that she missed her most. She missed Fudgie too but her cat was more of a creature unto herself, whereas Butter was perpetually glued to her side.

Her energy was drawn to the small table where her dad's journals sat. "Yes," she said, speaking directly to them. "I know I said it was time." After being with Brigid yesterday and drawing back to herself the fond and meaningful memories of her mother along with the guided journaling she'd done this morning, she knew she was ready for anything her father had to share.

As she picked up the first journal (her father had them all dated chronologically), she had one of her tingles go through her and a sudden knowing that life as she knew it was about to change. She hesitated briefly, took a deep breath, then opened the journal and sat back in the comfortable chair by the hearth to read.

Em had never read anything her father had written before, and it turned out that he was as exacting a man in his writing as he had been in life. He wrote methodically of his daily comings and goings, his work, his parents, and his impressions on the state of the world. She found herself skimming through many of the pages, wondering what it was that her eyes were meant to see, that her heart was meant to know. Then came an entry in April on the day that Eva and Jonathan were married.

April 22, 1973

Eva is the most breathtaking woman I've ever met. In all of my life I could never imagine that a woman as perfect as she, so beautiful, so fun and smart, so full of life, would ever want to marry an ordinary man like me. Today was our wedding day and when I saw her in her dress and veil, standing outside the justice of the peace, I thought my heart would burst out of my chest just looking at her. I'd told her that we should get married properly, in the church, so that her family would accept me as her husband, but she said no self-respecting priest would marry them now.

As I looked down at her broad belly, swollen with new life inside it, I had to admit she was right. It was 1973 and the Catholic Church still didn't look favorably upon women getting married after the fact.

Em closed the book and her eyes at the same time, trying to stop her swirling thoughts and still her pounding heart. Her swollen belly? She was already pregnant with her when she married her father? If that were true, surely either her mother or father would have told her. There had to be an explanation for all of this, there just had to be. She looked once more at the year. 1973? Wait a minute, that wasn't right. Eva and her father were married in 1972 because she, Emerald, was born in June of 1973. Em just couldn't comprehend it. She steeled herself to read a little more.

All in all, though, it doesn't matter in the end because there's no way I could be happier than I am today. As for myself, I don't give a whit what any church thinks because I'll take Eva O'Shea on any terms, for she is the best thing that's ever happened to me.

She read the words over and over. What did he mean when he said that he would take her on any terms?

An inner knowing threatened to shut her down completely at that moment. She sat and breathed into the feeling that was rooted deeply in her gut, realizing that she'd come here with a resolve to know the truth, a resolve she'd been building on since her arrival and one she felt was being supported by Pete. She opened her eyes and read on, searching for more entries about her mother. It would seem that a man who was so in love would write constantly about her but there were still a number of entries about mundane things. Em was impatient to learn more and quickly thumbed through the pages, looking for Eva's name.

June 1, 1973

Eva is uncomfortable all the time now. The baby is so huge that I don't actually know how she can stand upright. She is so petite. I worry about the delivery but she doesn't seem afraid, only excited about having this baby. Her gold eyes flash with excitement when she talks to me about the things we still need to get before the birth. I am working all the time now and when I have the evenings with her, we sit on the couch and I rub her sore back and feet. This is the closest she has allowed me to be near her in two months. It seems as though the nearer she gets to her delivery date, the further away from me she gets. She continues to write those damn letters and asks me to mail them each week. I don't ask who the man is that she is writing to, though in the pit of my gut I already know the answer. I don't say a word about it. I must confess, though, I haven't had the heart to mail them just yet. I'm just going to hold onto them for a while and see what happens. We have time, Eva and I. She is growing fonder of me each day I think. I just want us to work so much. I would lay down my life for her in a second and for this baby too.

Letters? What letters? And who is this man her mother wrote to? The gnawing in her stomach had turned to nausea and her hands were shaking now. Her father called the baby *this baby*, not *their baby*. Was it possible she was not her father's child? Her mind tried to deny it but her heart was telling a different story. No matter what came next, she had to know the whole truth at last. This time she read every word as she didn't want to miss a thing. She thought of her father's words to her when they cleaned out his house. "Read these journals before you go back to Ireland." He knew. He'd known all along.

After many laborious pages in which Jonathan Watts chronicled the many cases that he dealt with in his medical practice, the improvements and repairs he was making to their apartment in Brooklyn, his discourse on the weather and his nightly walks, sometimes with Eva and sometimes not, she finally arrived at the next entry about Eva.

July 18, 1973

The baby has those big oval eyes just like her mother's, though hers are green while Eva's are a curious gold. Her hair is ginger instead of black like her mother's, but the resemblance is still striking. I've never seen such a devoted mother as Eva nor one so beautiful. She is so protective of the infant that I can barely get near her most of the time, and in truth, she spends a great many hours now sleeping or being at her mother's breast. But I don't mind so much. I get my joy from watching them, being with them, and doing the things that make both their lives easier. When I'm home and not at the clinic, I'm washing clothes, making beds, preparing food for the next day, and sterilizing things for the baby. I want Eva to conserve all of her energy and I know she is exhausted. Eva is grateful to have me with her, I know, but sometimes when she strokes the soft red fuzz on the baby's head, she gets that distant look in her eyes, as though she is trying to transport herself elsewhere.

She's been too busy to write any more letters to "him" since the child's birth, which was a difficult one, with her developing toxemia late in her pregnancy. I've seen this in a few of my own patients, and I know full well that it takes time for the body to recover from it. Eva's doctor advised her not to have any more children due to this condition, which can repeat itself, so I don't know what that will mean for our intimacy. I wouldn't expect her to want to have sex when she's nursing, but she doesn't seem much interested in that anyhow. She treats me more like a brother or a best friend than her lover. Most of the time I don't mind but I have to admit to hoping for a bit more the longer we are together. They say love grows in time and even arranged marriages can bloom into something real. Not that ours was arranged exactly, but it may as well have been.

Em sat very still. His words confirmed something she'd always known deep down—that her mother did not love her father in the same way he loved her. While it saddened her, it also brought clarity. It explained why her father's eyes shone when he looked at her mother, while her mother seemed to busy herself with other things whenever he approached. It explained so many things that Em had observed growing up and didn't quite understand. Until now that is. But the part she now needed to know with absolute certainty was if someone else was actually her father.

She looked down for a moment at her hands holding the

journal and it suddenly seemed she was not in her own body but in that time and place with them, hovering over the scene as she read. Yet this was no fictional story and she already knew there was no happy ending.

I remember the night I asked her to marry me as if it were yesterday...

$$\sim 33 \sim$$

April 2, 1973

"Y ou're saying you want to marry me then?" Eva asked
point-blank as we sat in my car after the movies one
night. We'd been dating only about two months. "Don't
you think it's a bit sudden?"

I touched her stomach softly. "Sooner might be better than
later."

"You think I care about what people will say? Well, I don't!"
But as she spoke her ivory skin turned pink around the edges. "They can
all go to hell, they can!"

"Eva! Calm down now. It's not good for the baby."

"But why do you want to marry me?" She turned in her seat to
face him.

"Because I am in love with you. I've never been so smitten in all
my life, Eva. And I want to take care of you. I will take care of you,
you'll see. You won't have to worry about anything. I've got a good
position at the clinic and eventually we can move to a small town and

buy a home..." Eva put a finger to his lips to shush him.

"Jon, you're a good catch, as my da would say, and no doubt he'd approve if he knew not that I care what HE thinks!" Eva's father was still in Ireland and she hadn't spoken to him in months, ever since he shipped her off to America to live. She was on her own now and no one was going to tell her what to do any longer.

"And?"

"And I would be blessed, truly, to have such a kind man as you to marry, I would, I would, Jon. But..."

"But what, Evie?"

"But I'm in love with another man. The father of this baby. I like you very much but I'm not in love with you."

Em dropped the journal to the floor then, feeling the air whoosh out of her body. This was the confirmation of everything she'd already felt was true almost as soon as she'd begun reading. But seeing it in black and white was still an overwhelming truth to face alone. Once she felt like she could breathe again, she picked up the phone in the cottage and tried to call Sophie, not knowing or caring what time it was.

"Pick up, pick up!" She willed into the phone and when it went to voicemail, she hung up and sat, staring into space. Though her body was still, her mind raced. How could she not know this? Why? Why would her parents keep this from her, her entire life? She suddenly remembered what Brigid had said at the ringfort about leaving secrets alone. What else had she said that day? "Carry you inside her she did, against all odds of it working out."

So—Brigid knew, and likely Muriel and Jack too. Maybe even Conor? Why hadn't anyone said anything?

The words she'd read rang over and over in her head—*I'm in love with another man. The father of this baby.* The man she'd adored all her life, the man she'd looked up to, was not her real father. The thought crossed her mind that somewhere out there was her biological father, but she instantly dismissed any thought of that. It was too much. She could hear her father's voice when he gave her the journals. "These are for you, daughter. All for you. Promise you'll read them when you go to Ireland and not before." Her father was no coward so it didn't make sense why he hadn't told her himself, instead of insisting she find out this way. Nothing made any sense right now.

It was then she thought of Pete and she spoke as if he were right beside her. "Oh Pete, I need you here now more than ever. You would know exactly what to say, what to do." She wished more than anything to be able to feel his comforting arms around her. She felt so broken and so alone.

As if in response to her thoughts, there was a sudden knock on the door. She ran to it and yanked it open, half expecting to see her dear departed husband, but it was Conor's face she saw instead. Of course it would be Conor. She gestured for him to come inside and no sooner had she closed the door behind him, he looked at her and said, "Something wrong?"

That was all it took and once again, like the day she'd had tea at Aunt Brigid's, she fell into his arms.

For a few moments, Conor had the great presence of mind

not to say a word. He just held her, stroking her hair and gently patting her on the back. She shook with anger and cried all at the same time. "Why did he want me to find out like this? Why is it only now, after all these years that I am finding out about these things?" His arms might not have been Pete's arms, but they felt comforting and strong, safe and gentle, and he smelled of the sea.

Conor knew not to ask any questions. "It's okay, you're okay." He kept saying the words over and over. "It's okay, it's going to be okay." When her sobs subsided and she'd stopped shaking, he gently eased her back a little to look into her eyes. "You're shivering! Let's go sit by the fire, yes?" Em nodded mutely and allowed him to lead her over to the two chairs nestled in front of the wood stove. But the journals were there too, on the chair where Conor was to sit. He looked at her as if to ask where to put them.

"Please put them out of my sight. I don't want to look at them!" Conor took the journals, including the one that had fallen to the floor when Em ran for the door, and quietly tucked them into a cupboard along the wall. He added some wood to the fire and sat beside her, taking her hands and warming them between his own.

Em started to feel calmer, the touch of his hands soothing and safe. She looked at him with a tear-stained smile. "Thank you for being so kind to me."

He stared at the fire as if to cover up his own emotions. "Nah, that's what ya do here. People look out for one another. It's just the way I was raised up." Then he faced her squarely, with that same kind and open expression she was coming to appreciate so much. "I don't like seeing you this way is all."

Em nodded but was silent for a long moment. "I've just received a big shock, and I'm feeling as though my world is falling apart... again."

Conor nodded as if he understood.

"Oh goodness, I must apologize. I'm sure you didn't come over here just to rescue me a second time." I don't even know what time..." she looked down suddenly at her green robe and slippers and her cheeks pinked. "I'm not even dressed." In her distress she hadn't even thought about what she was wearing until now.

He smiled, his blue eyes glinting with the firelight. "They match your eyes."

She realized he was trying to lighten the mood but her thoughts were only on one thing. The journals. "Do you have to go yet? I mean would you mind staying for a bit?"

"I'm off today as it happens. I'm headed into Cork but not for a while."

She looked at him gratefully. "Would you like some tea or something to eat maybe?"

"I'm fine thanks. I'm more concerned about you right now. I'm happy to listen, to know what's gotten you so upset, if you want to tell me, that is."

"The books you put away for me? Those were journals that my dad," her voice caught at the word dad, "wrote over the years." She explained to Conor about how she came to have the journals. "I finally had the courage to begin reading them this morning only to discover things about my own life that I should have been told all along."

"Whoa. You've had quite a morning. What made you decide to read them today?"

"That's a good question. I've been trying to read them ever since I got on the plane to come here but kept putting it off. As I spent more time here, I came to understand that one of the biggest reasons I had come was to heal my relationship with the past. But when I met Aunt Brigid, the one person who I thought could help me make sense of things, she just bristled at all of my questions, going on about how some secrets are better left alone." Em paused for a moment, thinking about her time with Brigid at the ringfort the day before. "That is, until I saw her at the ringfort and she opened up a bit more. And after talking to Muriel again, I knew the time had come for me to read them, to take it upon myself to find the answers I was seeking."

"It seems those answers have brought the sadness upon you."

The quaintness of his expression along with his compassionate tone eased her of any doubt that Conor was the person she needed to be with her just now. She knew what she had to do. "Yes." Em's eyes caught his. "Just a few pages in a journal have turned my life inside out." She got up and walked to the cupboard where Conor had put the journals. She picked out the one she'd been reading, opened to the entry in question, and held out the book to Conor. "I know it's a lot to ask, but would you be willing to read this out loud? I think it would help to have you here."

"Are you certain it's me you want to read this?"

Em gave a half smile to cover up the tears she held in tightly. "Other than Muriel, you're the closest friend I've got here. I trust you and right now I don't trust myself to finish it alone. If you wouldn't mind, that is. If Sophie were here, I'd ask her to do it, but she's not. I know it must seem strange because we've only known each other a matter of days, but… "

He gave a small nod, reached out his hand, and took the book from her. They both settled in next to the fire again and he began to read. His rich soothing voice calmed her and settled her nerves. She felt held by that voice. When he got to the part where Eva stated that she was in love with another man and carrying his child, he looked up at Em. "You never knew?"

Em shook her head, the tears streaming down her face, but quietly this time. "Go on please. I didn't read past that point."

"Em, are you certain it's not too much?" He held her gaze.

She nodded. "I'm positive."

Conor stared at the page, cleared his throat, and continued reading.

"If you are so in love with this other man, then where is he? Why aren't you with him?" I was angry and didn't want to give up. I knew in my heart that Eva and I would be good together.

"He's far away. He's in Ireland and things were… broken… between us. But it doesn't change how I feel and it never will! I will always want to be with him, my true love, the father of my child. And I'm willing to wait if that's what it takes!"

I braced myself. I wasn't going to give her up for some phantom lover.

"How long?"

"How long for what?"

"How long do you think it will take?"

"I don't know. Maybe forever."

"It seems to me that while you are waiting, your child needs a father and you need someone to be by your side. Surely raising this baby alone with no money is not what you want, is it? Babies need lots of nurturing and care and how can you do that if you're broke and working all the time?"

"My father would want me to give the baby up for adoption if he knew about it."

"Is that what you want?"

"No!!! Of course not!"

"Well then, I'm offering you a solution to your problem. All I ask is that you say yes to marrying me. If this man comes along to take you back... well, I'm willing to take that chance. But in the meantime, let me take care of you and this baby, Eva." I took her small hand and watched it disappear inside my large one and she gave me the hint of a smile, considering what I said. I could feel her hand trembling inside mine.

"You won't hold me back when my beloved comes for me? Because he will, you know!"

I can still feel my heart thumping in my chest just as I did that night in the moment she said those words. What kind of a deal was I making? But then I looked straight into the golden depths of her eyes and I knew where my destiny lay. "No. I won't hold you back. All I ask is to love you as long as I can have you."

And so we were married. And after the baby was born and she first opened her eyes, I said to Eva, "Her eyes are as green as emeralds."

"Then we shall call her Emerald, after the island from which she came." Though it hurt me to hear her say those words, knowing she loved another man, I was still happy she was with me... that they both were with me. And I swore to myself to be the best father the child would ever know.

Conor stopped reading as he reached the end of the entry. He let the book fall gently into his lap and looked across at Em.

"He was too. The best father ever. Still is... even though he doesn't remember much anymore."

"And this is the first time you've been told any of this?"

Em nodded. "In the last hour, I've learned that my father isn't my biological father, my real father is presumably somewhere in Ireland, and my sister Sophie is... my half-sister!"

"No wonder you were so upset. I'm sorry, Em. That's a lot to digest and an awful way to find out."

Em nodded, staring straight ahead into the fire. "It certainly is. I just don't understand it. I don't understand why neither of them ever told me. Especially my dad. He and I talked about everything. I feel like my whole life has been a lie."

Conor just sat quietly, allowing her to process, getting up to stir the fire and add more wood. He went to the kitchen and made them each a cup of tea. They sat silently for a time, watching the flames. Finally, he spoke. "Is there anything I can say or do to help? Do you want me to get your Aunt Brigid?"

Em nearly choked on the tea she was sipping. "No thank you! I don't think Aunt Brigid would be of much help. In fact, I'm sure she knew about all of it." Brigid's words rang in her head then. "Eva was so brave, despite all the things that happened to her... " What had happened to her mother? Why was she separated from her beloved, the man who apparently was Em's biological father? She now knew part of the story, thanks to her father's journal, but there was obviously so much more she didn't know. Something shifted inside her. The "sadness upon her" as Conor had put it was replaced with a different feeling. A feeling even stronger, a resolve to uncover all that remained of her mother's, and indeed her own story. Despite her emotional state, she was made of strong stuff and she knew it. She didn't care what it took. She would see this through, and she would need the cooperation of these people she'd met in Ireland. She turned to Conor. "He wrote this journal for me, at least part of it anyway. He made me promise to read it because he didn't have the heart to tell me himself. It actually explains a lot about my childhood."

"What do you mean?"

"Well when I think about how my mom and dad were with one another, it really was an unbalanced relationship. He doted on her and she was sweet to him, but more like a friend than a lover. Just like he said in the journal. I accepted it when I was young as being the way things were but as I grew into my teens, I always had a feeling that things weren't quite as they should have been.

So many things make sense now. She must have felt so desperate being part of one life while wanting to be part of another. A life with her true love."

Conor remained silent, and Em felt supported by his compassionate presence. "Conor, tell me, did you know about this?"

He hesitated briefly before answering. "I did know there were secrets about. There was a lot of talk before you came that everyone hushed up about whenever I came round. But I didn't pay much attention. I figured it was not my business to know."

She took him at his word. "Well, I'm going to find out exactly who knows what and I'm not going to be so polite about it anymore either. I have less than a week left here and I'm not leaving without answers."

"Yes of course. Muriel's been a close friend of the family a long time. She's older than Brigid and she knew Brigid's father and mother, your grandparents. My guess is that if you can't get anything out of Brigid, maybe she can help."

"Thanks, that's good to know. I know that my mother was just a baby when her own mother died, but she never wanted to talk about her father to me, except to say he was a busy man and didn't travel much. I never felt she had much of a relationship with him at all. I've seen pictures but that's about it. There's so much more I need to know."

Conor nodded empathetically and, after a long and rich moment, as understanding flowed silently between them, he got up to stretch and stir the fire. "I hate to leave you but I should get on if I'm to make it to Cork and back before dark. Will you be alright then? Can I bring you anything?"

Suddenly her head felt very full and she was so tired. She stood, placing a hand on his arm. "Thank you for everything. Yes, I'll be alright. I just need time." He reached his own hands out to hold her arms gently. They stood like that for a long moment, she holding his arm and he holding both of hers and he didn't seem to want to let her go.

"You are a good friend, Conor."

Conor simply nodded his thanks, gently releasing her and, turning to go, he opened the door of the cottage and walked down the path.

As Em closed the door behind him, Conor heard her words ringing in his head. "You're a good friend." *Yes*, he thought, *just like Jonathan Watts was a good friend to Eva*. He was beginning to understand what that man must have felt. *It's tough to have feelings for an O'Shea woman.*

◦ 34 ◦

Em hadn't the heart to read anymore after that. She needed time to process all that she had discovered, but she did feel calmer now, thanks to Conor's supportive presence. Her thoughts turned to Sophie. Though her first urge had been to share what she knew so far with her younger sister, she felt it might be best to wait a bit. Just until she knew the whole story. Her protective instincts towards Sophie were strong, especially now, faced with this, and she wanted to be able to present it in the best light. She would deal with this on her own, at least for the moment. She decided to get dressed, have something to eat, and go to the barn to see Bea. She hoped no one was around so that she and "her" lovely four-legged friend could have some time together. After that, well, after that maybe she'd come back and read more of the journals. "One step at a time" were the words ringing in her head, just as Pete would always say to her when she got overwhelmed by life. One step at a time.

The barn was quiet, save for the sound of the horses munching their noontime hay. She spent a long time brushing Beatrice and fussing over her, talking to her and telling her about everything that was going on. She felt so supported and soothed by being in the barn this way and she realized how much she missed this. After Magpie had died of colic some five years before, Em had busied herself with her work at the vet clinic and teaching riding once a week. She loved what she did, but it wasn't the same as spending time with your own horse. Pete often asked her if she wanted to get another horse, but with her dad's health failing and Pete's construction business growing busier all the time, Em had always said no. She didn't think she would ever have the time to truly spend with a horse. She didn't even know until today just what a big hole that decision had left in her heart.

There was something different too about being alone with Bea. She loved riding with Conor and Jack. They were great fun, but being alone with a horse, not having to talk or be any certain way except who you really were, was a feeling she hadn't experienced in a very long time. The stillness allowed her to think calmly and deeply about those years when she was young and her mom had stopped being a mom.

During the period that she thought of as the "sad years," when her mother spent a great deal of her time in bed, Em had taken Sophie to the park a lot, made her after-school snacks, helped her with homework, and often saw her to bed at night. It wasn't every night—Mom had her up days but, looking back on it, she also remembered lots of down ones as well, and everyone in the family just had to cope as best they could.

Thinking of her dad, the man who raised her, just made her heart ache. She didn't believe it was possible that he wasn't her real father. He'd never made her feel for a second that she was anything less than his own child. He was a damn good father and she wondered how in the world he'd held it together for so many years, knowing what he knew. Her dad had never been a prideful man, but it must have been impossibly difficult for him knowing that her mom was in love with someone else. But then again, it would seem he had known this from the start and he married her anyway.

As she continued to brush Beatrice, her head full of thoughts, it was as though the mare could read her mind... so quietly did she stand there, allowing Em to brush her endlessly, emanating serenity. After a long while, Em had run out of thoughts and began to feel the quiet strength that Bea was sharing with her. She remembered something she'd learned long ago when she was in vet tech school, that the electromagnetic charge of a horse's heart radiated up to 45 feet around them and that they could entrain a person's heart to be in coherence just by being close to them. She knew that this was exactly what she was feeling right now. Her heart was entrained with Beatrice's heart and it gave her a tremendous sense of "all is well." This was why she chose the work she did, to remind herself of that feeling, to be entrained to their giant hearts. It always reminded her of her own strength, that quiet reserve that had stood her well through all she'd experienced in life so far.

She became very calm and clear about what she had to do. Tonight she would finish reading the journals, uncovering all that they contained about her past. Tomorrow she would go and have a heart-to-heart talk with Brigid. The thought of it made her nervous but the knowledge she had gained from what she now knew gave her renewed courage. She was no longer just asking Brigid questions into the empty air, hoping for some kind of revelation about her mother. Now she knew enough that Brigid surely would have to tell her the other side of that story. The secret would no longer be a secret to her. It was time for her to take charge of her own life, instead of being a victim of circumstance. Only she could change things for herself.

She reached up to wrap her arms around Bea's neck and give her a kiss. "Thank you, my sweet friend. Thank you for listening to all of my thoughts and making space for them. You are the best, you know that?" As if in response, Beatrice stretched out her neck and blew a long sigh through her nostrils. That made Em laugh. "Yes I agree! It's about time someone noticed just how special you are!"

That night Em read as long as she could but didn't find any more entries about her mother. When she finally gave in to her heavy eyelids and climbed into bed, she spoke out loud. "Pete, stick around please because I'm going to be needing you for this next bit." Within seconds, she fell into a deep sleep.

❧ 35 ❧

T he next morning, just before Em opened her eyes, she experienced the strongest feeling of Pete beside her, so much so that when she did open her eyes she looked over at the other side of the bed and all around the room, half expecting that he was there with her in the flesh. He wasn't of course, but even so, the feeling of him was so present, she could almost smell him. She wept tears of joy, knowing in that moment he was still with her! She felt that same strong connection as she'd had when she saw the rock in the field under the hawthorn tree. She felt the warm glow of safety and rightness, of all the world being somehow okay. A memory rose from the depths of that feeling, a memory of another time. She could see and feel the scene so vividly in her mind and she imagined Pete sitting beside her, seeing it as well, the two of them remembering together.

Christmas Eve 1992

Em and Pete dragged the tree back to the car, laughing the whole way.

"I love snow! It came just in time for Christmas! Don't you

think it's...Woah!" She'd suddenly skidded on her riding boots and nearly fell.

"Silly shoes!" Em said to him as he grabbed her around the waist with one arm, still managing to hold the tree steady with the other. "What was that about snow?" He let out a low hearty laugh that gave Em goosebumps.

"I told you I didn't have time to change my shoes after my riding lesson!" Em leased a beautiful chestnut mare named Lucy from the local stables. She usually worked there one day a week helping the owner who was a vet, and she was learning a lot in addition to being able to ride Lucy. Pete had picked her up today at the barn and now, as they tied the tree to the roof of his Jeep, she looked around in pure delight. "I was saying that the snow makes everything seem so much more..."

He stopped her in mid-sentence with a kiss as she slid into the passenger seat. "Romantic right? I think it's you that makes everything romantic." He winked at her and started the engine.

On the ride home, Pete turned left at the road to her house instead of right. "Where are you going? My house is that away," she giggled.

"I want to take you someplace first."

"Where?"

"Come on, Miss Nosy, you don't have to know everything! Just hold onto your britches," he said, taking a playful tug at her riding breeches.

"Stop it, you brat!" she said but was laughing as she sat back in her seat. "How far?"

"Not far... take it easy, will you? You're worse than a jittery

horse." But Em heard the slight quiver in Pete's voice and thought he was the one who seemed jittery. She looked at him but said nothing, sitting in silence until, about ten minutes later, he pulled into a driveway with a For Sale sign next to it.

"Hey, isn't this private property?"

"Hang on, Em. It's alright, I know the owners."

Em thought she knew everyone that Pete knew, but she definitely didn't know anyone who lived here.

As he pulled the Jeep off the road, Em could see Lums Lake in the distance, the moon shining brightly on it, giving it a beautiful glow. There was no house—just a grove of trees with a small clearing in the middle. Pete turned off the ignition and came around to get Em's door for her.

"We're here."

"Where?"

He said nothing but took her hand, gently coaxing her out of the car and towards the center of the clearing facing the lake. He turned to her and took both of her hands in his.

"Do you like this place?"

"It's beautiful. But I don't understand why we're here."

"Emerald Grace Watts, I have loved you since the day we met and you dropped that ridiculous bowling ball on my foot." Em looked at him, suppressing the urge to laugh when she saw the earnest look on his face. "To put it simply, Em, I really hope you'll agree to marry me so we can spend the rest of our lives together."

Em just looked at him, wide-eyed and, for once, speechless.

Pete pulled a ring out of his pocket and bent his right knee to the ground. He looked up into her eyes and with a voice that shook with emotion, he asked, "Will you marry me and make me the happiest I could ever hope to be? Please?"

It was the "Please" that made Em lose it altogether. She started to sob and laugh all at the same time. She couldn't get out any words at all, so instead she pulled him to his feet and held tightly to his shirt with both hands, as if she never wanted to let go. "Wow, oh wow," she finally whispered, her eyes brimming with tears.

He brushed away the tears from her cheeks with the gentlest touch of his thumbs. "Is that a yes?"

She simply nodded and then grabbed him tight to her and kissed him.

When they came up for air, he reached for her hand and placed the ring on her finger. It had a delicate setting of tiny green stones around a small but beautiful diamond, held together by a strong band of white gold. Strong yet delicate, just the way she liked to think of herself. She smiled, admiring the ring.

"Do you like it?"

"I love it, Pete. I couldn't imagine anything more right."

"It was my mother's. It's one of the only things I have of hers. Now it's yours." The fact that both Em and Pete had lost parents was something that held them together in a way not many people could understand. Though Pete had lost his parents in a different way than Em had, not through death but through abandonment, a loss was a loss all the same. They both knew that some things never really heal, they just develop a cushion around them that makes them not so prickly and sharp anymore. Em's loss of her mother was much more recent, however,

and still felt quite prickly inside.

"Do you think we're too young, Pete? I mean I don't know what my dad is going to say."

"I've already talked to him, Em. He made me promise that we would wait at least another year, until you are out of vet tech school and we have some money saved."

"You thought of everything! But I can't believe you kept this from me!"

"It wasn't easy, I was dying to tell you. But I wanted it to be right!"

"So why are we here at the lake, standing on someone else's land?"

"Not someone else's, Em. Our land. This is the place where I'd like to build a house for us when we have enough money. What do you think? Would you like to live here by the lake?"

Em looked all around her, out at the lake and back at him. "Are you kidding? It's a dream come true. But neither of us has any money. How can this be our land?"

"Uncle Walter. He got the land in a deal he made with the next-door neighbor to build his house as part of the down payment. He and Aunt Patricia have given it to us as an early wedding present."

"But surely that's too much for a wedding present!"

"That's exactly what I told them, but they are just so thrilled that I want to spend my life with someone as wonderful as you that they insisted on giving it to us. Uncle Walter is even going to help me build our house on our days off."

Em's eyes welled up with tears and she turned slightly away from Pete.

"Em, what's wrong? You do... want to marry me don't you? I

mean... I haven't got this wrong have I?"

At the frightened tone of his voice, she knew she had to be brave, for his sake. "No."

"No? Do you mean no, you don't want to marry me?"

"No silly, I mean you don't have it wrong. You have it so right it scares the heck out of me. I'm scared, Pete!"

"Scared of what, Em? I tried to think of everything. I just want to take care of you. I just want to be your safe place."

"You are my safe place, Pete. And I love you for that. But it scares me because of what happened to my mom. I mean I never saw that coming, not really. I knew she was sad and she spent a lot of time in bed, but I never expected her to just up and die. Pete, she was only 36 years old! If that could happen to her so young, what if something happens to one of us like that?"

"It won't, Em, I promise it won't." He put his hands on her shoulders and looked down into her eyes. "We are going to be together for a very long time. Believe me." He leaned down to kiss her lightly on both cheeks and then on her lips.

Em sat back in her bed, fresh with the memory of Pete's proposal and his promise of a long life together, her eyes streaming with tears once more. All of a sudden, through her tears, it was as if she heard his voice in her head saying, "You're right, it wasn't nearly long enough, but Em, I am still with you." He *was* here, he truly was. She could still feel his presence as if he were beside her and her sadness began to be replaced by something else. Her body felt charged with new energy. She needed to get out of the cottage and do something physical. She decided to take a walk. Maybe she would go see Muriel. First, Muriel, and later, Brigid.

~ 36 ~

Jack woke that morning with a smile on his face as he reached across the bed to where Brigid lay. He'd managed to convince her to let him stay the night, after a long and heated discussion about Em. He'd insisted that it was time for Brigid to come clean with the girl about everything. Brigid had been cross with him, but he'd soothed her with sweet words and Irish whiskey until she was smiling again just before they'd fallen into each other's arms and went off to sleep.

"Morning, beautiful," Jack said as he snuggled up against her, kissing the back of her neck. He half expected her to swat him at any moment, since she hated having her neck kissed. She always said it tickled and brushed him away. But this time she didn't resist. In fact she didn't move at all. Jack continued to kiss her, working his way up her neck and around to her cheek. Suddenly he stopped and looked down at her. He thought her skin looked pale. "Biddy?" he nearly shouted in her ear. "Biddy? Can you hear me? Are you alright? Oh God, Biddy!"

Jack jumped out of bed then and raced around to her side to grab the phone on the bedside table. As he waited for an answer, he put one hand on her neck and was relieved to feel a pulse there. He dropped the phone onto the floor a moment later when he heard her voice.

"What are you fussing about, Mr. O'Reilly?" Her grey-green eyes were open then and she was looking at him with an impish grin.

"Woman! What do you think you are doing? Were you havin' me on? You gave me the fright enough for two lifetimes, you cheeky devil you! I'd like to...."

Brigid laughed and threw back the covers, springing from the bed with the air of a much younger woman. Her night with Jack had done her much good indeed. She stood to her full height in front of him, while he stood and stared at her, his mouth open. Sometimes she liked to remind him of her height, especially now when she was feeling young and mischievous. "You'd like to... what? Whatever it is, you'll have to catch me first, Mr. O'Reilly!" She flung on her dressing gown without tying the long strap and practically trotted towards the bathroom.

Jack was so stunned by her behavior that all he could do was burst into laughter. Then suddenly he cried out, "Biddy, your strap! Watch that you don't..."

In horror, he watched her fall down, uttering a sharp cry as she did so. Jack tore around the bed to her side. "Darling, are you alright? Are you hurt???"

Brigid was holding her head and Jack could already see swelling underneath her hand.

"Rosaleen!" he shouted. He ran his hands lightly over her

body and she cried out when he touched her right ankle.

Rosaleen knocked on the door. "Rosaleen! Ms. Brigid fell. Ring for an ambulance right away!"

"NO AMBULANCE, Jack!"

"You are a stubborn woman, you know that?"

"Takes one to know one," Brigid said but her voice sounded strained.

Jack turned to Rosaleen, who was awaiting instructions. "Rosaleen, please call Conor instead and tell him to get here as fast as possible. Then get some blankets and an ice pack, will you? Quickly please!"

Jack was former military and he knew a bit of first aid. It came in handy at a time like this.

⚜ ⚜ ⚜

Jack insisted on staying at the hospital overnight with Brigid. Conor agreed to bring them both some clothes and essentials the next day. When Conor arrived back at the farm, he checked in with Rosaleen to give her an update, and then headed up to the barn to check on the horses. They would have been missing their nighttime feeding and be restless.

As he walked into the barn, though, instead of being greeted by the sound of whinnying horses clamoring for their food, he could hear a soft voice crooning to one of them. "You're so beautiful and perfect you know that? I don't know why people are so much more complicated. Why can't they be simple to understand, like you are?" Conor smiled wearily as he saw Em inside Beatrice's stall, brushing her and talking all the while.

"Hello! What a surprise to find you here."

"You're here!" Em moved quickly out of the stall, closing the door behind her and standing in front of him. "How's Aunt Brigid? Is she alright? Where's Jack?"

Conor, usually unflappable, rubbed his hand across his forehead. He sat down heavily on a straw bale just outside of Beatrice's stall. "How did you know?"

"Rosaleen."

He nodded and sighed deeply. "It's been a long day. Brigid will be alright. She hit her head and broke her ankle." At Em's gasp, he quickly added, "It's just a hairline fracture, no surgery required. She will just have to wear a boot for six weeks and stay off her foot. Of course, trying to keep Brigid immobile could be more dangerous than the fall itself." He broke into a tired grin and Em suddenly, irrationally, felt tempted to smooth his hair back from his face. She resisted.

"And Jack?"

"He insisted on staying the night with her at the hospital." Conor lifted his eyes to Em's. "You do know they're a couple, right?"

"Of course! I've known since the first time I saw them together. I don't know why they try to cover it up."

"Yeah, well, they've had this thing for decades where they pretend to be just employee and employer but everyone has known about them for simply donkey's years."

Em smiled at his turn of phrase. "Why didn't they ever marry or have children?"

"I'm not sure really. Neither of them ever wants to talk about it, but does that surprise you?" He grinned, and his face looked as though it had sprouted a few new lines that day.

Em laughed but shook her head at the same time. "People around here keep secrets like some people keep cats."

Conor looked out the barn door straight ahead of him, gazing blankly at the green fields beyond, rubbing his head as if to rub away the worry inside it.

"What is it, Conor? Something else is wrong. I can tell." She sat down on the bale beside him.

He shrugged, still looking straight ahead. "It's just, I don't know, well, they both aren't that young anymore and I guess I just realized that today. I mean they've always been just Brigid and Jack to me, two strong, ornery people who happen to love each other. But today, with Brigid lying in a hospital bed and Jack looking like he was ready to fall apart himself, it just made me realize how fragile they really are. They're the closest thing to parents that I have now." She knew exactly what he was saying.

Em put an arm lightly around his shoulders. "I get it, Conor. My dad back home, he used to be so strong and in charge and now, well, some days I can't even bear to visit him. It makes me so sad."

"Yeah, that must be tough." He looked into her eyes and they just stared at one another for a long moment, sharing a truth without words. Something stirred between them in the quiet of the barn, their faces close together, and suddenly Conor was leaning in as if to kiss her. She quickly jumped to her feet, feeling her pulse racing. She wanted to kiss him but... she didn't... she couldn't.

"I know what you are going through is difficult." Em widened the distance between them, moving towards the door. She chose her next words carefully. "I just wanted you to know I understand. You've made me feel so at home here, as if I'm not alone and I want to be here for you too." She meant what she said.

"I don't ever feel alone when you're around." He stood up, walking over to where she stood, lightly touching her elbow as he spoke. "What I mean is, you do know how much I like being with you, don't you?"

"I like being with you too. You're a good..."

"Friend right? A good friend is that what you were going to say? Well, to be honest, I've been feeling a bit more than just friendship."

She took a deep breath and steadied herself. He was such a dear sweet man and she didn't want to hurt him in any way. "Conor, if we are being honest I'm feeling things for you too." *So many things*, she thought. "But I'm also just so torn right now. I don't know if I'm ready for this. It still feels so soon after... I mean, I didn't expect... well, I didn't expect you when I came here."

He nodded. "I get it. You've been through a lot and besides you're dealing with all of these mind-blowing discoveries about your family and all. Hell, I wasn't expecting you either." His eyes caught and held hers for a moment, and then he looked away, staring out the door into the growing darkness. "I don't need to put myself out there only to have my heart smashed up again." His vulnerability touched her and she found it difficult not to want to console him.

"I would never do that to you."

"Sometimes women say those things but it doesn't always happen that way." His voice was bitter. He kicked at a clump of straw on the floor. He looked so worn out.

"Conor, please." Her voice begged him to look at her. "I know you've had your heart broken but I'm not her, Conor. I was married for twenty years to the same man and I never even looked at another man. Not all women lie or cheat. But I don't know how I feel from one day to the next right now and I don't want to hurt you."

His face softened then, resembling the Conor she was coming to know and care about. "I know you're right. Sorry I said that. I'm just completely exhausted is all. Don't pay any attention to me, okay? You don't need anything else to be stressed about." He gave her a half smile. "Can we forget about this? I really do like spending time with you."

She smiled and nodded. "And I with you."

"Good." Then, changing the subject, he said, "So... about Brigid. Muriel should know."

"Should we call her?"

"No, it's late now. It can wait until tomorrow." Conor ran a hand over his head once more. He looked around him, seeing the horses as if for the first time, munching their hay contentedly. "Did you do this?"

"Well it wasn't Rosaleen," she teased. "Horses are what I do for a living, remember?"

"Thank you. Could I ask one more small favor?"

"Anything."

"Tomorrow morning, after I do the chores, I'll take Jack some things. And I was wondering... would you mind going to see Muriel?"

She reasserted her place in this. "You look like you could use a lie in. I'll take care of the horses in the morning, and I'll go see Muriel. You just get some sleep and focus on Brigid and Jack."

"Are you sure? You're meant to be a guest here."

"I'm not a guest, Conor. I'm family."

He stood up then and put a hand out to cup her face gently, and once more, his sudden closeness made her feel things, things she hadn't felt for many months, months that felt more like years. She gave him a small nod and a smile and gently backed away.

"Please don't worry about anything here, just let me know what all needs doing. I think everything is finished here for the night so I'm going to head back to the cottage."

"I'll drive you. It's on my way and it's dark and windy out there."

She didn't really want him to but she couldn't think of a good reason to say no and it seemed rude to do so. "Thank you, Conor." She walked ahead of him out to his car, not looking back.

As soon as he pulled up in front of the cottage, she jumped out quickly and bade him goodnight. "Have a good rest, Conor."

Conor nodded and waited until she opened the door and

turned on the light before he pulled away in his car. The house he shared with Jack was just down the road.

She smiled and waved from the doorway, walking in and shutting the door behind her. The whoosh of the heavy door felt the same as the heavy whoosh of her heart. What in the world was she doing? Suddenly she felt so tired she could fall asleep standing up, and all she wanted was to lie down, close her eyes, and make the world fade away.

∽ 37 ∾

E m showered and changed the next morning after she'd finished with the horses. She grabbed a bit of breakfast and headed on foot to Muriel's house. Walking along the quiet country roads felt grounding and it was just what she needed right now. She looked longingly at the path that led to the ringfort as she passed by, promising herself a visit there soon.

Muriel opened the door before Em could even knock, waving her in warmly and encouraging her to sit in one of the comfy chairs by the fire, a spot that was becoming quite familiar to Em by now. It felt like a safe space and she was grateful for it and for the woman herself.

"I spoke with Conor this morning briefly before he left for the hospital. Tell me. How did it happen?"

"Well... I think... um, I think that Jack was there with her..." Em stumbled over the words, not knowing if Muriel knew about their relationship.

Muriel just nodded. "Go on."

"I'm not sure of all the details, but it sounds as though she got up to go to the bathroom and then she tripped over the strap on her robe, and fell, hitting her head on the dresser. Jack called Conor and they rushed her to the hospital in Cork."

"What did the doctor say? Is she alright?" Muriel's voice was filled with concern but her manner quite calm.

"The doctor said she had a mild concussion and a broken ankle."

"Ah the poor dear!"

"Well, I guess it could be worse. Her ankle should heal fine, according to Conor, provided she keeps her ankle immobilized."

Muriel laughed at that. "Immobilizing Brigid! Now that'll be a challenge!"

Em's lips parted into a grin that reached her eyes. "That's what Conor said too. They kept her overnight for observation so I'm not sure how long she'll be there. Jack insisted on staying with her."

"Aye, he would do. How are you doing with all of this?"

"I'm okay. Concerned of course, but okay."

"There's something else, isn't there."

"Does it show?"

"I can just feel it." Muriel calmly waited for a reply, all the while pouring the steaming tea from the pot that sat on the table between them.

Em reached out gratefully for the hot cup Muriel offered and felt a curious relief to have this kind, caring woman to talk to about it, especially since she hadn't yet felt it was time to talk with her sister yet. "Do you remember I mentioned to you the journals that I brought with me that my dad wrote?"

Muriel nodded and sipped at her tea.

"I started reading them just before all this happened. And I've got some answers— answers that I'm not sure I ever wanted or needed to know."

"Yes sometimes finding out answers can be more perplexing than having the questions in the first place." Muriel placed her tea cup on the table, folded her hands in her lap, and waited quietly. Together they sat in silence for a few long moments, until Em felt ready to go on.

"According to the journal writings, my mother was in love with someone here in Ireland and she got pregnant with me before coming to America." Muriel's eyes held Em's steadily and her head nodded as if of its own accord. Even though Em suspected that Muriel must have already known this, her reaction, or rather lack of one, angered Em.

"You knew this didn't you?"

"I did know... yes, I did."

Em struggled to get a grip on her chaotic emotions, standing up suddenly. "I don't understand. Why didn't you tell me? Why hasn't Brigid? Or my mother or father? Why didn't anyone bother to tell me?" Muriel sat quietly while Em paced around the room.

Muriel reached for her hand and motioned to her to sit once more. "Not everyone, no. It isn't like that. I've only just found out about... you... a few months ago. I knew, of course, that Eva had two girls in America, but I didn't know... the rest until recently. I didn't know the truth about you. I always wondered, but nothing was ever confirmed. Not until your visit was imminent."

"What do you mean, exactly, found out the truth about me?"

Muriel took a deep breath. "This was always meant to be for Brigid to tell you. She promised me that as soon as you got here, she would tell you everything. But now I see that it is up to me after all."

"Tell me what, Muriel? Please! Enough of these secrets! I want to know!"

"Let's go for a walk and I'll tell you a story." Em's eyes brimmed with tears. "A walk? You want to go for a walk? Now?" But Muriel was firm, leading her towards the door.

Out of respect for the older woman, she grabbed her coat on the way out the door. As they walked in the direction of the ringfort in silence, Em found herself waiting impatiently for Muriel to speak, but then she couldn't help falling into the beauty of the landscape—the twisting road lined with green fields, the promise of the sea ahead—and her edginess fell away of its own accord. This place, this land, continued to captivate her soul and take away all her worries, no matter how big or small. She couldn't breathe the air without feeling more at home, more at peace than any place else she'd ever been. No matter what Muriel was about to tell her, she knew she would never regret coming here.

As though Muriel could feel the peace settling over Em, it was then that she began to speak. Em knew that weaving stories was a big part of Irish culture and was not surprised when Muriel's voice became like the voice of someone retelling a faerie tale. "Fadó fadó a long, long time ago, there lived a woman named Eva, your own sweet mother, who was so beautiful and full of life that everything else around her seemed to fade in comparison. From the time she was a young girl, she embraced everything about her life with open arms and knew exactly what she wanted."

"She knew she wanted to travel, to see the world, to explore every part of nature everywhere. She loved nature more than anything else and was as in tune with it as any shaman or wise sage. She had dreams, but they were different than the kind her father had for her. He wanted her to go to school and get married to a proper young man."

"You see her parents were very wealthy. Though Irish born, her father had lived for decades in London and had adopted the ways of the upper class. He looked down upon the "common" Irish, as he called them, even though they were his very own people."

A raven flew overhead, squawking as if in response to her story. Muriel smiled. "But Eva had no intention of marrying anyone—she was far too independent and her dreams much too big for that." Muriel took a deep breath as they turned into the woods that led to the ringfort. "Yet as the expression goes, 'We make plans, God laughs.'"

"Is that when she met my... " Em stumbled over the words, "my father?"

Muriel nodded.

"And they fell in love?"

"The young man's name was Seán and no, Eva had no interest in him at first. But he, on the other hand, was smitten with her from the first second he laid eyes on her. She was riding her horse the day he first saw her, her raven hair blowing wildly in the wind, every line of her body free of cares as she galloped across the field towards home. Seán was working as a stable hand that summer on her father's farm and she mostly ignored him, not on purpose but just because she had no time for men. She was too busy seeing the beauty in every day. And then came the day when he rescued her after she'd taken a bad fall off a new horse. Seán helped her back to the stables and nursed her wounds, murmuring to her in Gaelic all the while. That was the first time she really noticed him. Soon after that, there was no separating the two, at least not when they could sneak off to spend time together."

"Why did they have to sneak off?"

"Because of Eva's father. Seán would never be good enough for his daughter. But young love has a mind of its own."

Em nodded, remembering what it was like to fall in love with Pete.

"One night they consummated their love in the barn loft. Your grandfather walked in by sheer chance and found them together. He completely lost his mind." Muriel's tone of voice changed with those words, no longer speaking in a storyteller's voice. Em felt a chill go through her.

They kept walking up the hill through the forest towards the ringfort, but Em's steps grew heavier and she wasn't sure she wanted to go on. Though the path of star-crossed lovers was a tale as old as time, this particular story was intimately connected to her. It was not only her mother's story but the story of her own beginnings in Ireland. Though she carried a deep sense of foreboding in her gut, she couldn't run from this... she had to know.

The two women reached the ringfort and as if by mutual consent, they stood silently, looking out over the beautiful landscape and the ocean beyond. Em found herself matching breath for breath with the older woman, as if to calm herself for what came next. After a time, Muriel chose one of the large flat rocks and Em another and they sat down, side by side, watching the waves for a time. Em found herself breathing in time with the waves. Finally she spoke.

"What happened next?"

Muriel turned to face her before she replied. When she spoke, her voice was steady and her words were delivered gently, without any emotional charge, in the way of someone who had lived with a truth for long enough that she'd had to make peace with it.

"He went into a rage and ended up pushing Seán off the edge of the barn loft. Seán fell to the ground and couldn't move. They had to take him to hospital."

"Oh! How awful!"

"Yes. It was. It was terrible for everyone concerned, especially for Seán, and for his... family." Muriel looked down at her hands and Em noticed they were shaking ever so slightly.

"Are you alright?" Em asked her, putting a hand in hers.

Muriel nodded. "It was many years before I spoke to your grandfather after that, but when he was dying, I came to learn that it was the moment in his life he regretted the most and it haunted him. A moment of irrational anger that could never be taken back. He died a very unhappy man. For that at least, I felt sorry for him."

"What happened to Seán?" It felt easier to call him that than father.

"He spent several months in a rehabilitation center in Dublin, learning how to walk again. The fall had left him paralyzed from the waist down."

"Oh my God!"

Muriel was silent for a moment and when she finally spoke, her words brought to light all of the repercussions of Em's grandfather's blinding moment of rage, a moment that altered many lives forever more.

"Your grandfather paid for everything of course. It was the least he could do. And yet, despite the damage he'd caused already, he made sure that Eva and Seán would never see one another again. He sent Eva to America to live with his sister Eithne, who ran a boarding house in Brooklyn." Muriel squeezed Em's hand gently. "No one here knew she was pregnant with you, you see, when she left for America. I don't think Eva herself even knew. As I said, I only recently found out from Brigid that when Eva was working at a restaurant in Brooklyn, near the boarding house, she met your father, and, well, you know the rest."

Em stood very still, letting go of Muriel's hand and saying nothing at first, trying to imagine her mother falling in love only to have that love shattered in an instant, watching her beloved, hurt and broken, sent off to Dublin, and she herself being shipped off to America. And then to find out that she was pregnant! Pregnant and very much alone. No wonder she fell into the safe and gentle arms of Jonathan Watts. He would make anyone feel cared for and secure. He was exactly what she must have needed. It made Em feel so sad for the woman she'd known as her mother and the girl she once was, full of hopes and dreams.

"You said that my mother and Seán were madly in love. Do you think it was that once in a lifetime kind of love?" She was thinking of the love that she and Pete had shared.

Muriel looked not at her but out into the expanse of the ocean, and smiled softly, as if remembering. "Yes, yes I do. They were young and oh so different yet they understood one another as two people do when they share the same breath, the same heart."

"I don't understand though. Why didn't they try to find each other? I mean once she got to America and he was well again."

"It was a long time until he was well and yes, he wrote to her from the hospital all the time, but she never replied, or maybe she never got the letters. I rather suspect the latter."

Em sat upright, remembering, and stared at Muriel. "And my mother wrote letters to him too! My father said so in his journal! And he also said he hadn't mailed them! But... but surely she could have called him or he would have found a way to call her?"

"Well, I'm not certain as I wasn't part of that story, but phone calls were expensive to another country then. It was the seventies. There was no internet or email. And I'm guessing that

Eva had no money to spare, not to mention she was pregnant and taking care of herself in another country. Seán, for his part, was busy learning to walk again. They were both going through major life events in different parts of the world."

Em took a deep soulful breath, and then, in a sad voice, more to herself than to Muriel, she said quietly, "They never got their chance." The enormity of the choices made by others for the two young lovers that sent them on completely different paths in life made Em feel such sadness for what was lost, what could have been.

The two of them stood there for the longest time, each with their own thoughts, watching the waves crashing far below them. Em tried to allow all of the information she'd been given over the last three days to sink in. She had a father in Ireland and, in fact, if her mother and Seán had been allowed to stay together, she might have been born here, in this place where she felt so at home. Everything would have been different. She would have never had Jonathan for her father nor Sophie for her sister. Would there even have been a Sophie? Unimaginable, all of it.

And for the first time she began to have an adult understanding of the woman she'd called her mother for seventeen years. For so long, she'd only been thinking of herself, and of Sophie, and what they had lost, both when her mother died, and during the years when her mother went into a dark place, forgetting about everyone else, even her children. What if she and Pete had been torn apart by a similar tragedy and they were never able to see one another again, to share the years and the memories they had? If her mother loved Seán with one half of the passion that she had loved Pete, then it made sense that having her heart broken, never to be mended, would, over time, tear her apart the way that it did. As she looked out at the waves, remembering Brigid's description of the young Eva, dancing at the ringfort and talking to the dolphins, she felt a deep sadness for the part of her mother she never knew until just now, for the heartache she'd suffered. She mourned too for Jonathan Watts, the man who had loved Eva as best as he could but could never replace her one true love.

"Muriel? Do you mind if we go back? I have a feeling there's a lot more to this story that I'm meant to hear, but I'm just not ready yet."

Muriel turned to hug her then, a hug that held her in place for a long moment, just long enough. "Of course, dear girl. You've been hit with a lot today, the last few days in fact. Let's get you back to your home." Then she took Em's hand and led her down the steps on the hill, taking the shortcut back to the little cottage.

⌒ 38 ⌒

Em was back inside the cottage and Muriel had gone on her own way home. She lit a fire in the stove and just sat for the longest time, staring into the flames. At first she simply felt numb thinking about all she'd learned these past couple of days. But the more she thought about her mother's story, what she'd gone through and what she'd lost, it was if the young Eva was in the room with her. Suddenly she remembered the book she'd found and she tore upstairs to get it. Once back in front of the fire, she opened the book and read once more the inscription inside the front cover. "To Eva, my Anam Cara, love always, S." S was Seán and his Anam Cara was her mother. She didn't know why but reading those words again opened up something in her. Her eyes blurred with tears and she began, at last, to release emotions that she didn't even know she'd been holding, as if her tears were coming from a place where they'd been hiding for a very long time. She sobbed until she was spent and the fire had gone out along with her tears. It was at that precise moment that the phone rang.

"Soph?" She was aware that her voice sounded rough from crying.

"What's wrong, Sis? Are you alright?"

Half-sister or not, she could never hide anything from Sophie. "It's been an emotional few days." Em took a long deep breath, dropping into her heart the way Muriel had taught her to do. "I have a lot to tell you."

"I'm right here."

Em began to share the entire story, beginning with finding out about them being half-sisters all the way through to their mother mourning a man she had loved and lost in Ireland, a man named Seán who was Em's biological father.

"I just can't believe it," Sophie kept saying over and over again. "Moo... do you want me to come there? I could probably get Chloe to stay with the animals and Dad would be..."

"That is so sweet of you to offer, but I'm really okay, that is... if you're okay." In spite of everything, she realized that she was. Jonathan Watts had always told her she was made of strong stuff, and she guessed he was right, considering all she'd been through and now this. "I know this is a lot of information to get over the phone, and all at once. I'm so sorry, Soph. I'm sorry for springing it on you like this. It's probably selfish of me. I really needed to hear your voice."

"It's not selfish, Em. It is a lot to take in! And let's face it. It affects us both, but it affects you more than it does me. Dad is still my dad and I know I have the best sister in the whole world. But for you this changes so much!" Sophie always had a way of compartmentalizing things, a trait that Em did not have. Sophie just seemed to carry on, no matter what life threw her way. This was one of those times when it felt to Em like Sophie was the big sister instead of the other way around.

"It changes a lot for us both, Sophie. I mean when I think about what might have been... what could have been, had things turned out differently, well, it blows my mind. I just know I love you more than ever and I'm so glad you're part of my life."

"I'm glad you're a part of mine! I don't know where I'd be without you! But what I don't understand is how is it that neither Mom nor Dad ever thought we should know about this?"

"I don't understand either. I guess the journals were Dad's way of telling us, but what a lousy way to find out, so many years later! I guess Dad was trying to protect her, to keep the family intact, but surely after she died... the saddest part is that now there wouldn't be any point in even trying to ask him about it. I guess we'll just never know why he didn't tell us."

"I guess so. I'm so sorry, Em. Look at what you had to go through just to find out the truth! And you and me... half-sisters?"

"Does that bother you?"

"Strangely enough, no it doesn't bother me at all. Half or not, you're still every bit my sister and you always will be, no matter what anyone says."

Em let out a huge sigh of relief. "I'm so happy to hear you say that, because you don't feel any less my sister than you did yesterday. And let's face it, we're all we've got! Aside from Dad, that is." Dad. Every time she spoke or thought of him, she couldn't quite work out how she felt. He was still her father through and through and a great one at that, but she did feel very disturbed by the fact that both of her parents had kept this from her and Sophie all these many years.

Her sister spoke up, reading Em's mind as she often did. "And you know what the weirdest part is?" Em could tell Sophie's mind was going 100 miles an hour. "We can't even be mad at them for not telling us!" Truer words were never spoken. Their mother was gone and they couldn't be mad at their father for anything anymore either. What good would it do? Still, it would take some time to sort out all of the emotions.

"I know you're right. I guess that means we just have to not be mad." Em's voice belied her words. "I'm just not there yet." Then she remembered something Muriel had said when they were leaving the ringfort about taking her back to her "home." "There is something really positive in all of this, though."

"And that would be?"

"We own a cottage in Ireland!"

"Okay... keep rubbing in the fact that you're there and I'm here."

Em suddenly felt the heavy weight of guilt land squarely on her chest. "Oh, Soph! Of course you should be here! If I had only known how life-changing this trip would be! It could have been, it should have been something we discovered together!"

"I was just teasing you, Em. I think we are both exactly where we are meant to be right now. Would I love to be there with you in "our" cottage? Of course I would, but I don't agree. I think this is something you were meant to experience on your own. Besides, if I'd been there, you wouldn't have been spending so much time with your hunky hunk!"

"Oh will you stop already with the hunky hunk! His name is Conor and it's complicated…"

"Now it's complicated? We went from "we're just friends" to "it's complicated?" Ok, spill! Did something happen? I need to know everything."

"Nothing happened exactly but… look I just don't want to talk about it right now. There's too much else going on, and besides I have no idea how I feel, except confused is at the top of the list. I haven't been spending too much time with him anyhow with Brigid in the hospital and all."

"Woah, Aunt Brigid is in the hospital! Wait a minute! What happened there?"

Em began to talk, filling her sister in on the events of Brigid's accident and everything that transpired since, but leaving out the more personal bits she wasn't ready to share about her growing feelings for Conor. Normally her sister would have been the first person she'd have told, but in this case, she needed to sort out how she felt first.

"Are you sure you are alright, Sophie? Again, I'm so sorry you're not here with me and I promise we'll come back here in a few months so you can see the cottage and meet everyone."

"I'm fine, Sis. Totally. But please keep me in the loop, will you? It feels like so much has happened since the last time we spoke."

"Believe me, so much has happened and it just keeps happening! I promise to keep you updated from now on. It's just that I felt as though I needed to have all the information and some time to process it before I shared it with you."

Just then, a knock came on the door of the cottage. "Soph, I gotta go. Someone's at the door and I think it must be Conor come to give me news of Brigid."

For once Sophie did not tease her about Conor. "Please let me know how she is, okay?"

"Yes of course! Love you. Love to Dad and the fur kids."

～ 39 ～

onor had come by just to let her know that Brigid and Jack were staying together at the hospital for another day or so. Brigid did have a slight concussion and she needed to be where the staff could keep an eye on her.

"Do you think I should go and see her tomorrow or whenever next you go?"

"Definitely not if you want to keep your head. She's in a foul mood. She hates hospitals more than anything and only Jack knows how to deal with her right now. I'm surprised the entire nursing staff hasn't quit!"

She laughed at that—it lightened her mood just to see him, but when he didn't return the laughter, she noticed how tired his face looked. She realized that he was the one who needed the comforting now. "Would you like to go with me into the village for a quick bite to eat then? Are you hungry?"

"Famished. My stomach thinks my throat's been cut," Conor said.

Em couldn't help but laugh at his expression. "That sounds like a yes! Just let me wash up and we can go."

"I could do with a bit of a wash myself. Can I use this one?" Conor pointed at the half bath near the entrance to the cottage's kitchen.

"Of course. There's clean towels and soap in there. Help yourself."

"I've got another shirt in my car. I'll be back in a tick."

Em nodded and dashed up the stairs. She kept telling herself it was just a meal shared between two friends. It wasn't a date. But when she came back down and saw Conor in a pale blue shirt with his copper waves brushed back off his face, it felt like a date even if it wasn't.

They decided they both needed the walk so off they set side by side down the middle of the road. It felt so familiar to her now, as if she'd walked this road all her life. They laughed and talked of light things over dinner at the pub, and it felt good to let go of everything for a little while. Looking into Conor's clear blue eyes and watching his face wreathed in smiles helped too. But on the way home, it was as if the present circumstances caught up with them, and their talking led to more serious subjects.

"I hope Jack's okay. He can't be getting too much sleep in the hospital," said Em.

"Oh don't worry about Jack. He has them all eating out of his hands over there. They set up a cot for him next to Brigid and are feeding him day and night. I think they're all scared he'll leave them alone with Brigid."

They both laughed at that and she became keenly aware of their arms swinging in rhythm, their hands almost touching. She felt the timing was right to share with Conor about her visit with Muriel and the pieces of the story she'd found out that day, about her real father Seán and what had happened in the barn that night.

He stopped and turned towards Em. "And?"

"And what?"

"Well is there more to the story?"

"Well, yes, I think so, but I couldn't hear anymore today. I just couldn't take it." Em thought she saw a shadow pass over Conor's face. "Did you know about this?"

He said nothing.

"I can't believe it. You knew too?"

He looked down at his shoes and then at her. "I told you before, there was a lot of talk."

"This whole time, you knew and you didn't bother to tell me?"

"I overheard bits and pieces, Em, not the whole story. It wasn't my place. You have to understand..."

She cut him off mid-sentence. "Well, I don't understand. Everyone, even you, wants to keep me in the dark about my own life, my own history! I thought you were my friend." Her face was set in a grim line. This man who she had trusted had lied to her. She turned to walk back towards the cottage.

"Em, wait." He caught up with her easily, his long strides getting ahead of her. He turned and faced her, forcing her to stop in front of him. He reached out and took her arms. His eyes were earnest and his hands on her arms were warm. "It wasn't my story to tell."

She had to ignore the shiver that went through her at his touch, even in her anger. She looked at him, her lower lip trembling slightly. "But you lied to me."

He shook his head. "I didn't know the whole story, just bits and pieces like I said. And it wasn't my story to tell."

"It still feels like a lie. I have to go home now. I'll speak to you later." He took a step back and she moved around him, walking away and this time he didn't follow.

That night she tossed and turned. She didn't call Sophie. She didn't read the journals or write to Pete. She just wanted to wallow for a while and even that wasn't satisfying. Her heart hurt. She felt betrayed by Conor even though she knew he was right. It wasn't his story to tell, and yet she had that awful feeling of others knowing something she didn't. It made her feel sick inside. When she did finally fall asleep, she was plagued even in her sleep. She dreamt of Conor, a dream in which he was reaching for her, again and again, as she slid backwards down a steep hill, but she kept sliding just enough so that he couldn't take hold of her until finally, she fell. At that moment, all went black and she woke up with a start.

Though it was still early morning, she got up immediately to soak in the tub till the water turned cold, trying to wash away at the dream. She felt her fury rising at all the secrets that had been kept from her for so long. She was angry at her father, her mother,

Brigid, Conor, even Muriel. There was only one thing she could think of to do and that was to go to the ringfort, to be near her mother.

～ 40 ～

Em picked up her father's journal on her way out the door, the last one, and took it with her. She nearly ran to the stables, a swirl of emotions pushing her along like a current. Cautiously, she approached the barnyard, but thankfully Conor was nowhere to be found.

She grabbed Bea's halter and walked out to her pasture, speaking to her softly, her anger disappearing at the sight of the beautiful horse. "Sweet Bea, you would never lie to me, would you." She felt fresh tears spring to her eyes as the mare rubbed her shoulder and breathed against her face.

"Can we go somewhere together? Would that be alright?" Em slipped the halter on easily and the mare walked beside her all the way back to the barn.

Once they took off from the farm, Em rode for a while without a destination. She knew there was a trail through the woods that also led to the ringfort—she'd walked it with Muriel the other day, but she'd never ridden it.

Sitting on Bea's back, feeling the sway of her hips as the horse moved in rhythm down the road, Em felt as though she could start to breathe fully again. Somehow being on a horse's back, especially one as loving as this mighty little horse, it was difficult to feel anything but good. Her heart slowed down its racing and fell into a rhythm that matched the horse's hoofbeats. Clop clop, clop clop. She wished more than ever before that Pete was by her side now. "I guess there's always a part of me that will feel that way," she said to the mare, who simply bobbed her head up and down as she walked.

At first Em couldn't find the entrance to the woods that led to the ringfort at the top of the hill. She'd gone a long way down the road before she realized it, and then turned around to head back the same way. Suddenly, she had an idea. "Beatrice," she said, leaning forward toward the mare's neck, "take me to the ringfort—you know the way, don't you?" She said a little prayer and let go of the reins, letting the mare lead this time. If Bea was like most horses, she would have taken that invitation to return straight back to the barn, but then she wasn't most horses. She was Beatrice, bringer of joy. Jack had told her once that this was what her name meant.

Em closed her eyes, focusing her attention on the movement of her own body matching her horse as Bea's hips dropped and lifted as did her own. She knew quite a bit about the therapeutic effects of riding and how many people used the wonder of Equus to relieve their traumas. She'd even worked with vets for a while at a place called Horses for Hope and had seen miracles happen. She didn't need a miracle, but some peace of mind and heart would be welcome. She let Bea carry her and almost forgot where she was or wanted to go, keeping her eyes closed and putting complete faith in her horse to carry her for a while.

Then she felt the mare's body turn to the right and the footing changed; she could feel the unevenness of it by the way her hips swung wider as the horse stepped right. She opened her eyes and they were in the woods heading through the thickness of trees and over rocks. It was a good thing she opened her eyes when she did too because she was just in time to duck under a low branch and that made her laugh. She reached down and stroked Bea's neck vigorously. "Atta girl! I knew you could do it!"

This forest was thick with the hawthorn trees that Em had come to know and love and being amongst them gave her a tingly feeling, almost as though she was being seen by something invisible. It wasn't scary yet Em was just as glad when they reached the top of the rise and came out into the clearing. Before her was the ocean and when she looked to the left she saw the ringfort some distance away, with an open path along the cliff that led straight to it.

"Would you like to stretch your legs a bit?" she asked the horse, clucking softly to her and pressing in with the calves of her legs, while lifting herself slightly out of the saddle into a galloping position.

Beatrice didn't wait for a second invitation. She took off in a gentle canter from a walk, a graceful transition that continued to pick up speed the more Em encouraged her to be free. They moved as one across the vast expanse of open space and Em felt all of her cares flying out behind her with the wind. This was her mother's special place and it was quickly becoming her own as well.

Once they got close to the fort and the three flat rocks for sitting along the sea where she'd met Muriel that first day, Em settled back into her seat and the horse slowed to a walk, both of them catching their breath.

When they reached the rocks, she jumped off the horse's back slipping off the bridle and allowing the mare to graze freely. She knew Bea would never leave her. She sat on the middle rock, watching the waves for a while, looking for dolphins, eventually retrieving the journal from her jacket pocket and sitting with it, unopened.

After a long time, she heard a voice. "Hello, Emerald." Somehow not surprised by her appearance, she turned to see Muriel, a vision in purple, her cloak long and flowing with her hood up around her head, strands of her white hair escaping and blowing around her face. Despite feeling angry at everyone for keeping the truth from her Em realized that she couldn't be angry with Muriel, not ever, and she stood up to greet her.

"How did you know..."

"I saw Conor. He was worried about you and I told him I'd find you. He left early for the hospital and stopped by my house on the way there."

Em sighed, her heart aching as she thought about Conor and how she'd walked away from him in anger the previous evening.

Muriel moved to stand in front of the rock next to Em.

"Shall we sit?" When they were both settled, the older woman spoke. "I know you are upset with Conor right now. I understand why you would feel betrayed by all of this."

"And you think I shouldn't be?"

"I don't think I can presume what you should or shouldn't feel, my dear. But I want to help you sort it. And there are a few more bits you need to know."

She looked at Muriel, feeling a mixture of excitement and trepidation. "Yes. Please! I want to know it all. I'm tired of knowing that everyone is keeping things from me, thinking they have the right. I feel like I'm walking around with blinders on and everyone else can see things clearly—everyone but me. I've just found out that I have a different biological father who was my mother's true love, along with a host of other things. I need to know how I fit in here, who I am."

"Oh yes. I do understand exactly how that feels," Muriel spoke as if from experience. "It isn't right to be kept in the dark about your own life."

Em nodded in agreement, pausing at her words, wondering who had kept Muriel in the dark and under what circumstances, yet she felt compelled to ask the question that had been so much on her mind. "You know, there's one thing that I don't understand, Muriel. How is it that you know so much about this story? I mean I know it's a small village and people talk and all that, but when you told me about my mother and Seán it was as if you were..."

"... there," Muriel chimed in. "As if I were there."

Em looked at her then and understanding dawned. "Because you were, weren't you?"

Muriel nodded and reached out to take her hands, her eyes glued to Em's. "I'm Seán's mother. Which makes me your..."

"My grandmother." They both spoke the word grandmother at the same moment and Em just stared, not sure how to feel about this earth-shattering news. Should she be angry? Delighted? Or something in between? At the moment, she was mostly confused.

"If you are my grandmother, why didn't you ever come to see me or write to me or even tell me I had a grandmother? Why didn't my mother ever tell me I had a living breathing grandmother, for god's sake?"

Muriel squeezed her hands, imploring her with her eyes to stay connected to her words. "I know this is a lot to digest. As I told you before, I did know about you, at least I knew that Eva had two children, but I always assumed that they were conceived with her husband. I never knew you were my granddaughter until recently when you were coming to visit here. Brigid kept that secret, even from me, all these years. I can tell you I was fit to be tied when I found out! And then she made me promise that she be the one to tell you all this, but fate had another plan in mind."

Em looked across at her, realizing that Muriel certainly did know what it was like to be kept in the dark. "So I wasn't the only one then. A big part of this was kept from you too."

Muriel nodded. "Yes there were many secrets on all sides, it would seem. As for your mother, I'm guessing she didn't tell you about me because then she would have had to tell you who your real father was."

"I guess I understand that part. Sort of. She was carrying on the story of me being Jonathan's daughter." Even as she spoke those words she still almost didn't believe them. It all seemed so oddly surreal. "But that doesn't explain why Brigid kept it a secret from you all these years. Surely things could have been different had you known about it, especially after my mother's death. Why would it have mattered then?"

Muriel shrugged. "I don't know. I guess because she felt that one secret would open up a whole pandora's box, and it was better left the way it was."

Softly, as if to herself, Em said, "Incredible. All of this over a child." Em looked down at her own hands as if for the first time. "And that child was me."

They sat then for a long time in silence. Em was feeling the gamut of emotions—disbelief that her birth caused so many secrets to ensue, sadness for her mother who never got to be with the man she loved, and, finally, a sudden growing sense of wonder armed with the knowledge that she had a grandmother, one who was alive and sitting right beside her. It was impossible to hold all the feelings she had right now. She knew she had to stay focused on getting the answers to the questions and then she could deal with processing her emotions more deeply later on.

"So many secrets intertwined around one another. What I still don't understand is why they didn't try harder to find one another. Surely if their love was as strong as you say, they would have tried? I know from my father's journals that my mother wrote him letters that never made it to him, but what about Seán's letters to her?"

"I'm not exactly sure of all the details. Seán has never wanted to talk about it. I know he mourned for her for some months, but he was also busy fighting to get his life back too. He couldn't exactly show up at her doorstep without the ability to walk on his own. Eventually he found out from Brigid that Eva had married a man in America, your father, and that's when he knew had to let her go."

She felt a deep pang of sorrow for this man, the father that she never knew existed until today. Until that very moment, she'd been pushing aside any thoughts related to the man who was her biological father, but as the story unfolded he became more and more real. Wait a minute... Muriel just said that Seán *has* never wanted to talk... has never, not *had* never. That must mean... "What happened to your son, what happened to... Seán? Is he still alive?"

Muriel paused before answering. Em waited, knowing that her answer would change the course of her life once more.

"Yes, he's alive and living in Dublin. During his two long years of rehabilitation in which he learned to walk again, he befriended a woman, a nurse named Maeve, who cared for him and eventually they became more than friends. They married three years after Seán's accident."

Em just sat then, looking out at the sea and thinking about Seán, married to Maeve and living in Dublin. And for the first time, she felt a real curiosity about him. She began to wonder if she looked like him and if he was the kind of person she would like. She recognized, for the first time, that instead of feeling angry about all of these secrets, she could look at it another way. She'd gained co-ownership of a cottage in Ireland. She had a grandmother, and she had a man who was her birth father. Her life had become richer for this visit and she wanted to know more.

"Do they… do they have children?" She suddenly started imagining how it would feel to gain even more family members.

"Unfortunately, as it turned out, Seán was not able to father children after the… accident." Her voice landed heavily on the last word. "They looked into adoption for a while but it never happened somehow, and then they just became so comfortable with one another that it didn't matter so much." Muriel looked over at Em. "I'm sure that he would want to know about you though."

"You mean… "

Muriel shook her head. "I was waiting until you came. I thought it best to see how you felt about the whole thing, if you would want to see him, to know him or not."

Em sat staring at the sea, saying nothing, and then, "I'll have to think about that. I mean I just found out that I have a grandmother!" She looked at Muriel in amazement. Then it struck her. No wonder she'd had that feeling of knowing Muriel before! Even though they'd never met, something in her had felt the bond, an energetic bond that couldn't be denied. She smiled at Muriel and the woman smiled back. "I still have so many questions!"

Muriel reached out and took Em's hand in her own. Their rocks were just close enough to do so without straining. "Ask away."

"How well did you know my mother?"

Muriel's smile grew wider, and her blue grey eyes sparkled with the memory of Eva. "Your mother used to come to my house a lot when she was a child. Seán was away at boarding school at the time and they didn't know one another yet. She knew I had healing medicines and she wanted to learn them all. She was fascinated by the essences I made out of herbs and she always wanted to get onto my healing table even though she had a hard time lying still for it. She always had the energy of a nymph. Floating free, moving fast, that was Eva."

Em smiled then frowned again. "I still don't understand why no one ever told me any of this—my mother, my dad, Aunt Brigid..." She thought of Conor then. "How much did Conor know?"

"Not much really. He just knew there were secrets afloat and he knew about my son Seán. I think he suspected that you might be my granddaughter, but I don't think anyone outright told him. Jack and Brigid kept him out of it. Conor is such an honest young man, Emerald. He wouldn't hurt you for anything. He feels really awful."

"But that doesn't explain Aunt Brigid or my parents keeping it a secret."

"I guess sometimes when something is kept secret for a long enough time, it becomes like a great big ball of yarn that is tangled and twisted. It just gets more and more difficult to untangle it. Sometimes it's just easier to keep the secret." Muriel sat still, both her hands now quietly in her lap, her body relaxed but her eyes intent on Em.

"It's a lot to take in."

Muriel nodded her agreement. "May I offer you some healing energy?"

"Here?" Em looked around as though they had an audience and Bea looked up momentarily from her grazing.

"Why not?"

"Ok, yes, thank you."

Muriel came around behind her and gently laid her hands on Em's head.

Em felt a little awkward at first, receiving healing in this place outdoors, but in no time at all, she went into a peaceful space within herself. She knew that in spite of everything, she trusted Muriel, and she wouldn't have wanted to be here with anyone else right now.

A little while later, as Muriel finished, Em opened her eyes, raising her head to look up at the woman she had come to so admire in the short time they had been together, and the corners of her mouth turned up just a smidgen. She had a grandmother. Once again she acknowledged all she had gained here – a grandmother, a cottage in Ireland, a dear friend in Jack, an aunt she was getting to know, a new friend in Conor, and a father she never knew existed!

Muriel finished and walked around to face her, her back to the sea. Em looked up at her with a smile. "When I was little and I didn't feel well, Mom used to put her warm hands on me. Was she a healer like you?"

"Oh, yes. She definitely had the healing touch. She could

see things too—colors in the sky that no one else could see. She could see magic in what to others seemed ordinary. I always believed she was part girl and part fey."

"There's a part of my father's journal I still need to read but I'd like to read it with you. Would it be okay with you if we do it now? I feel like I just want everything out in the open, once and for all."

"I'd be honored indeed."

∽ 41 ∽

March 15, 1993

Eva never let go, never stopped believing that the day would come when her Seán would show up, never stopped loving him or waiting for him. Though it pained me greatly, I knew that deep down he was her soulmate. And when she found out from Brigid, years later, that he too had married and moved on with his life, it was more than she could take. That was when she gave up wanting to live. I still remember everything about that day, the day the life washed out of her beautiful gold eyes, the way her shoulders drooped low and her neck jutted forward suddenly as if it had a life of its own. The feeling of the energy in the room as if someone had sucked all the air out of it. It was as if, in that moment, Eva, the dreamer, my beautiful dreamer, had lost her ability to dream and with it her ability to live as well.

She withdrew into herself and was never the same after that. About two years later, I began to notice that she was losing weight and her color was off. I took her to the doctor and he confirmed what I already suspected. As the life had drained out of her, the cancer had grown in its place. The doctor wanted to start her treatment, but no matter how much I argued with her I couldn't convince her to do it. In the end, I guess you can't make someone want to live.

Em stopped reading for a moment and wiped at her face with her hand until Muriel handed her a tissue. Muriel's eyes were glassy as well. And in the midst of her own emotions, Em realized that this was the first time that Muriel was hearing this story as well. There was something sadly poignant about the two of them, grandmother and granddaughter, learning this sad truth about the one who connected them to one another.

I should have known—I've seen it before with my patients, usually the much older ones though. When I suggested that she talk to a therapist, to help heal her heart, all I got in return was a blank stare as if to say, "I'm Irish."

Her illness dragged on for three years, her body fighting to live even as her soul asked to let go. The only thing that comforted her were Em and Sophie. I don't believe she meant to leave them—she just didn't know how to stay.

Em's hands were shaking now, so much so that she handed the journal to Muriel, her eyes holding a silent appeal.

"Are you sure?"

Em nodded and dropped her eyes, no longer able to hold the woman's compassionate gaze.

Muriel put on her reading glasses and gently fingered the

pages of the well-worn journal. Her voice, soft and low, broke the silence, the sound then carried off by the sea before them.

In the end, it was Emerald who I felt the worst for. She did everything for her mother—laid with her, read to her, brought her food and extra blankets, brushed her hair. She never gave up. Sophie was too young to really comprehend it all and Emerald split her time between the two, except when she was at school. She was far too young to carry such a burden. But I couldn't dissuade her from it and I knew better than to try. It was what she had to do. She loved her mother so much.

Hearing these words broke Em open. She was sitting on the ground then and she stretched her body over the rock, sobbing. "I did, Muriel. I loved her so very much. I've spent all these years trying not to remember."

Muriel simply stroked her hair and let her cry it out. "There, there Gariníon. There, there."

When there were no more tears left, Em sat up, wiped her eyes and looked at Muriel.

"What's that word you just called me?"

"Gariníon. It means granddaughter in Irish."

Em mustered a small smile. "I like the way it sounds." Her grandmother's use of the Irish word for her gave her the strength to want to continue. It made her feel.. supported and loved.

"Please go on. I want to hear the rest."

Muriel adjusted her glasses back over her eyes.

And it was on one of those days that Emerald was at school when my dear wife decided to let go. Sophie, home sick from school, found her "sleeping" and called me at work.

"Daddy?" she said. "It's Mommy. She's sleeping and she won't wake up." Those words are seared in my memory forever. I was in my office in between patients. I remember the soft click of the blinds against the window sill when the breeze hit them just so. I held a pen in my left hand and just kept clicking it on and off, seeking some sense of normalcy, some way to escape what I already knew. I remember the ache in my gut and was sure someone had stabbed me when I wasn't looking.

But I had to stop thinking about me. I had to get Sophie out of there and I had to reach Emerald. And I had to take care of their mother, this one last time.

Em had shifted position and was now lying in the soft grass, looking to the sky as if to separate herself from the words— these words her soul needed to hear, but her heart could not bear to listen to. Muriel came to snug in beside her in front of the flat rock facing the sea, the rock where Eva had sat many a time as a young girl growing up here. She placed a warm hand on the younger woman's shoulder, allowing them both the time and space to be with their own thoughts and emotions.

Em spoke silently to her mother then. *Mom, why didn't you tell me? I might have been able to help! I wasn't a little girl. I would have understood.*

She looked up at Muriel. "Maybe if she had talked about it, she could have gotten better. Things might have been different." The wind swept at her words, bringing with it a feeling of her mother swirling around both women. They stayed like that for a long time, each feeling the loss of Eva O'Shea in those moments in a way that neither of them had been open to before.

Sometime later, it could have been minutes or hours, Em suddenly sat bolt upright, startling both Muriel and the horse, who was still contentedly grazing nearby.

"I'm not doing it, Muriel."

"Not doing what, dear?"

Em turned towards her, coaxing the same intensity from her grandmother's eyes as she felt in her own. I'm not going to be like her. I'm not going to die of a broken heart. I'm going to live in the now."

$$\sim\!\!\circ\ 42\ \circ\!\!\sim$$

Em made sure that her grandmother was composed enough to make it home on her own, and then hastily climbed onto Bea's back, riding swiftly back to the farm. She needed to see Conor and hoped he would be back from Cork. She rode up to the stables but he was nowhere in sight. She untacked Bea and turned her loose into the large pasture. Where was he? His car was parked by the barn so she knew he was there. She had to find him.

The day was cold and she grew tired of searching and was about to turn back, when she heard it—Beatrice's shrill whinny across the field. Conor was way down at the bottom of her field, fixing the fence, his back to her. She didn't know how she'd missed seeing him before. She ran, climbing nimbly over the fence and calling his name, feeling foolish but doing it anyway. She felt she had no control right now, over her emotions, her body, anything.

"Conor!" The third time she called his name the wind took it and sent it right to his ears. He looked up and saw her, his hammer in his hands. She sprinted across the long stretch of grass as if her feet wore wings, landing in a heap on his chest.

He didn't ask her what she was doing there, or why she'd launched herself at him. He just held her. It felt like the safest place in the world and she wanted to stay there forever.

She felt something at the back of her neck, rubbing back and forth. Hearing Conor chuckle softly, she looked back over her shoulder and saw that it was Beatrice, standing right behind her, brushing her with her nose, wondering if she was alright. She laughed and turned to touch her forehead to Bea's nose, looking into the mare's liquid eyes.

Conor was now speaking to the back of her head. "I'm so sorry, Em. Truly sorry."

She turned back to him then and put a finger to his lips, shushing him. Her eyes searched his face, willing him to understand what she was about to say. She didn't know that she could feel so much. "I'm not going to be like her, Conor. I won't, you hear me? I'm not going to go through life with a broken heart. And neither should you."

Inexplicably, he understood. With his free hand he moved her hair back from her face, wiping her tears with the back of his gloved hand. He reached forward to kiss her forehead gently, ever so gently and as he began to pull back, she moved just enough so that his mouth could find her own. Tentatively, trembling, her lips sought the relief of his full soft ones. She longed to dip her lingering sorrow into the well of love that those lips held and for a long moment, she did. And then she remembered. She was Pete's wife, or rather his widow, not someone who should be kissing this Irishman in a field. But just then she felt Bea nudging her closer to Conor. It was as if Pete were there, telling her it was somehow okay. That it was okay to move on, to feel something for someone. And instead of breaking the kiss, she deepened it... and the world went away.

She didn't know how long they kissed, but when she pulled back to look into his eyes, she saw nothing but love there. "I don't know what this is, Conor. I don't know what I'm ready for yet. I don't know if I'm ready for anything at all."

"Fair enough. Still, that was some kiss." As he spoke he smiled and his cheeks pinked a bit. She would not have noticed if she weren't so close to him, so close that they were still sharing breath. Reluctantly she slowly stepped back and almost fell over Beatrice, who was still standing right behind her. She looked then at the only place left and that was straight up at the sky, the place where she imagined Pete to be, and she silently said thank you because she knew something then in that moment that she hadn't known before. She was going to get through this and she would love again. Maybe it would come slowly, bit by bit, but eventually it would come. If Ireland had taught her anything it had taught her this. Her green eyes met his blue ones and she smiled. "Thank you, Conor." There was nothing to explain or apologize for. They were just two people, standing in a field, sharing a tender moment.

He held her gaze and then nodded, a small gesture that sent chills along Em's spine. In that nod, she felt everything that was in his heart. Then, as if he knew this visit was over, he turned, picking up his hammer from the ground, and, with a parting smile, walked over to continue fixing the fence, lining up the wood and nailing it back into place with the same precision and care that he did everything.

<o 43 c~

Em left Conor and walked to the village for some dinner, relishing the time alone to mull over the events of the day. She felt giddy from kissing Conor and everything had a different quality about it. She walked back slowly to the cottage under the light of the nearly full moon. When she found herself finally turning down the covers and climbing into bed, she sighed and curled up next to her photo of Pete and the one of Eva at the ringfort.

Her father's journals sat on the nightstand and she picked up one of the earlier ones, thumbing through the pages, skipping the entries that talked about his practice and his patients and stopping whenever her mother's name was mentioned. Then she came across an entire section about her mother that she'd somehow missed the first time and her heart skipped a few beats.

Sometimes I look at her in sleep and wonder what it is that I have done. I knew what I was getting myself into at the time, or at least I thought I did. But I was still young and foolish and I thought I could change her mind. I thought I could make her let him go. But the truth is

I love her, she loves him, and now she's learned that he loves another. It's all such a damn shame. Why does it have to be this way? I sit and stroke her hair now. I can do that when she's sleeping and she doesn't pull away from me like she does in wakefulness. I can sit and pretend that she is really my Eva, that I have her heart as she does mine. I can imagine the life we could have had if... if things had been different.

I try to remind myself how lucky I am in so many ways, how much I have to be grateful for. For Eva and for my beautiful perfect Em, who could not be more my daughter if she tried. She says and often does things that remind me so much of myself that I cannot believe that she isn't of my blood, because in every way that counts, she is. I know she is and no one can tell me otherwise.

Em smiled when she read those words.

And Sophie, the little miracle child that Eva brought to me. She is already as smart as a whip and wants to know everything about everything. I worry about her though because she will never know her mother in the way she should. Eva has already gone away from us, though her body is still here.

Her spirit's been gone ever since she got the news of Seán's marriage, news that she should have had a long time ago. For that, I am to blame. Maybe if I hadn't kept her letters from him in the beginning he wouldn't have married another—maybe they would have ended up together. Perhaps if I had truly loved her I could have helped her find him—even if it meant I'd have been left with a broken heart. It is only now that I can begin to understand the ramifications of my actions and that keeping those letters from him was not only cruel; it was dishonest. And I've always prided myself on being an honest man. I carry the guilt of it every day, even more so now that Eva has slipped into a deep depression.

All I can do is tend her in wakefulness by keeping her comfortable, warm, and fed, and soothe her in sleep as I do now. And love those children with every breath in my body. If this doesn't kill me, it will indeed make me stronger and I pray for the strength to bear it all.

Reading these words and hearing her father's voice in her head left her feeling less angry with him for not telling her the whole story. Having an understanding of what really happened back then, she could see the situation for the first time from an adult's point of view and knew then just what loving Eva O'Shea had cost her father. His love blinded him so much that he had fallen into a web of deceit, first by keeping her mother's letters from Seán, and then by not telling Em who he loved so much that she had a different biological father. She wondered at his motives. Love for the first and, she supposed, protectiveness for the second. She knew from the earlier journal entries that Eva had made him promise not to tell her about Seán being her real father. But after that? After Eva's death? It would seem there would be no reason for it then, unless... she thought of Jonathan's words, "... I would have been left with a broken heart." Maybe he was worried that the same thing he feared would happen with her mother would also happen with her—that if he told her, she too might have cut him out of her life.

Em sat for the longest time, holding the book against her chest, thinking about the father who had loved them all so fiercely and suffered so much in return, mostly for his own omissions. It was little wonder then, she thought. Little wonder why his mind was going. Forgetting was easier than remembering.

"Yes, Dad," she spoke out loud as if to the man who'd written the journal, "forgetting is sometimes easier than remembering." Forgetting is what she'd practiced for so many years. Forgetting the good parts about her mother, shutting out the bad parts, just pretending she'd never had a mother. Choosing to forget instead of remembering. And that's what this trip had shown her—that remembering, while painful, also opens the door to understanding and growth. She didn't want to forget anymore and she didn't want to be angry either. She would do her best to accept the truth, whatever that truth might turn out to be, find forgiveness through understanding, and move on. She sighed and at long last in the wee hours fell into a deep sleep.

44

Em spent the next two days alone, journaling, talking to Sophie on the phone, shopping for gifts in the village, and visiting with Bea. She'd seen Conor briefly here and there, mostly in passing, and they did manage one ride together, but he was busy with Jack and Brigid. However, they were all planning to have dinner together the following evening.

She was in the cottage thinking about what to wear for dinner, which Rosaleen had told her would be held in the formal dining room. She wasn't sure what that meant in terms of attire, but she wanted to wear something special to celebrate Brigid's homecoming and her own departure in just two days! She was looking forward to going home to her family in North Carolina, but she wasn't ready to leave Ireland by any means.

She couldn't believe the time had gone so quickly and that so much had happened in the past two weeks. She was a mix of emotions. She did what she always did when she couldn't contain her thoughts. She called her sister.

Sophie picked up on half a ring as if she were expecting the call. "What deep dark family secret are you about to reveal this time? More relatives? Or wait a minute—we inherited a sheep farm next to Brigid's house!" Em laughed for a moment. Sophie had been so amazing about everything, sharing all the emotional twists and turns as Em continued to discover them and taking it all in stride.

She'd already told Sophie about Muriel being her grandmother and many of the details in Jonathan's journals, but she felt that Sophie should read them herself when she returned. "No more dark secrets, at least I don't think so. I hope to finally get some time to talk to Brigid tonight after dinner. There are still parts of the story I need answers to."

Sophie already knew the questions—the two of them had discussed every aspect at length on their calls. Em could not get over her sister's generosity of spirit throughout this whole time. All of this had to be difficult for her, too, though she didn't show it. She knew that while Sophie had been young when their mom died and so claimed to have few memories of her, that surely wasn't the whole truth. After all, Sophie was the one who had found her "sleeping" on the day of her death, though she claimed she didn't remember it very well. She suspected that her sister was equally as good at avoiding things she didn't want to look at as Em herself had been. She hoped that when she got home they could talk more about all of it, and then when Sophie came to visit Ireland and meet more of her family, she might begin to unpack her own feelings in similar ways. She thought of what Muriel said the other day— sooner or later, we all have to revisit our stories and make peace with them.

Sophie's voice jolted Em back to the present. "So—big

dinner tonight, right? And your hunky hunk will be there?" That was the one thing she hadn't shared with Sophie. The kiss. Ever since the kiss, things had changed between her and Conor, even though she had no idea what exactly was happening. Though they hadn't had any real time to be together since the kiss, there were looks exchanged and a subtle touch here and there. He didn't press her for anything more and for that she was grateful. She liked him, a lot, and at the same time Pete was still occupying a great deal of space in her heart. Curiously enough, Conor seemed to instinctively know this, but it didn't noticeably alter how he felt about her, and that made her feel happy, even though she hadn't a clue what she wanted or even felt.

She wondered if Brigid and Jack would notice anything tonight at dinner. It would be the first time that they saw them together since the kiss. Conor, for one, wore his feelings all over his face and she wasn't sure how adept she was at hiding her own feelings either, but, in the end, did it even matter? Surely she and Conor weren't going to be like Jack and Brigid, hiding their relationship for years on end. And yet, as of now, she wasn't even ready to talk to Sophie about it.

"Hello... Earth to Em... did you hear me? Are you still there?"

Once more, Em had to stop her own swirling thoughts long enough to answer her sister. "Yes, Conor will be there and Muriel too. The whole cast of characters."

"Sounds like fun! Especially you having dinner with your Granny!" Sophie laughed.

Em laughed along with her. "Once you meet her, Sophie, you'll see why I don't think I could call her that! She called me Gariníon the other day. It's Irish for granddaughter but I'm not sure what to call her yet so I'm just sticking with Muriel for now."

After a short pause Em said, "I just don't know what to wear! We're eating in the formal dining room, according to Rosaleen."

"Ah, just be yourself! Wear a nice sweater and clean jeans. If they don't like it, what are they going to do, make you eat in the kitchen?" The sisters both laughed at that and said goodbye.

In the end, Em chose a soft red wool dress with black leggings. Though her hair was a rich auburn, the red worked for her, bringing out the green of her eyes. She had brought it along just in case there was an occasion to wear it and she guessed tonight was it.

Conor had insisted on picking her up and she was happy he did, as the rain started just minutes before he arrived. She greeted him cheerfully, her dress covered up with her long, dark navy raincoat and hat, complete with wellies. She'd brought along her indoor shoes to change into when they got to Brigid's.

When Conor took her coat in the hallway of Brigid's home and got a good look at her in the red dress, he whistled long and low. "That's not fair," he said, smiling.

"Whatever do you mean, sir?" she teased, fluttering her eyelashes. She smiled, just allowing herself to feel light and happy without any worries—it had been too long.

He leaned in close as Rosaleen approached them in the

hallway. "I mean with you in that dress, a man might be tempted to whisk you off into a side room to steal a kiss." It was the first time he'd openly flirted with her and it sent a delicious shiver up and down her spine.

Muriel arrived shortly after, looking beautiful in a long sage colored dress adorned with a dark purple shawl. Em kissed her cheek and happened to look Brigid's way as she did so, noticing how closely she was watching the two of them.

Dinner was fun and lighthearted. Everyone was in a good mood, including Brigid. "I am so very glad to be out of that awful place and back in my home," she said as she raised her glass. Jack nodded at Rosaleen, who brought an opened bottle of champagne from the sideboard and poured a little into each of their flutes.

Jack raised his glass and cleared his throat, getting everyone's attention, "A toast."

Em and Conor looked at each other and smiled, sharing their own private toast with their eyes alone.

Jack stood up ceremoniously. "At this table tonight we have much to be grateful for. The return of our beloved Brigid to her home safely. The time spent with Emerald, ahem, I mean, just Em," he smiled at her, "has been wonderful. And today we also have one more thing to celebrate."

All eyes were on him, including Brigid's, as he reached down to take her hand before speaking again. "I'd like to announce that this beautiful woman, who I have been in love with since I was a boy, finally agreed to be my wife."

An intake of breath moved around the table, followed by

exuberant smiles. Brigid sat stock still, looking slightly embarrassed and raising her chin to cover up her feelings.

Before anyone had a chance to speak, Jack continued. "Everyone, allow me to introduce you to Mrs. Brigid O'Reilly."

They all just looked at the two of them with wide eyes as Jack leaned down to kiss her softly on the cheek. And then, everyone began speaking at once. "What? You got married? When? How? Do tell!" Finally it was Muriel who posed the question they were all thinking. "Surely there's a story?" Em had learned by now that in Ireland, there was always a story.

Jack sat down then, not letting go of Brigid's hand. "Go on then, Mr. O'Reilly, you're the one who likes to weave a good yarn." She spoke to Jack in her usual brusque voice, but the tenderness in her eyes and the way she squeezed his hand back softened the effect of her tone.

"Aye, will do, Mrs. O'Reilly," giving her an impish grin. "Well I'm sure it's no secret that I've been asking this woman to marry me for decades." He smiled as he caught her disapproving look, which made his smile grow wider. "But when she went into hospital, we were both faced with the idea that life doesn't go on forever. And somehow, in her weakened state, I managed to convince her this time that we shouldn't waste another moment." Brigid said nothing.

"But I was there every day," Conor said. "How did you pull it off?" Conor looked happy but confused and Em reached under the table to hold his hand.

"There happened to be an Irish priest in the room next to

us and he and I got to talking one day. He was in for minor surgery and, as it turned out, he was feeling up to performing a wedding. I nipped out the next day to get the license and he married us the following morning, just as the sun was coming up through the window of Brigid's hospital room. Two of the night nurses who knew what we were up to acted as our witnesses. One of them surprised with us with a proper Irish breakfast following the ceremony and the other one, bless her, managed to sneak in a few drams of Irish whiskey for us to toast with afterward!" He looked at Brigid, love simply streaming from his eyes. "It was perfect." She didn't comment, which was unusual for her, but the corners of her mouth turned up ever so slightly.

"And you're stuck with me now, hey, Biddy?"

She slapped his arm then. "Ah go on with you, you daft sod." Em could have sworn she saw Brigid's cheeks turn pink for a moment.

Congratulations were on everyone's lips and the mood couldn't have been brighter. Muriel stood up as the last of the champagne was poured.

"I have a toast as well." Everyone drew silent. "I'd like to say how overjoyed I am to finally connect, after all these many years, with my beautiful granddaughter, Emerald. Welcome to the family, Emerald. I am so very glad you came."

"I'll second that," said Conor.

Em's eyes glistened with bright tears of joy. She looked at Muriel, standing to hug her and as she did so, her gaze once again came to rest on Brigid who was looking intently at the two of them. Muriel told Em earlier that day that she had visited with Brigid and had filled her in on what had transpired in her absence. But it still all felt awkward somehow, as if the cat had jumped out of the bag without Brigid's permission. She could imagine that the older woman must feel uncomfortable and out of control. Brigid's gaze gave away nothing, but shortly after, she excused herself, retreating to her drawing room, saying that she was feeling lightheaded from the champagne.

Perhaps tonight was not going to be the time she spoke to Brigid after all. She only had one more full day here... tomorrow. She hoped it would be long enough.

❧ 45 ☙

Em awoke frequently during the night, wondering if she would indeed get the chance to talk to Brigid. Somehow, even with all she'd learned from her dad's journals and from Muriel, she still felt as though there were pieces of this complex story that didn't quite fit together. She got up early, before the sun was even on the horizon, and started packing for her departure tomorrow. Every time she thought about leaving, she felt a tightening in her chest. The uncertainty of not knowing whether she'd get a chance to talk with her aunt made her feel anxious. She knew she should quiet her nerves, maybe by writing to Pete, but her body wouldn't settle down to do it any more than her mind would. And it was way too early to call Sophie.

It was still dark outside after she had packed and cleaned up the little cottage, so she rolled out her yoga mat, needing something physical to calm her nerves. As she stretched her limber body into the poses that were so deeply familiar to her, she thought about Pete. Even though there was still a hole in her heart where he used to be, something had changed in these past days in Ireland. Instead of a gaping hole, full of hurt, it was as if a soft blanket had been laid there. Her thoughts shifted to Conor and she couldn't deny that his presence in her life was soothing to her heart as well.

Intricately connected to all of this was opening up to let the memories of her mother in again. It seemed as though, once she opened her heart to Eva, she could open it more to everyone and it made her feel powerfully connected to everything in this world and everything in the world beyond her physical senses. She felt that the gap between the two worlds was narrowing, at least for her. In the past days, she'd begun to connect with Pete's energy at almost any time just by thinking about him. She didn't have to sit and write to him anymore or wait for him to appear in a dream. He was just around in a myriad of little ways when she paid attention and tuned in. She still missed him and wished he were with her in a physical sense, but the longing, the yearning to have him back—that had changed. For the first time in many months, she could see a way forward, that life could hold the possibility of love again.

She'd only known Conor a short time but she felt such gratitude and... yes... even love for him. She felt a love for him that was different than the way she'd loved Pete, but there was such goodness about the man. Pete may have been her first and only love but she knew enough of the world to know that love came in many different types of packages. But... was she really ready to love someone in that way? She realized that it was a good thing she was heading home to North Carolina for now. Later would be soon enough to ponder all these new feelings.

She thought then about the other two significant people

she'd met here – Jack and Muriel. She didn't actually know how she'd gone this far in life without either of them, or quite how she would leave them. In fact, she'd grown a whole new family. Even Aunt Brigid, with her prickly ways, was part of her Ireland family now. At least she would be spending another few days with Muriel. They had put their heads together and mutually agreed that they would go to Dublin so that Em could meet Seán. Muriel had phoned him at long last to share with him that he had a daughter he'd never met. His first reaction, quite understandably, was one of complete shock, but once he'd had time to digest the news, he was overjoyed at the idea that something of his Eva still remained. Jack would be taking Em and Muriel first thing the next morning to the bus station.

With all of this still buzzing around in her head, she'd decided she could wait no longer. She would go up and see Bea. She and Conor had a date to ride at noon today but she couldn't stay inside any longer. She dressed and was about to open her door to leave when she heard an unexpected knock. She was very surprised to find a smiling Rosaleen on her doorstep.

"Hello, Rosaleen. Do come in," Em said.

"Oh, thank you, Miss Emerald, but I'm just here to deliver a message from your Aunt Brigid. She'd like very much if you would come by to have lunch today with her. At noon please."

She hoped Conor would understand that their ride would have to wait. She had to go. Brigid was inviting her—this time *she* was making the first move. This had to be a good sign. Maybe she was finally ready to talk.

After she changed, she dashed off a quick note to Conor and left it at the stables for him, asking if he could meet her later that afternoon and, by then, it was nearly noon so she headed up the hill to Brigid.

Even before she raised her hand to knock on the massive door at Brigid's home, Rosaleen opened it. How did she know she'd arrived?

"Miss Emerald, please do come in. You're right on time. Miss Brigid, I mean, Mrs. O'Reilly, is waiting for you." Rosaleen smiled shyly. "That may take some getting used to," she said with an embarrassed laugh, referring to the change in Brigid's surname. Em reached out a hand and placed it on Rosaleen's arm, the two of them smiling at one another in understanding. Rosaleen led Em to the drawing room where Brigid and Em had shared their first cup of tea, a day that had ended in disaster. It was hard to believe that was only two weeks ago. It felt like both a blink and a lifetime.

Her aunt was sitting in her chair with her leg up, the one that was in a cast, and Em guessed that the excitement of last night's dinner had worn off because Brigid looked none too happy about her current situation. Or at least that's what Em presumed to be the reason for her scowl. She hoped it wasn't her arrival that was the cause. But no matter—she was here.

"Hello, Aunt Brigid, how are you feeling?" As she spoke, Em presented her with the bunch of flowers she'd picked along the way, placing them on the table next to where she sat.

"I'm fine, just about the same as I was last evening when you saw me." Brigid's voice was gruff. "What are those for?"

Em caught her breath, which had creeped up to settle in her throat. After last evening's dinner, somehow she'd expected a different Brigid than the one she found now. She started to feel defensive but then caught herself, remembering her decision to stand in the strength of who she was, no matter what Brigid threw at her. She would be loving and allow Brigid to be Brigid. "I just thought they were cheery."

"Cheery. Yes, unlike me. Ach I didn't mean to sound so harsh. It's just frustrating having this bloody cast on that's what! But, as Jack reminds me, it could have been worse."

"Well that's true. It could have been way worse." Em watched as Brigid raised one eyebrow at her remark.

Rosaleen wheeled in a cart with a tray filled with tiny sandwiches with the crusts cut off and, of course, a pot of steaming tea on a smaller tray. She placed a small folding table in front of Em, while Brigid had a similar one next to her.

Brigid gestured to her leg, which was up on a chair. "Doctor says I have to keep it elevated so we'll be eating this way today." She didn't sound apologetic but Em didn't mind. She was more focused on all she had to say to her aunt.

They ate in relative silence, except for the odd polite remark, and then Brigid took her cup in her hands and spoke. "So what is still burning in your gut that you need to know about this family?"

Em guessed she should have expected nothing less than a direct approach from Brigid. She decided to follow her lead. "I want to talk about Seán. I want to talk about my father." Em heard the words come out of her mouth and was surprised to hear that her voice did not sound hesitant, but instead rang with an assertiveness that matched her aunt's. She was not asking a question. She was seeking information.

"Didn't Muriel tell you enough about him? He is her son after all." Even now at the very last, Brigid was trying to evade.

"I know some of the details from Muriel. What I really don't understand is why you've kept all of this from me, Aunt Brigid."

"I'm not entirely to blame, young lady." Brigid's words were clipped and harsh.

"I'm not placing blame. And I'm not a young lady! I'm a grown woman who has lost a mother and a husband and just found out I have a different birth father and a grandmother that I never knew about! I'm just trying to understand everything that happened back then. I've spent most of my adult life not knowing what drove my mother's sadness or what her life was like or even how I fit into all of it." Em's voice crackled with something between anger and despair, but she held herself steady. Muriel had advised her to remain calm and direct, to keep emotion out of it. "I would like to understand why you have been so determined to keep me blinded to my own family history."

Em's words fell silently between them. Brigid sat back in her chair, allowing her head to rest against the high back, looking out at the sea, as if bringing back the past from the water and waves themselves. "Yes, I can see it is time you knew these things." She paused and took a deep breath. "I always liked Seán. He was kind and a hard worker and he was handsome, oh so handsome. But good too, very good. And he fell in love with Eva the first time he laid his eyes on her. I was there, I saw it."

Em felt her breath slowing down, lulled into story now. She imagined transporting herself back to when it all began for her mother. "And my mother? Did she feel the same?" Even though Muriel had already told her this part of the story, she wanted to hear Brigid's version, especially now that she was finally opening up to her.

"Not at first. Eva was like a hummingbird, always flitting here and there. She didn't notice him right away, but he made sure that she did notice eventually. And once it began, their love became like a runaway horse. They were together every moment they could be. All behind my father's back of course."

"But why? Was she too young? I know he was a hired hand and all of that, but surely your father could see they had feelings for each other!"

"My da had this way of seeing only what he wanted to see and what he saw was someone inappropriate for his daughter to be dating. Up until then, Eva was always his favorite, but when he refused to let her be with Seán, it caused a terrible rift between the two of them. After that, everything changed."

"What changed?"

"She and my da argued over him. He threatened to fire Seán but Eva begged him not to do so and promised she would stop seeing him. I remember the day she told him. I was standing behind her in the library and I could see her fingers crossed behind her back as if to wipe out the lie."

"Was that when she started to sneak around in order to spend time with him?"

"Yes. They found moments together for a while. Until that night in the barn when everything came apart. It was all so horrible in the end."

Em caught hold of the sadness in her own heart as it emanated from Brigid. They were both silent for a few moments, each of them in deep contemplation.

Brigid shifted in her seat, moving the leg with the cast painfully. She frowned, but continued on. "After that, things changed so quickly—Seán sent off to the hospital in Dublin and our Eva shipped off to the States. Do you know I never saw her after she left? All those years we spent apart, and then... she was gone." Em thought Brigid was as near to tears as she'd ever seen her. Her sadness was palpable.

"Why, Aunt Brigid? Surely you had the money to visit her in America. I'm sure you missed her terribly."

Brigid nodded her head. "Oh yes, I missed her so very much. Still do, every day of my life." Brigid cleared her throat and took a gulp of her tea to cover up her emotions. "But soon after she left Da started drinking a lot. Someone had to look out for things, for the farm, for him. It was up to me. I didn't feel I could leave. And by the time he died, it was too late."

"Why didn't my mother come back here to visit?"

"A lot of reasons I suppose. Our da for one. She didn't want to have anything to do with him. Also, she was a young mother and then there was Seán. She couldn't bring herself to revisit all those memories of him." She paused as if to let her words sink in. "We wrote though, she and I."

More letters? Although she didn't dare hope she'd ever see the letters that Seán and Eva wrote to one another, she would give anything to read the letters her mother had written to Brigid all those years ago. She wondered if Brigid had kept them. But now was not the time to ask. Right now what Em wanted to know most was where Brigid had fit into the events that unfolded. "Aunt Brigid, if they were so in love why didn't they try harder to find each other?"

"Once Seán was in the rehabilitation center, he wrote to me for a few months, always asking after Eva. He didn't know she'd been sent to America, you see, and he always said the same thing. He wanted her back. He wrote her letters too you know, for those first several months. But our da destroyed them."

"And my mother wrote to him too. But my father didn't mail them. He kept hoping... well, it's all in my father's journals. They were kept apart by two people who didn't want them to find each other. But *you* knew! You knew about Seán's letters."

Brigid's face hardened then. "Yes I knew. I knew he wrote her and I knew she wrote him. I was stuck in the middle of them both. But you have to understand how it was. She was in another country, alone and pregnant with a man's baby who our da would never accept. If my da found out, who knows what he would have done! I had to protect her and the baby. I had to protect you." With those words, she looked at Em as if asking for some understanding.

"And I thought that the only way I could do that was by keeping my mouth shut." Looking at her now, Em could see the toll it had taken on her. She still carried it—the guilt, the shame, the sadness and the loss. Em could see it all on her face, in the tight line of her mouth, the way her eyes were half closed and her chin had dropped ever so slightly.

"So my grandfather never found out that my mother was carrying Seán's baby?"

Brigid shook her head. "No, he never found out. Somehow she convinced our Aunt Eithne at the boarding house that the father of her unborn child was Jonathan's. But Eva never forgave our da."

"That must have been so hard for you... to keep a secret like that. And for all these years. And you had to keep it secret from Muriel as well?"

"Yes. That was the most difficult part. Muriel and I.. well, we're friends and that made things so much worse. At least I didn't have to see Eva face to face." She cleared her throat then. "But it's in the past now. Everything is out in the open and that's what matters. Thank goodness Muriel doesn't hate me."

Em spoke with true compassion. "Aunt Brigid, I'm so sorry." She suddenly understood her aunt's gruff exterior. She was merely hiding her pain. She waited a moment and then, "The part I don't understand is that once your father died, why didn't you tell Muriel then? Why didn't she ever know about the cottage? Or after my mother died, why didn't you tell me?"

"Why didn't I suddenly after all those years tell you that you have a father who isn't your father and a sister who's a half-sister?" Brigid bristled. "Tell Muriel that I've been keeping her own granddaughter from her? Tell Seán he has a daughter with a woman he had been madly in love with, a woman he nearly lost his life over? What right did I have to turn people's lives inside out like that? Besides, it wasn't up to just me. Your father, the one who raised you, he could have told you too. Who was I to step in? I barely knew you. It's not that I didn't think about it. I thought about it all the time, but in the end I thought it was better left alone. And as far as the cottage was concerned, my da stipulated in his will that Eva or one of her offspring had to come here in order to lay claim on it." Em raised her eyebrows. "It's true, I know it seems old-fashioned but I think he was just hoping against hope that she would return." Suddenly her aunt visibly deflated, looking frail in the light coming through the windows. Her hands trembled slightly and she grasped one with the other as if to still them into silence.

Em spoke very tenderly then. "I know what happened to my mother, but what about Seán?"

"Well it turned out that Seán wasn't easily deterred by her not responding to his letters. He still planned to follow her to America when he got better. But by then, she'd already married Jonathan Watts. I had to tell him that, and at the time I didn't know you were his. Even if I had known... well, he'd already been through enough."

Em spoke quietly, without any judgment in her voice. "Those were big decisions for you to make, decisions that affected people's entire lives."

"You think I don't know that? You think it hasn't eaten me up all these years? I had my own problems here too, you know! Da was getting worse by the day and he'd developed cirrhosis of the liver. I was already managing the farm for him." Brigid paused then, a pained look crossing her face. "As for my sister, I thought that not saying anything was better than saying something, that I was doing the right thing. I told myself it was just a fling, just a teenage romance, that they would both forget about it in a few years' time. But I was wrong. So very wrong about all of it." Brigid slumped in her chair, chin drooping towards her chest. Em had never seen her look so vulnerable. It scared her.

"We can stop talking about this if you want."

"No." Brigid sat up as if suddenly challenged by Em's words and set her chin. "Let's get it all out once and for all. Seán and Eva both married other people, went on with their lives."

"But I don't think she ever did."

Her aunt's voice was flat and hollow. "No. I suppose she never did get over him." Brigid turned to look out the large windows then. "I've sat here on so many nights, looking across the sea, thinking about her and wondering what would have happened had she known about the letters? If he'd known about you? Would they have both walked away from their relationships and lived happily ever after with one another?" And with Brigid's next words, another piece of the puzzle fell into place.

"In the end, I tried to ease my own guilt and pain by finally telling her, after you were a teenager and Sophie was a little girl, that Seán was remarried. I thought that at last I'd be free and she would let go." Brigid's eyes filled with tears then, and it was difficult to watch this strong, ornery woman show such raw emotion. "And let go she did, just not in the way that I thought she would." Brigid lowered her head and let the tears flow freely down her cheeks.

So that was it, thought Em. That must have been when her mother took to her bed. She remembered her father's words from his journal... "*... when she found out from Brigid, years later, that he too had married and moved on with his life, it was more than she could take. So she just gave up wanting to live.*" It all made sense now. As much as she felt sorrow for what her mother had experienced, she looked at the woman before her, in the present moment, alive and feeling the pain and guilt of the past and felt her heart fill with compassion for her. Brigid was feeling such grief over something she could never go back and change. She reached out and laid a gentle hand on her aunt's arm. "You must miss her so."

Brigid nodded her head over and over. "I loved her more than I ever loved anyone. I could have done more to make sure they got to have a life together. All this secrecy, all these lies. It's as if our whole family life has been one great big web of lies." She raised her eyes to Em, watery grey-green meeting emerald sparks of light. "I missed her so much when she left. I wanted her to be happy. That's why I couldn't tell her about Seán. And when I finally did, it broke her heart in two. I guess she just couldn't find the courage to live after that." Em nodded in complete and utter understanding.

As her aunt continued speaking, she seemed to gather herself once more. "Seán moved on, or at least he seemed to do. He knew, as soon as he'd heard that she was married to Jonathan, that he didn't have a choice. But she just wasn't as strong as he was I guess. She was made of too much faerie dust and dreams."

And just as Em was about to respond, Jack appeared at the doorway.

Em looked at him and back at the woman before her and she felt a sense of peace wash over her. The past had been revealed, and at the end of the day, it was just the past. She knew that she belonged here just as much as she did in North Carolina with her dad, Sophie, Butter, and Fudge. "I know you might find this hard to believe, Aunt Brigid, but, despite everything, I'm really glad you told me, I'm not upset with you. In fact I'm happy that I came and we met again after all these years. I would like to get to know you better."

She got up then and walked over to her aunt, gently hugging her and whispering in her ear at the same time, "Whatever happened, Auntie, it doesn't matter now. Please don't blame yourself for what's past. I know Eva wouldn't want you to." She heard the older woman whisper back, "Bless you."

When Em straightened back up to a standing position, she noticed that Brigid's eyes were glistening once more... and then she did the most remarkable thing. She closed one eye in a conspiratorial wink before turning to address Jack, who'd been standing by silently. "Well, Mr. O'Reilly, since you've gone and interrupted us, are you at least going to help me to bed?"

"With pleasure, Mrs. O'Reilly, with pleasure," Jack said, approaching Brigid with the wry smile that he reserved just for her.

$$\backsim\ 46\ \backsim$$

Conor took Em for an early dinner that night at the Strand. It was a Sunday and the place was full of families and good cheer. Afterward, they walked the beach as the day gave way to night. "I don't know how to say goodbye, Conor. The time we've spent has meant so much to me."

He stopped and took both of her hands in his, turning to face her. "Then don't say goodbye. Wait until you come back and say hello instead." He looked at her with a certainty that it would indeed happen. She felt that way too, although they both knew, deep down, that one never really knew what life would bring.

Then he dipped his head towards hers and, ever so slowly, he came closer and closer until he could touch her lips with the whisper of a kiss, almost a question. She moved towards him, closing the space between their bodies and their lips met once more, this time exploring, giving and receiving until she could barely catch her breath. He pulled away first.

Em spoke. "I want to ask you to come home with me tonight... so much, but..."

He shook his head, reaching up with one hand and

stroking her hair, smoothing it down along the side of her face. "But it's not time yet for that." He smiled and pulled back from her gently. "Although you leaving tomorrow makes me wish otherwise."

"I just... can't."

"I know. You're not ready. I get it. I do." He placed both hands on her shoulders and kissed the top of her head tenderly. "When you are ready, you'll know where to find me."

She smiled, even more torn by his sweet acceptance, but she would honor her feelings, no matter how difficult it might be for them both. The kissing was glorious but the thought of more intimacy just felt too soon.

"Till next time then, yes? And planes go both directions you know." She smiled playfully at him.

"I've not been to the States in a long time. Might be fun to see this North Carolina of yours."

"I think you'd love it, Conor. I mean it isn't Ireland, but..."

"If you are there, it will be Ireland for me." With that, he reached out just to hold her in his arms, and they stayed like that for a long time, until the sky turned deep black and was lit with stars.

~⚬ 47 ⚬~

Em and Sophie had already made their plans to come back together in a few months, yet even so saying goodbye to Jack at the bus station was harder than she'd expected. Muriel smiled at the two of them and climbed onto the bus first, giving them some time to themselves.

Em looked up at Jack. It was difficult to understand how she could love this man so very much after knowing him for such a short time, but there was no denying it. She wrapped her arms around him and hugged him tightly, then stepped back to look into his eyes.

"I want you to promise me that I'll hear from you, Jack. I want to know how Mrs. O'Reilly is doing and we both know she won't be as likely to call. And please don't let Bea forget about me."

"Ah, Beatrice will be missin' you, but I'll tell her every day that you'll be back soon." She'd spent the morning with Beatrice in the stable, brushing her and talking to her. She didn't know how she'd get along without seeing her sweet face every day. That horse had healed her in so many ways.

She held Jack's gaze. "Jack O'Reilly."

"Emerald O'Shea," he replied with a wide grin and a twinkle in his eyes. "Now you know what they say about Ireland don't you?"

She smiled back, trying to memorize every endearing laugh line on his face. "What do they say?"

"Once you've fallen in love with Ireland, she'll always call you back. Make sure she does, lass."

"You can count on it, Mr. O'Reilly," she teased him, turning reluctantly and stepping onto the bus, turning back to wave at him once more before heading to her seat next to Muriel.

As the bus pulled away from the tiny village in West Cork, Em watched through the window for as long as she could see Jack and the station. Then she turned to her grandmother with a small smile.

Muriel put a reassuring arm around her. "Not to worry. You'll be back. Ireland's in your blood now. And besides, my dear, we have one more adventure ahead of us."

❀ 48 ❀

Em and her grandmother were meeting Seán at Phoenix Park, Dublin. She saw the little dog first, a golden ball of fur yapping furiously at another dog who was passing. The fog was lifting over the park and the sunlight shone on the reddish salt and pepper hair of the man sitting on the bench with the small dog beside him. She didn't know how she knew it was her father—she just knew and her eyes stayed glued to his figure as she and Muriel closed the gap between them on the long path.

When he saw them, he stood, his cane in one hand, his figure erect. Muriel took her arm, both to steady herself on the wet leaves and in solidarity. Em felt her smile growing wider as her heart began to beat in a similar rhythm as it had that day in the barn brushing Beatrice. As she approached her biological father for the very first time, she felt that same electromagnetic charge long before she reached him, as if her heart knew, and by the time she drew close, he'd dropped his cane and his arms opened wide. She found herself moving easily into his embrace, resting against the steady beat of his heart.

When she finally pulled back to look at Seán's face, she saw two eyes as green as emeralds looking back at her and it was almost like looking into a mirror, only one that saw into her soul. As they smiled at one another with unmistakable recognition, she thought to herself that somehow, in the midst of her grief and confusion, by crossing an ocean she had found the way home to herself once more.

Acknowledgements

As with any book, fiction or non-fiction, much of what is written is either researched, experienced or in some way acquired through life's teachers. This book is no exception.

Much gratitude is extended to the following people for helping to birth this book.

To the Irish horse who was my faithful companion on my first trip back home to Ireland many moons ago and to Lenora for taking me there.

To the people of West Cork and their warm welcome during my winter's stay there, especially Ann S.

To my writing partner Annie, without whom I would have given up on Em's story years ago.

To my editor Rosie who pushed me to dig deep and make the writing better.

To my writing coach Alyssa Johnson, who, unbeknownst to her, started the seed of this book, a scene created from a simple writing exercise.

To my friends who have encouraged me—I am so blessed. And to my beta readers, especially Becky, Emma, Sanchi, Valzora, and Karen H.

To Rebecca Austill Clausen, who taught me how to believe in after-death communication.

To my Irish teacher and soul sister Karen Ward who generously helped me to give the book an authentic Irish feel.

To Slí an Chroí and its teachers, Karen and John, who continue to teach me both the earthly and the mystical ways of being with Ireland.

To Adrienne Morella Photography for her beautiful author photo.

To Eva Polakovicova for understanding the importance of feeling into a great book cover and the artistic ability to create it.

To Rachel Bostwick for her superb and detailed formatting skills.

To Rebekah B. who helped me with the back cover description and author bio.

To my precious daughters for always supporting me in everything I do. And to my husband Joe, for patiently walking this particularly long footpath with me.